FATAL SECRETS

SHADOW CITY: DARK ANGEL

JEN L. GREY

CHAPTER ONE

THE ANGEL AZBOGAH glared at me. I stood in front of my preordained mate, Levi, his father, Bune, and his best friend, Zagan. Azbogah's black suit blended in with his dark wings and emphasized his heaving chest as he landed directly in front of me. His spiked caramel-colored hair was messy from the wind, and his winter-gray eyes were trained on me.

Whispers hissed among our people spread out behind him and framed by the shining beauty of the pulchritudinous Shadow City. The angels had flown here from the angel condominium in the center of the city to determine what to do about the demons that had flooded through a portal into our world. But I could only concentrate on the anger coursing from Azbogah. Even the sound of the demons pounding against the city gate was lost on me.

Right now, the threat was Azbogah and the secrets he'd kept from *everyone*. Considering how long he'd been alive, he should've known the truth never stayed buried. It always came out...eventually.

Given all I knew about him, I shouldn't have been surprised that he would consider himself above the Divine plan. He must have thought that Fate believed his lies as much as the angels did.

The angels behind him were spinning into confusion not only due to the demons pummeling the gate but also from my return after I'd escaped prison and the city. I'd been imprisoned for stealing three rare artifacts from our well-guarded building. Not to mention the fact that everyone gathered here had just learned that I was preordained to a demon.

Breena and the Shadow City witches continued to chant spells to strengthen the gate and ensure the demons outside didn't get through, adding to the chaos.

"What is she talking about, Azbogah?" Munkar, a warrior angel and trainer, asked in a low voice. His dark brows furrowed, and he hovered about ten feet in the air, slightly behind my mother, with his arms crossed, making his hulking form seem even larger.

Mother's face was lined with worry, and her forest green eyes appeared darker than normal. Even her hair had dulled, lacking its usual sheen and thus appearing only a few shades lighter than her black wings. My father, Pahaliah, hung next to her. His usually soft white feathers seemed a little brittle, and his butterscotch hair appeared almost golden brown in the dark. His all-white suit still looked pristine, but his sky blue eyes were wary, as if he knew that whatever I was about to tell them would change our entire world.

He wasn't wrong.

I'd hoped that Mother or Father would question Azbogah, but they were in a strange state of mind. The composed parents I'd always known weren't present.

"I..." Azbogah started, but stalled.

Bune chuckled darkly as he stood straight. He and Azbogah were both nearly seven feet tall. He stroked his bronze beard as the moonlight reflected off his golden skin and coffee-brown hair. His normal hickory eyes were a deep brown. "Choose your words carefully, Yelahiah and Pahaliah—you don't want anyone to smell your lies."

He thought Mother had been involved in forcing the former archangels to fall and turn into demons because she'd been dating Azbogah when a witch had performed the spell to take their wings and set them on a path to Hell. Five of the seven archangels falling and the elimination of all angels' preordained bonds had been the cost for the remaining angels to become more powerful.

Even still, I didn't understand why the demons thought she'd been involved. She was the angel of Justice and an archangel. She wouldn't have compromised her morals...but maybe her disdain for Azbogah stemmed from more than him overseeing her brother Ophaniel's execution. The thought crushed my heart, but I couldn't keep hiding from the truth.

"Me?" Mother placed a hand on her chest. "I have no idea what you or Rosemary are referencing."

I cringed, waiting for the sulfuric stench of a lie, but the air remained clear. My eyes burned with tears, and some of the tension inside me uncoiled. She didn't know, thank the gods.

"Do you take us for fools?" Bune scoffed. "You two were preordained—of course he confided in you."

My world stilled as I struggled to breathe. "What?" Surely that couldn't be right. I knew my mother and Azbogah had been together romantically for centuries—Mother had told me that much, which meant she would have told me everything...right? Them being preordained mates seemed like something worth sharing.

The picture of her and Azbogah, which I'd found hidden in her bed frame with the stolen artifacts, flashed through my mind. They had been in a lover's embrace and had looked so happy—like Fate had brought them together.

No.

But that would answer so many questions, such as why she would stay with someone who had threatened her brother and manipulated others for his own gain. Something had always felt off...missing. The foggy picture finally cleared, showing me the entire view.

She hadn't worried about Ophaniel because she'd never considered that Azbogah could do anything to hurt her at that magnitude. Now her mistake made sense, though I doubted I would've understood it before meeting Levi. I couldn't have fathomed the love and emotion that preordained mates had for one another until I'd found my own. I would *never* do anything to hurt him. Not on purpose.

The judgment I'd reserved for my mother for so long vanished.

Her face paled, and her attention flicked to me. "I...I..."

The sting of betrayal sliced through me.

You didn't know? Levi asked as his mocha eyes turned to me. His shock mixed with mine, and my chest tingled with more discomfort. He squeezed my hand, and the slight buzzing where our skin touched made me feel less alone.

There was no point in lying. *No, she never told me. I had no idea. They always disliked each other.* Which should've been my first clue, but I'd been raised with them disliking each other as the norm. Gods, I felt so stupid.

That wasn't a plausible excuse. I was a warrior, and part of my training included picking up on subtleties that could alert me to the bigger picture. I'd always prided myself on that ability, but I'd been blinded to the truth before I'd even begun my training.

Then of course you wouldn't think to question it, Levi assured me, but the sentiment fell flat. He ran his free hand through his short espresso-brown hair, and the iridescent swirls of the city's special lights revealed that his chestnut scruff was slightly longer than normal. My stomach fluttered. He looked even more ruggedly handsome.

"I've been by her side for the past thousand years, and if she had known anything, she would have told me," Father said as he moved in front of Mother.

Azbogah winced as if Father's words pained him.

My chest heaved with bitter laughter. Once again, the odd reaction caught me off guard, but at least I was breathing again. "I wouldn't be so confident about that, Father. After all, she failed to tell me they were preordained, which begs the question of why no one has asked why their preordained halves have fallen."

Maybe changing the subject was to my benefit, but I needed to concentrate on the truth...not the betrayal swirling inside.

"They didn't—" my trainer, Isham, started, but he paused, and his eyes widened.

Angels' belief that we were smarter than most others was ironic. Our kind had suffered the worst kind of devastation, yet no one had picked up on the devious plan behind it.

Well, the false reality ended now. "Azbogah has lied to all of you," I said.

"Do *not* listen to her," Azbogah commanded as his face twisted in anger.

Eleanor scoffed and tossed her dark golden hair over her

shoulder. My angelic rival's dark blue eyes locked on me. "There's one way to silence her: kill her demon friends, and lock her back up in jail."

I clenched my hands so tightly that my fingernails cut into my palms. She wanted to anger me and knew how to get the reaction she desired.

Zagan grunted in disappointment as he and Eleanor stared at one another.

A low warning growl came from Levi as he sneered. "Love, you never told me someone was so insanely jealous of you. And here I thought angels were unfeeling."

Eleanor's smug expression vanished.

"Her comment was irrelevant, much like she is to me." Though the words sounded cruel, I didn't mean for them to be. If anyone understood, it would be my fellow angels.

"That's enough." Azbogah chopped the air. "Jailing Rosemary isn't a priority since the artifacts are back in place and demons are attacking our city. Three are inside our walls. That is our focus. Munkar, Isham, and Phul, deal with the three demons she's protecting."

The warriors moved toward us, and I stepped in front of Levi, Bune, and Zagan. The towering buildings of downtown jutted behind the warriors, the purple dome acting like a dramatic backdrop. Though the three approaching angels were my trainers, I wouldn't hesitate to fight them. I would stop at nothing to protect these particular demons.

"Of course you couldn't allow your *daughter* to go back to prison," Eleanor scoffed. "Everyone here adores her, including her father—who chose to give her up."

Air whooshed out of me. Even the three warriors stopped and turned to Azbogah.

Mother gasped and jerked back. "Eleanor, why would

you say such a thing?" She tucked a piece of hair behind her ear, one of her nervous tics—the same guilty twitch she displayed whenever she spoke about her brother.

As if that wasn't enough, Azbogah closed his eyes.

A lump formed in my throat, and something hard settled inside me. I wanted them to say it wasn't true, but their silence only confirmed my worst fears.

It *was* true.

Eleanor was unwavering. "Oh, please. I was old enough to hear what happened the last night Azbogah came to visit. It was the same night you sent me away with him. I heard the whole conversation where you told him you were pregnant."

My feathers fluttered, and I concentrated to still them. Though I'd always found his attention odd, I'd never pondered it much. The closest I'd come to this revelation was when I'd been imprisoned and he'd been desperate for me to admit I hadn't stolen the artifacts, but I'd let the idea slide because of the impossibility. Because I hadn't wanted to address it in case it was true.

Levi touched my arm and linked, *I'm right here.*

His touch and presence eased part of me. I hadn't realized I needed his comfort, which was silly. Of course I did. He was the person who completed my soul, literally and figuratively. I needed him especially at this moment. *The man I detest...the angel who caused the angels to fall and created demons...is my biological father.* The realization ripped through me like a tidal wave. If it hadn't been for my anchor, Levi, I'd have drowned.

How could I not have confronted it before?

What did that say about *me?*

"That's *enough*," Azbogah snapped. "Who Rosemary's

father is has no bearing on this situation. Now, take care of the demons."

I had to control my heart and push away the sense of betrayal. This wasn't the time to deal with it. We were under full-fledged demon attack, and Azbogah was threatening my mate, along with his father and friend. If I allowed my feelings to overtake me, this situation would grow even worse.

With every ounce of self-control I could muster, I ignored the storm raging inside and focused on what mattered most. "Before you act, think. If he can deny his own child, what else could he abandon?" Every angel coveted having a child. Our kind struggled with fertility, and over centuries, angels had at most two or three children. Even one was rare. There were cases where an angel couldn't reproduce at all, so if Fate blessed one of us with a child, it meant she favored them.

Though the words had tasted foul passing my lips, they'd hit the mark. The three warriors didn't move.

"Don't push me!" Azbogah snarled.

But I was done being complacent. All my life, I'd straddled the line between fighting for what was right and not making waves lest Azbogah find out. I wasn't afraid of him, but I hadn't wanted his attention more than I already had it. He'd had a way of cutting his enemies down at the knees even when he hadn't been popular among our kind. It was easier to maneuver when his wrath was focused on someone else, but the time had arrived to stop bending to his will.

I pointed at *my father* and wrinkled my nose. "Azbogah is the reason the angels fell. He wanted to make us more powerful, so he made a deal with a witch to perform a spell. The price for the power was that everyone lost their preordained mates, which slowly took away our emotions until we couldn't feel joy, pain, sadness, or happiness. *He* is the reason we're under attack—the demons want retribution."

Placing a hand on her stomach, Mother leaned forward. "That can't be true. He couldn't have."

"Oh, it is, Yelahiah," Bune interjected. "Marissa told me everything. And until now, before seeing your reaction, I fully believed you knew all about it."

Azbogah laughed loudly and jerked his head at Bune. "Are you going to believe a *demon*? Don't be a nincompoop like Rosemary."

"Do *not* talk about my *mate* that way," Levi said as he stepped beside me. His irises darkened, and his lips curled. "They may listen to you and worship you here, but I won't tolerate disrespect."

"You're in Shadow City and angel territory. There's not much you can do to back up that threat." Azbogah cracked his knuckles.

For a moment, I forgot I was with angels instead of shifters. They were doing a dominance dance. With shifters, the animal within always wanted to move up the hierarchy, whereas angels were usually complacent with how things were. We had status and a role, and we rarely deviated from expectation. The only angel who had animalistic tendencies was Azbogah, but that was because he thought Fate had slighted him. Having demons inside the city was causing an uproar.

Things would escalate if I didn't step in, and if we wanted to set the truth free, we had to stay on topic. *I love you for making it clear that we're a unit, but Azbogah will twist anything into a distraction.*

Levi's fingers dug into my skin as the warmth of frustration floated from him into me. *You're right. I was being foolish.*

No, you were being a mate. His first instinct was to protect me, and I would have done the same thing if the situation had been reversed. However, it was time to get the conversation back on track. "I find it odd that you're avoiding directly answering the question. How hard is it to say yes or no to whether you did what Bune and I accused you of?"

"I do *not* have to answer to a demon or..." He trailed off as if he wasn't sure what to call me. I wasn't a demon, despite being mated to one, and I definitely wasn't his *daughter*. Then he cleared his throat. "Or you. I don't need to waste time on foolish allegations."

"If they're foolish, why not address them so we can put them to rest?" Pahaliah arched a brow, and he glanced at me with concern.

Why was he concerned? So much was going against our family, but he was such a good father, especially with the way he'd taken me in. I wished I could ease his worry.

My blood ran cold.

What if Father hadn't *known*? Would this change things between us? Ugh. These emotions were hazardous.

Without thinking, I stepped closer to Levi, needing his support even more.

Azbogah straightened his shoulders. "Why should I humor them? Demons are attacking us, and they're stalling, probably to buy the demons time to get inside."

He was doing everything possible not to answer, and I wouldn't allow him to continue to manipulate the situation. "The witches are reinforcing the spells, and the gate's angel wood will hold up for a long while. Knowing *why* the demons are attacking is critical to understanding how to *defeat* them."

Azbogah jabbed a finger at the door. "They *hate* us. That's the *reason*. Nothing else is relevant."

"Rosemary is right." Munkar waved a hand at me. "Part of any effective strategy is understanding the mindset of the opponent. *Everyone* knows that." His attention flicked from Azbogah to Bune. "And the demons here can provide us with some insight. We can ask a witch to spell them if the truth is in question, but we should hear them out."

Jerking his head in Munkar's direction, Azbogah crossed his arms. He squeezed his shaking hands under his armpits to hide the quiver, but the damage was done. Munkar, Mother, Father, Isham, Phul, and I had already noticed. That was a sign of guilt, and his blatant refusal to answer reinforced that he'd done something horrible.

I glanced at Bune and nodded. If Azbogah wouldn't speak the truth, I knew someone who would. It shouldn't be me. This wasn't my story to tell but Bune's. Of all the people here, he'd been the most impacted.

Bune nodded and stood straight as he told the events of the past, almost verbatim to what he'd revealed to us back at the hidden neighborhood of the silver wolves. When he spoke of Marissa, his heartbreak cut deep. No one was that good of an actor, not even Azbogah. When Bune was done, Azbogah closed his eyes.

He had to know he was finished.

"You did *all* of that?" Mother asked, her voice broken. "You had our brethren turned? You had the preordained separated? You fractured our souls and made us unfeeling and unable to connect with our humanity in order to perform our jobs more effectively...for *what*? What could have been so important?"

Angels murmured, and I tore my attention away from Azbogah, my mother, and the angels closest to me to take in our surroundings. A chill ran through me, and the hairs at the nape of my neck rose.

The city no longer looked beautiful. Yes, the golden buildings still glistened, and the lights swirled like dancing rainbows, and the smell of fresh flowers filled the air. However, it had all been built on lies. Anything built on evil had a way of crumbling, and I feared this city was no exception.

I exhaled and squared my shoulders. There had to be a way to salvage this...to make this right. We just needed time.

Shifters in nearby condominiums peered out of their windows, staying out of angel business because that was the *law*. A stupid law that should've never been put in place.

Times were changing. Fate had begun to unfold her plan by bringing my friend Sterlyn, the silver wolf alpha, into our lives. Sterlyn and her circle of friends were bringing the supernaturals together the way we always should have been. But Azbogah—and all the angels, really—had worked against the vision of the founders of this city from the very beginning.

Azbogah sucked in a breath and turned to stare at the angels behind him. His face reddened as he bellowed, "I did it for *us*. I did it to ensure we would be in control and as strong as we needed to be to fulfill the destiny Fate had chosen for us. Those who fell were the very ones who would have held us back from all we could achieve. I made each of you *strong*, and I refuse to let these demons come here and destroy everything for which we've sacrificed." Azbogah pounded his chest. "We will remain strong and take down every person who tries to ruin our great city."

The words hung heavy in the air, reminding me of the humidity outside these walls on a hot summer Tennessee day. But no one here would understand that comparison.

The angels had been forced to remain in the city because of the truce with the demons.

Yet another control mechanism we'd fallen for without questioning the validity of Azbogah's statements.

When no one spoke, Azbogah lifted his head. "If you want to defeat the demons, you need to stand with me."

The angels glanced at one another, unsure of the right decision.

"We're already in this situation." Ingram, an unfortunate past dalliance of mine, scratched his head, ruffling his ginger-blond hair. His tawny wings appeared slightly dingy in the darkness, and his moss green irises held no kindness. "So we might as well continue down the same road. It's not as if the demons will listen to reason."

"Yes, they will." Bune spread his hands. "At least the ones who are undecided—which is *half* of the demon population—will."

I wanted to scream in frustration, but I swallowed it down. Yelling would create more emotions and lead to irrational thinking. With a controlled voice, I said, "The right thing to do is to kill the ones who give us no option and make peace with those who will listen to our truth and be willing to start a new world where we can come together as one. Remember, some of those demons out there are your preordained mates. Can you throw away that connection after everything you've learned?"

Levi wrapped an arm around me as he stared down the angels and stated, "I would *never* give up on Rosemary. And I know your mates will feel the same way if they see your remorse. Don't allow *him*"—he pointed at Azbogah—"to continue to control a disaster he put into motion."

"Don't listen to him," Azbogah snarled at Levi. "Those who will stand by me and do what's right, raise your hand."

As soon as Ingram's hand lifted, darkness settled over the city. One not of the night but of unnatural causes.

Everyone tilted their heads up.

Demons swarmed the dome, their red eyes gleaming everywhere. Then the thrashing began with a loud screech.

If that wasn't an omen, I wasn't sure what was.

CHAPTER TWO

THE SCREECHING ECHOED ALL AROUND, and I wanted to cover my ears. However, I couldn't allow my guard to falter for even a second. That was all Azbogah would need to make a move.

I've never heard a demon screech like that, I linked with Levi as I moved closer. Not only did I need to feel him due to all the information I'd learned, but I also needed to ensure he was safe in this dire situation.

Levi glanced up at the dome. *They aren't screaming—it's their weapons. They're trying to cut through the glass.*

That's absurd. Under any other circumstance, I'd have loved to inform the demons that the weapons wouldn't break through the glass, but they should have known that. There had to be more to their plan, especially since there was something bizarre about the way they were working. The red eyes were constantly moving, and I couldn't lock onto a pair at any given time. They were like red streaks blazing by in the darkness, as if a current of dark, murky air or water had crashed over the city.

"We need to stop fighting one another and work

together to prevent the city from collapsing," I said. All the angels stood around in shock and, dare I say, terror. Though I suspected none of them would admit it, I wasn't arrogant enough to deny this discomfited me.

Azbogah pinched the bridge of his nose as his darkening irises focused on me. He rasped, "Little one, now isn't the time for you to try to become a leader."

My face burned. His assumption that I wanted to be like him and his use of the nickname he called me in private were equivalent to a slap in the face.

I refused to cower or become silent. "I'm not trying to lead." That was the truth. My skill was in battle strategy. Sterlyn and several of my other friends excelled as leaders. "I'm trying to prevent a war that has been brewing for over *one thousand years* because of *you*." If he was going to throw punches, I would return the favor.

A dark laugh escaped Zagan, and I went still. He'd been so quiet that I would've forgotten he was here if the angels hadn't continued to reference three demons. He and I had never been on the best of terms, but in fairness, I'd had a rocky start with Levi and Bune, too. Heavens, Levi and I had only of late become solid in our relationship, as Fate had intended.

Snarling, Azbogah glared at Zagan. "Do you have a *problem?*"

Now that was a foolish question. "Don't be daft," I scoffed. With all the demons attempting to get inside, Azbogah had decided to focus on the non-threatening ones here beside me?

"I've heard stories about *you*." Zagan smirked, his black diamond eyes sparking with mischief. He rubbed a hand over his face and pushed his raven hair to the side. "About how, despite not being an archangel, you had as much influence as they did, if not more."

What is he doing? I asked Levi. Zagan seemed to despise the dark angel, yet his words sounded complimentary.

Levi squeezed my hand. *Don't worry. He's getting to the punchline.*

No! He doesn't need to punch him right now. Though tempting, we'd already risked a lot by coming to the city. Chest squeezing, I readied myself to stop Zagan. *If he attacks Azbogah, he'll make the situation worse.*

Warmth spread through our bond, easing some of the tension inside me. Levi's adoration was coming at a very peculiar time, but I wouldn't complain.

He's not going to punch him. Humor followed his words.

I was lost, and I didn't have the extra mental capacity to solve the riddle. *Good. Don't scare me like that again.*

A huge smile filled Azbogah's face, boosting his narcissistic and arrogant aura. Despite Hell descending on Shadow City, he stood there, enthralled by hearing others speaking reverently about him.

And he was my *father*.

A sour taste filled my mouth, and I had to fight the urge to spit. I wasn't sure I'd ever recover from that particular truth.

"I'm not surprised that my reputation extends to Hell." Azbogah rubbed his nails along his chest as if to ensure there were no wrinkles in his black suit. "I've worked hard to stay relevant by doing whatever was necessary for my people."

"You mean I wasn't 'your people' once?" Bune challenged and waved a hand up and down his body. "Were the rest of us expendable? You never gave us a second thought?"

Father... my *real* father... hung his head. Pahaliah said, "Of course you were always in our thoughts. Each one of you who fell. None of us realized that Azbogah was behind it."

"If I'd known..." Mother inhaled. "I wouldn't have—"

"You wouldn't have *what*?" Azbogah bit out. "You are an archangel, and you let that power pass you by in the name of *justice*. You wouldn't do what was necessary but rather aligned yourself with the other supernaturals when it came to what type of place this city should be. I was the *one* making it a *true* safe *haven*." Azbogah tilted his head back and wrinkled his nose. "How else to best protect the *entire* world than to bring the strongest supernaturals inside the city so we could watch their every move?"

"We were never supposed to *rule* over them or *anyone*." Mother flew closer to him as her eyes narrowed. "Look at what happened every time *you* tried to do that. The silver wolves coordinated a full supernatural attack among our kind to overthrow you, and then they left. And now the silver wolves have returned, Rosemary's preordained is a demon, and there's a demon horde set on breaking through the city barriers to kill us. So please, continue lying to us about Fate favoring a world where angels are supreme. The Divine Plan doesn't want us to be in *charge*."

I'd never seen the two of them argue like this before. They usually stuck to underhandedness and strategic moves as if they were playing chess. Now they were discussing the true problems in front of everyone. I couldn't be sure if emotions had made this candor possible, but either way, this confrontation was long overdue. All of this should've been addressed centuries ago.

Azbogah tapped his chest. "This is the shortsightedness that makes me different from *you*. I'm willing to do what it takes to protect everyone, despite the consequences. The best way to do that was to get all the strongest supernaturals in one place and ensure we were strong enough to control them. We may be seen as rulers, but that gives us the last bit of leverage we need."

He was insane. "So you were willing to sacrifice the majority of the angels to override Fate and make us rulers so we could protect the outside world?" I countered.

"I should have known that if Yelahiah raised you, you'd become just like her." Azbogah inhaled sharply and frowned. "I should have kept you close."

I couldn't tell if he was feeling remorse or frustration, but the sentiment didn't matter. He'd made his choices, just as Mother had. "That doesn't answer my question. Look at what your decision has done." I gestured at the gate and the dome. "No one can change Fate's plan. It's called *Divine* for a reason. Was it all worth it?"

Silence was his answer, though I didn't believe he remained speechless on purpose. He stood there, mouth opening to speak before closing again, reminding me of the horrible times I'd flown beside squawking birds. Thankfully, he stayed silent—not that anything he said would add to the turmoil.

Each moment we stood here gave the demons more time to get into position. Since I couldn't speak telepathically to anyone except Levi, I needed to go to the vampire side of the city to check on Sterlyn, Griffin, Alex, and Ronnie. Sterlyn and Griffin were staying in the vampire mansion while the shifters' former home, the Elite Wolves' Den condominiums, was being rebuilt. The construction was taking a while due to the challenges of working with the city's angel-sourced materials, even with the witches' magic aiding in the building process.

What's wrong? Levi stiffened, becoming more on guard. *Suddenly, you're more stressed and upset, though frankly, I'm not sure how that's possible.*

Sometimes, I hated how he could read me so clearly. I liked to process things in my own time, and Levi sensing my every mood was one of the things I struggled with the most as we acclimated to the bond. He knew *everything* and understood what I was feeling even before I did. *We need to check out the situation on the other side of the city.*

Good call. Levi glanced to the right, toward the vampire side of the city, where the other city gate was located. The darkness seemed just as thick there.

My heart sank. I wasn't sure how we were going to get out of this unscathed.

Then I cringed.

My emotions were affecting me again.

The truth was that we *wouldn't* make it out without casualties. They were unavoidable. Though we now had a way for shifters, vampires, and witches to *see* the demons, the demons could still fly, which meant the angels would have to do most of the fighting. Either way, lives would be lost on both sides, and I could only pray that the loss of life was limited.

The original demons hadn't chosen to fall, and the demons who *had* chosen to lose their humanity had been under the influence of those who had been forced. It was a horrible situation. I was certain if I'd been raised in Hell, I wouldn't be recognizable as the person I was today.

"When you determine a diplomatic way of answering that particular question, let me know," I said to Azbogah. "Until then, my *preordained*, his father, and my..." I wasn't sure what to call Zagan, but the answer came to me quickly.

"My *friend* are going to head over to the vampire side to check on things there."

Zagan's head jerked in my direction.

Though the word hadn't come to me at first, I realized it was true. If Zagan was Levi's friend, that made him mine, too. Not necessarily a close one, but a friend just the same. That must have been how Levi felt about Sterlyn and our entire group, seeing as they didn't treat him the same as me but were coming to tolerate and maybe even trust him.

Eleanor snickered. "You stole artifacts and broke out of prison, but you think you can just fly around as you wish *with demons*? Your arrogance is showing."

Though I had my faults, my current actions didn't stem from arrogance. "The truth is—and I think everyone who knows me is aware of this—I *didn't* steal the artifacts. I found them, and before you ask where, I will *not* tell you." I was tired of taking the blame, but that didn't mean I would make it easy for Mother to *re*take the blame. Azbogah's hold was weakening, and now was the time to make him squirm. After everything I had learned, I had no doubt that he and Erin had planted the artifacts in my parents' bedroom. Though I wished I could blame him for the picture as well, I was certain *that* was Mother's. "And yes, I escaped from prison, but only because I accepted the blame for something I didn't do. I feared what would happen if I didn't.

"But I'm tired of being afraid and allowing things to continue the way they always have. Protecting the city is more important to me than arguing with you, Mother, or Azbogah. And if your focus is on capturing *me* when there are demons *surrounding us*, then you're letting your disdain for me get in the way of everyone's safety."

Her eyes widened, and her jaw quivered. "Ingram, do something." She placed a hand on his shoulder, and a slight smirk fixed on her face as if she thought touching him would bother me. "She clearly has feelings for you, even after your breakup, and must be sleeping with the demon to get back at you."

"Breakup?" Levi snapped. *Did you sleep—*

He's irrelevant and not worth wasting time or anger on. Ingram was a mini-Azbogah and wanted to be seen as more than he was, no matter the cost. *Don't act as if he's important, or you'll inflate his ego.*

Levi's displeasure coursed between us, allowing me to feel just how unhappy he was. He linked, *If a woman I'd slept with was standing before you—*

I'd want you to make her feel as if she'd never existed. Though the thought wasn't comforting, Levi pretending as if he didn't know her, let alone acknowledge her, as if she were nothing, would be the way to comfort me.

He glanced at me. *You're a cruel woman...and I dig it.*

Dig it? That was impossible. He could dig a hole in the ground, but not a woman. However, I bit back my confusion. We were under attack, and that required our entire focus.

"Rosemary is right," Mother said as she flew to Azbogah. She held her body straight and with confidence like the woman I'd always known.

The two of them standing so close together caused goose pimples to spread across my skin. I wasn't sure how I'd never seen it before, but I was an almost perfect combination of the two of them. I'd always wondered why I didn't have lighter features and feathers with Father being so pale, and now I knew.

Ignorance was bliss.

I'd always scoffed at that saying, but it worked perfectly in this situation. Knowing Azbogah was my biological father didn't help anything—okay, that wasn't true. I'd learned that Mother had never been honest with me. She'd failed to tell me one huge fact. What else had she kept from me?

The question settled hard in my chest.

"We have a battle to prepare for, due to the many horrible decisions that were made for us in the past." Mother's tone was bitter, and though she didn't look at Azbogah, she didn't have to. Her insinuation was clear.

I was glad Mother was back to normal and coming across as a leader. Someone besides Azbogah needed to make the decisions, or he'd do whatever he could to turn the situation in his favor. It would be easy for the angels to continue following him—then they wouldn't have to admit their misjudgment.

"Let's go," I said to Bune, Zagan, and Levi. I refused to leave any of them behind.

Azbogah snarled, "That's not a wise idea."

"Neither was having a witch perform the spell that created demons." Levi mashed his lips into a line and shrugged. "Yet here we are."

Zagan chuckled. "When I said we talked about him in Hell, he thought it was a compliment. Little did he know it was the princes of Hell determining all the ways to kill him. They want it to be painful and slow, and I think they've determined the most skillful way to butcher him so he'll stay alive for as long as possible." He sneered, and his eyes twinkled. "We all despise him and call him the Impotent One, so I'm rather disappointed to hear he created a child."

Face reddening, Azbogah glowered. Not only had Zagan highlighted his poor decisions, but he was mocking his manhood as well. For some reason, men grew extremely upset over people making jokes about their penises.

Tearing my gaze away from the angels, I turned to the

witches and the wolf guards at the gate. Erin stood in front
of the coven, next to Breena, as they chanted the same
words over and over. Her black hair with scarlet highlights
appeared like a target and looked unnatural compared to
Breena's long, dark brown hair. Sweat beaded on their
upper lips, showing me they were growing tired. More
witches were running toward them from the witch neighborhood at the edge of the city. From what I could tell, there
were approximately one hundred of them on this side. That
was about a seventh of their population, which meant they
could work in shifts if needed. I hoped an equal number
were at the gate on the vampire side.

The two wolf guards were pushing against the wooden
gate to offset the impact of the pounding on the other side.
A few more wolves rushed over to help. I wasn't sure how
effective they would be, but if they could offset some of the
pressure, there was no reason to stop them. However, we
needed to find a more permanent way to reinforce the gate.

I wanted to reach Sterlyn and the others and check in
on that side of the city.

As if the demons realized we were rallying our forces,
the banging on the door strengthened, and a female wolf
screamed, "We can't hold it much longer!"

CHAPTER THREE

EACH MOMENT THE ATTACK PROGRESSED, more demons arrived. Yet all the angels were hovering and arguing as if we weren't under attack. Even with the wolves asking for help, they were standing around as if they didn't know what to do.

And we'd proclaimed ourselves warriors.

"The gate will fall—the witches can't spell it quickly enough," I declared. If no one else would take charge, I would. "Munkar, Phul, Ishim, and Ingram, go assist the wolves in holding the gate while Eleanor, Morael, and Laylah find something to put against it. We'll tire out otherwise. Whether it's glass tables from your homes or whatever, get some sturdy things to barricade the gate." I turned my attention to Mother and Azbogah. "And no more fighting. Azbogah has to determine a way to fix this."

I motioned to Bune, Zagan, and Levi, indicating we should go. We'd wasted more than enough time on stupidity.

The angels I'd commanded jumped into action,

including Eleanor. Though her face was twisted in disgust, she didn't argue. She might hate me, but she was smart enough to realize that we had to act to survive. The angels were the demons' targets—not just Azbogah, but all of us. They viewed us as traitors, some worse than others.

To fly, my three demons had to change into their shadow form, which wasn't ideal. But we didn't have much of a choice. We'd reach the vampire side faster that way.

As if they'd heard my thoughts, all three of them flickered into shadows.

Azbogah made a choking noise, his disdain clear. I wished the sound hadn't been for show and that he was actually suffering.

Even with everything he's done, he has the audacity to act like we're the ones to blame, Levi linked, his revulsion causing my stomach to harden.

I had to remind myself that Levi didn't know how things worked in Shadow City. *It's more about maintaining his position to make himself seem credible.* Azbogah had realized he'd made a huge blunder, which was why he hadn't responded to my question. He was struggling to determine how to save the situation, but that was impossible. *Just ignore him. Your reaction will only give him ammunition against us.*

With angels, any type of attention was deemed positive.

For a moment, I worried Bune and Zagan would react, but Bune shook his head marginally at the younger demon, and nothing more was done.

That was one nice thing about Bune—he understood both angels and demons. With his guidance, I was able to understand both sides *and* the past.

As we flew down the road that bisected the city, more

wolf shifters rushed toward the gate. Sterlyn and Griffin must have been directing them, which was reassuring because they weren't rushing toward the vampire side.

The streets and sidewalks were littered with shifters and vampires, their faces twisted in confusion as they stared up at the demons attacking the dome.

A large, dark brown–complected man's lime green eyes narrowed. "I can see the floating weapons that are causing the sounds, but there is *nothing* holding them up there."

Another panther shifter nodded. "What the *hell* is going on?"

Little did they realize that *hell* described the moment perfectly. However, I didn't stop to explain. It would be best if Griffin and Sterlyn handled the shifters to help cement their positions as the shifters' council representatives and leaders, especially since Azbogah had worked vigorously to make them look inept.

Soon, the white capitol building came into view. It resembled many of the nation's state buildings, adopting the shape of a white rectangle with a cathedral-like domed roof. The building was huge, covering an entire city block. I had yet to confirm why it was so big, given that only the council utilized the building. In my opinion, it had been made that way to reinforce the importance of the council—as if they'd ever allow the citizens to forget it.

Should we say something? Levi asked with concern. *They're unsettled.*

That was a nice way of putting it. *No, we need to decide as a collective before we do anything. I want us to think this through and not add to the panic.* The fact that my preordained—a *demon*—was concerned with the wellbeing of the residents of a city he'd grown up hating proved he wasn't like the malicious ones attacking us. *Let's not forget they can't see you. If you speak, it might freak them out.*

Fair point. He chuckled, and a nearby shifter looked at me strangely.

Not only was the laugh deeper than normal, but the woman probably thought I was laughing at their fear. This day was progressively getting worse, and I was terrified that more danger would come before it was over.

As we continued toward the vampire side of the city, the crowds began to thin. The busiest section was around the capitol building at the city's heart. Most of the businesses there were frequented and run by a mix of supernatural races. Whenever you approached a less central area, the majority of the residents wandering about were of a particular supernatural race. Here, a few vampires were out, but they were all rushing toward their homes. I wondered if Ronnie and Alex had instructed them to go home, which was probably the safest place for them at the moment.

When the four-story, Neo-Renaissance-style royal vampire mansion came into view, I exhaled with relief. The demons weren't swarming this gate. I'd take whatever blessings Fate bestowed upon us.

"That's Alex and Ronnie's home," I said, informing Levi and Zagan since they hadn't been in the city before. I wasn't sure if Bune knew that or not.

Flapping my wings harder, I continued straight.

"Aren't we going there?" Zagan asked. "Because we're passing it."

I could see why it might be confusing. "They won't be inside during an attack. They'll be at the gate." There was no doubt in my mind that if we knocked on the door, we'd be wasting our time. My friends were fighters and wouldn't ask their people to do something they wouldn't do them-selves. It was one of their most admirable traits.

"They're not just leaders but warriors in their own right," Levi added as we flew over a few vampires, who glanced up at me and stilled.

Quiet, remember? I linked, and continued forward. The vampires were going through enough with the screeching weapons and claws on top of the dome; we didn't need to terrify them more.

Regret floated from him. *You're right. I just added to their tension.*

It wasn't on purpose. Mere months ago, I would have said that was irrelevant, but I'd learned that intent mattered. If someone messed up, they deserved the benefit of the doubt. I cringed at all the times I'd made a mistake without apologizing because it hadn't been intentional. No matter what, if you hurt someone, you should let them know you regretted it. Otherwise, you came across as heartless. And I was certain that was exactly why we angels didn't get along well with others.

That was changing. From the way Mother and the others were reacting, I suspected they were becoming more like humans, and they were struggling with the onset of emotions just like I was.

The gate came into view, and as expected, Griffin, Ster-lyn, Ronnie, and Alex were there, along with fifty of the vampire guard. Diana, a witch council member, was on this side with close to a hundred and fifty witches. That made sense since Erin, Breena, and Diana were the strongest coven members, so having more witches with Diana here would balance out Erin and Breena at the other gate. I could only pray to the gods that more coven members were on their way.

Just like on the Shadow Ridge side, the pounding was loud as the demons used their brute strength to attempt to pummel their way through.

I pushed myself harder to reach my friends. Even with their excellent hearing, all the noise would drown out the sound of my approach. The cacophony was at an excruciating level for me, so I couldn't imagine how painful it was for their shifter ears.

I focused on Sterlyn's silver hair and flew toward her. She, Griffin, Ronnie, and Alex were standing at the guardhouse, where an angel-glass window was set into the wall near the crank so that the guards could monitor who was requesting access into the city.

When I reached them, I followed their gazes out of the window...and the view was more horrible than I'd expected. Demons were *everywhere*.

All of Shadow Terrace was cloaked in the same darkness as our city, and I feared Shadow Ridge might be blanketed as well. We could confirm that since Sterlyn could link with the silver wolves in the area, and she and Griffin could both link with our other friend, Killian, the alpha of the Shadow Ridge pack, due to Killian having submitted to them out of mutual respect. No doubt they were monitoring the situation in both towns.

Not wanting to startle them, I said, "Hey," as I landed beside Sterlyn.

"Rosemary!" Some of the panic etched across her face smoothed as her iridescent purple eyes examined me. "You don't know how much I needed to see you."

The situation must have been worse than I realized. My head spun. I asked, "What do you need me to do?"

Flickering into view beside me, Levi wrapped an arm around my waist.

I'm okay, I assured him as the world began to slow. *I just thought something was horribly wrong.*

The vampire guard that stood with them stumbled back a few steps, his eyes wide. "How did *he* get here?"

"He's a demon friend of ours. There are two others with him that you still can't see," Ronnie told him. "They're three of the good ones. I promise."

That appeased the vampire enough for him to focus his attention back out the window.

Skin buzzing, I tried not to allow Levi's touch to affect my mind more. He always made me dizzy but in a pleasant way. This situation was dire, and I didn't want two sensations mixing. However, I didn't want to step away for fear that I'd fall.

Still not moving, he replied. *I would've wrapped my arm around you earlier because in all this chaos, your touch is the only thing grounding me.*

My heart swelled, surprising me that my love for him could still increase.

"That's not what I meant. We don't need you for anything in particular—we were just worried," Sterlyn said as Bune and Zagan changed back into their human form.

The vampire guard closest to us gasped. "I knew they were there, but it's *still* unsettling."

"Well, get used to it. The demons we're going to inevitably fight can do the same thing," Zagan countered with annoyance.

I came close to slapping him. Though it was something we would need to address, the poor vampire needed time to adjust to what was going on before we made him realize he could be fighting an enemy he couldn't see.

Laughter bubbled in my chest.

Needed time to adjust. Ha. That was how mortal I'd become.

The guard's hands shook with fear, and I couldn't blame him. If I had been in his situation with the same information on hand, I'd have been ready to shoot the air just in case another demon was close by. He was prepared to strike down the threat.

Spreading my wings, I stepped in front of the demons to put his mind at ease over not being able to see them. "They're on our side, and we're working on a plan." I only hoped that the witches were willing to share their plans with us.

"How can you say that?" The guard waved his hand at the gate. "They broke into the city and are attacking us from outside!"

"Orpheus," Alex said sternly, his blue eyes tensing, "these three are *not* a threat. They're our friends. We will figure out a better solution before the gate opens." He stood tall, remaining regal and portraying all the confidence a vampire king needed to have.

Orpheus's brows furrowed, but he kept his eyes locked on the demons. His light brown bangs hung in his eyes, but he didn't budge to move them. He was on high alert.

He was a good soldier.

"We're not far from being taken over." Orpheus sighed. "But if my king says they're friends, I won't wield my weapon unless provoked."

Appeased, Alex swung his gaze to me. "We were worried you'd be thrown back in prison and we'd have to deal with that *and* this attack." His sun-kissed brown hair blew in the faint breeze.

"I wouldn't have allowed that to happen." Levi's anger swirled between us, and my heart picked up its pace.

Bune shook his head and crossed his arms, making it feel as though he were towering over us. "Son, we're three demons and one angel against hundreds of other angels. Don't be arrogant like Azbogah and the princes of Hell. It's unbecoming."

Bune had been more fortunate than many angels inside Shadow City. Using Marissa's archangel abilities, they'd restored their preordained-mate bond. He'd never lost his emotions, unlike the rest of us, which might be why Levi didn't struggle with his feelings as much as I did.

"None of that matters since we're all standing here right now," I said. We couldn't be too assured of the decision not to harm Levi, Bune, and Zagan. Angels were fickle, and though Azbogah had taken a hit by us revealing the truth, he had an uncanny way of getting out of trouble. That was why we were in this predicament, after all. "However, we need to determine a solution to this mess."

Griffin lowered his voice. "Do the angels know the truth now?"

He didn't want to inform others of Azbogah's perfidy before the angels learned about it.

Griffin had become a completely different man since Sterlyn had appeared in our lives—a man I never would've imagined he could become. A true alpha.

"Yes, but I'm not sure what the angels will do. For now, we need to remain resilient and see where things settle." I hoped Mother would gain traction with any angels who were questioning Azbogah's actions before the dark angel could lure them back to his side.

Bune *tsk*ed. "That angel has a way about him. I'm not sure if I prefer believing that the angels turned their back on us or learning they're this naive."

Though Bune wasn't saying enough to influence those

around us, we didn't need Azbogah to claim we were trying to sway judgment in our favor.

My stomach soured.

Unfortunately, I *knew* that was what he would do, and the fact that he was my biological father made me want to vomit.

Needing to change the subject, I raised my voice so no one would think we were discussing secrets. "Are the other towns under siege?" I glanced out of the dome again and saw only darkness. With the density of the demons swarming the city, I couldn't make out Shadow Terrace.

"Cyrus and Darrell report that they're inundated on both sides of the river," Sterlyn growled, sharing news from her twin brother and the silver wolves' beta. "The silver wolves have split up so they can keep an eye on both towns since no one else on either side can see the demons."

Griffin sighed. "And Killian's pack is trying to protect Shadow Ridge while helping the vampires as well."

"Are the demons terrorizing anyone?"

"No," Ronnie said as she laid her head on Alex's shoulder. Her copper hair stood out against the white of Alex's shirt, and her emerald eyes were full of concern. "The last time we checked in with Joshua, they weren't."

Joshua was a friend they trusted and whose vision of the vampires' future aligned with theirs.

"At least not yet." Alex's jaw twitched.

That was my fear as well. However, we didn't need to dwell on what-ifs. I looked at Sterlyn. "Please tell me you have more shifters heading to the other side of the city." I was confident that she and Griffin had been apprised of the grim situation across the city, but I needed to ensure they understood the horror of it all. "The gate is struggling to hold."

"Now that we know you're all safe, Griffin and Ronnie should go to the Shadow Ridge side." Sterlyn fidgeted like she didn't like her own suggestion.

Griffin shook his head. "No way. I'm not leaving you."

Gesturing to Griffin, Alex said, "I'm with him. You two can handle the wolves while Ronnie and I handle the vampires. We can monitor the demons on both sides."

They were allowing their mate bonds to influence their decisions. Maybe now that Levi and I were bonded, they'd take my words more seriously. I lifted my chin and said, "Griffin is the alpha of the city, and he needs to be on the Shadow Ridge side. Ronnie can see the demons and link with Alex to keep this side informed of what's happening over there. If Sterlyn and Griffin both go, communication between the two sides will be slower and more challenging."

Alex rocked back on his heels. "Does that mean you'll go with Griffin and Ronnie and Levi will remain here?"

He had a valid point, but unfortunately, it wasn't feasible. "If the situation were different, I'd agree. But angels will eventually come to help this side, and I need to remain with the three demons to protect them. The angels are more likely to listen to me than any of you." Though I was glad Levi and I had a reason to stay together, it would have been a better strategy for me to go with Griffin and Ronnie.

"Rosemary's right, and Sterlyn's suggestion makes the most sense," Ronnie said, then kissed Alex. "I won't be gone long. Just until we get the other gate under control."

Sterlyn followed suit and kissed Griffin. "I'll head over to you as soon as we're certain things aren't getting worse here."

"Fine." Griffin focused on me. "Please make sure nothing happens to her."

He and Ronnie took off for the other side of the city just

as bright red eyes appeared at the gate's window. A shiver of warning ran down my spine as the eyes locked on mine, and maliciousness wafted toward me in such thick waves that my knees almost buckled.

That had to be a prince of Hell, and he was ready to wreak havoc.

CHAPTER FOUR

LEVI STEPPED in front of me to block some of the negativity. He bared his teeth, reminding me more of a shifter than a demon.

Don't make yourself a bigger target. Though the princes of Hell knew he was alive, we didn't have to broadcast his location.

He chuckled darkly, not sounding like the loving man I knew. *Better me than you, especially where Lucifer is concerned.*

Lucifer.

The archangel of intelligence.

I'd heard stories about his endless knowledge. He had helped begin the construction of Shadow City, which meant he knew its weak points. *Why would he target me?*

When I was in Hell and felt your injuries, I lost it, which caught his attention. He smelled your scent on me and realized I had bonded. He glowered as he stared at the demon prince. *He knows what you are to me.*

Maybe Fate hadn't been helping me after all. It didn't

matter. We would either figure a way out of this or die trying. Surrendering or standing idly by wasn't an option.

The red eyes squinted as if Lucifer were smiling. My blood turned to ice, but I refused to let my body tremble. I wouldn't let the demon see that he had any effect on me, and so I lifted my chin in defiance, wanting Lucifer to feel my blatant disregard.

Don't challenge him, Levi warned. *He doesn't like being challenged. He's the demon of Pride for a reason.*

Pride.

Isn't everyone of angelic descent prideful, though? Look at what we did in the name of prosperity. I couldn't see how anyone could be worse than a certain person in Shadow City.

Oh, Lucifer's worse, believe me. Levi edged in front of me. *His intelligence makes him a worthy foe, and he hasn't lost a battle of wits yet. Anything that will give the demons more of an advantage, even something we think is inconsequential, might be of use to him.*

Lucifer disappeared, swallowed by the horde of demons, and my stomach revolted. *How do you know that was him?*

We can recognize each other in demon form. Levi became a statue. *It's hard to explain, but there's something familiar about each demon, even when we can't make out features.*

I hadn't considered that before. If they stayed in demon form in Hell, then of course they would be able to recognize one another.

"What's going on?" Alex stepped closer to the glass, narrowing his eyes as if that would make the demons magically appear.

"A powerful demon was there." Sterlyn turned away

from the window and moved closer to the witches. "He's gone now, but something didn't feel right about him. His negative energy stole my breath. It was that strong, even with this barrier."

Bune repeated the information about Lucifer that Levi had told me. As he informed the others, I surveyed the surrounding chaos. The witches were still chanting in unison, their hands lifted toward the gate as they reinforced the spell...or tried to. Sweat beaded on their faces as if they struggled, but I wasn't sure why. Their magic should have easily reinforced the gate, unless...I winced. The witches on the demon side could be using their own magic against it. Still, every witch I could see seemed determined to strengthen the barrier.

I wondered if it was because they knew the whole story and realized they were as much of a target as the angels. If I were a demon, I would focus my hatred on the angels first, but witches wouldn't be far behind. After all, someone had willingly performed the original spell.

I itched to end this war, but I didn't know *how*. To fight the demons, we'd have to open the gates, but that wasn't a possibility yet. The demons were still attacking with fury, and we needed to wait them out for as long as we could. We were grossly outmatched, especially with the angels divided.

My people needed to unite behind the *right* person. Not Azbogah.

"Uh, my king," Orpheus said loudly. "There's a person outside the gate, hovering in midair."

For a moment, I contemplated not turning around. Lucifer wanted a show. But my reluctance was asinine. The vampire was already an audience to whatever diabolical plan Lucifer had concocted.

"Oh, gods," Zagan sighed, but it sounded more out of frustration than shock.

Don't turn around, Levi commanded.

Any reservations I had about giving Lucifer more attention were gone. If Levi didn't want me to see, I probably *should* watch to understand what we were up against.

I pivoted on my heels and stared out of the window... and a lump lodged in my throat.

Lucifer stood on the bridge in front of the gate. Demons had moved out of the way so we could see him clearly from the window. His shadow hand was gripping the neck of a woman in her thirties. Her eyes were so wide that the whites showed all around her irises as they flicked back and forth, searching for whatever held her.

The demon fisted his hand in her long, mousy brown hair, and she looked frozen in fear. There were bite marks on her neck, and I assumed the demons had been using her to tempt the vampires, which proved one horrible fact.

She was *human*.

Lucifer jerked her head back as he released his hold on her neck. He reached to his side and pulled out a knife.

The scratching on the dome and the pounding on the gate ceased, and an eerie quiet enveloped the city.

They wanted to instill fear, and I hated to admit that it was working. The city was the quietest it had ever been. Even the witches had stopped chanting.

"Don't stop," Alex commanded. "Keep reinforcing the gate."

Diana glared at him but waved at the witches to begin chanting again.

I was glad he'd made that call because I had an inkling it would be harder to make it in the next few minutes.

Lucifer lifted the knife in front of the woman's face.

She screamed, but then her terror kicked in, and she went mute as the knife inched toward her neck.

He was going to kill her if we didn't open the gate. I suspected he would kill her even if we did open it, but I couldn't sit here and let an innocent woman die.

Angels were meant to *protect*, not stay safe and watch people being murdered.

I lurched forward, but even as I did, I knew it was futile. There was nothing I could do without sacrificing myself and, more importantly, risking everyone inside. But my natural instincts fought against logic.

Strong arms wrapped around my waist, anchoring me to my mate's muscular chest. The buzzing of our connection almost didn't register as I watched Lucifer slit the woman's throat. Blood poured from the wound, and her hands clamped over the cut as if that would stop the bleeding.

There was no going back.

A sob formed in my chest, but I swallowed it. I couldn't break down, not here in front of everyone.

I told you not to watch, Levi linked as he held me close.

He was right, but I couldn't appear weak, especially in front of Lucifer. His gaze was locked on me, probably because he could see my wings.

Blood spilled between the woman's fingers, proving that no amount of pressure could stop her from bleeding out. Her hand slipped, but she put it back up as she blinked rapidly.

"Every hour you stay locked in there, safe and sound, another person dies." Lucifer's voice boomed. "Every death is on *your* hands. Do as you see fit. Either way, I'll be enjoying myself." He released the woman, and she crumpled. As she hit the ground, her body began to convulse.

He rushed away without a backward glance, as if what he'd done was a normal occurrence.

The thought rattled me. It probably *was* in Hell.

I couldn't tear my gaze away from the woman. Her body stilled. Death was imminent. If only I could go out there and heal her...but if I did that, more than one person would be slaughtered. My heart fractured as guilt and indecision descended upon me.

If you leave, the demons will storm the city, Levi said, reiterating what I'd been thinking. *Remember, it's the price of one for the many.*

He was right, but that didn't make the decision easy. *That's still one too many. How can it not affect you more?*

It does, but they do this stuff all the time in Hell. He released his hold and moved beside me. *That's how they killed...*

He didn't need to finish. The memory had to be hard enough, so I interjected to prevent him from having to. *Your mother.* The princes of Hell had terrorized the other demons so much that they'd practically desensitized them.

The turmoil Levi had been repressing broke through at the memory of Marissa. Opening myself, I pushed the warmth of my love and comfort into him. I needed him to know I was here now and for as long as my heart remained beating. I hated that he'd watched his mother die. No one should have to go through that.

I despised that every single demon had been forced to live with the princes of Hell once they'd lost their humanity. They were miserable and numb and did anything, even hurting their people, to get some sort of high.

A puddle of blood grew under the woman's head. She'd bled out, and the demons surrounding her watched, enjoying every moment of our torture over her death.

That was when I realized that the enemy surrounding us was made up of demons that had truly fallen and chosen evil. So where were the undecided demons?

"Your Highness, that woman had bite marks. If the vampires are feeding—" Orpheus cut himself off, red bleeding into his irises. "They could be losing their humanity and causing more havoc."

I had the same fear.

Sterlyn inhaled sharply, and my head snapped to her as her eyes took on a faint glow. Griffin was connecting with her.

"Dear gods," Alex murmured next to her.

Panic clawed inside me, quickening my pulse. "What's wrong *now*?"

"Let me guess," Bune rasped. "They killed someone on the other side as well."

Sterlyn nodded as she turned to us and exhaled shakily. She'd been smart to ensure that none of the demons could see her reaction, but this was hitting us hard. This attack had been sudden and overwhelming, and I could feel the panic increasing around us with each passing second.

My brain worked overtime. "Who did it?"

"Lucifer left in a hurry." Zagan shook his head. "I'm betting he had them capture someone else, and he went to the other side to perform the same type of execution."

"It's happening now." Alex clenched his hands into fists. "Ronnie and the others moved away from the window after learning what happened here. He doesn't have an audience."

That wasn't good. The demons craved an audience, and I suspected Lucifer would do whatever it took to get one. "Did Ronnie know whether it was Lucifer?" If Lucifer was working on both sides, there had to be a reason for his madness.

"The demon is in his shadow form. They can't tell who it is." Alex arched an eyebrow.

His message was clear. If one of the demons had gone with Ronnie and Griffin, we'd know whether it was Lucifer. But I couldn't risk being separated from any of them. To protect Levi, Bune, and Zagan, I might have to fight my own people.

"That must be why the demons haven't restarted their assault on the city." Levi looked at the top of the dome, which was still shrouded in darkness.

I wasn't being paranoid. Several pairs of red eyes were locked on us.

"Did the person on the Shadow Ridge side have bite marks, too?" Orpheus whispered.

"I'm not sure, and they don't want to look and give the demon holding the human the audience he's seeking." Sterlyn bit her lip and glanced at me. "The angels are heading back to their neighborhood to regroup. Things are tense."

Of course they were. After being numb for so long, the angels were finally feeling emotions, and now they weren't sure what to do. They'd always trusted and followed Azbogah without question. But the longer they remained indecisive, the more the demons could strategize. "I'll head that way as well unless you need me here," I told her.

"No, the witches are still performing the spells, and the shifters and vampires are rallying together," Sterlyn said, placing a hand on my shoulder. "Your people need you."

She was right. I hated to leave my friends, but the angels had to find a way to work together. "Make sure to communicate with Killian and the silver wolves. They need to escort every human out of town as quickly as possible."

"You'll have to coordinate brainwashing stations before they leave," Orpheus interjected. "They can't remember anything about the supernatural world."

Suddenly, I couldn't breathe. We didn't have time for that. "If we wait, the demons will kill more people." They had to be killing humans for a reason.

Alex's phone dinged, and he removed it from his back pocket. He hissed in frustration. "Well, it doesn't matter now."

"What do you mean?" Levi glanced at the phone, trying to read the message.

"It's Joshua. The demons have made several vampires lose control, causing mass chaos. A dozen humans fled for their lives before any brainwashing could commence." Alex clutched the phone, and the screen cracked.

We couldn't lose what was left of our calm. Taking action—any action—would make us feel more in control, which was exactly what we needed. "Where's Gwen?" I hadn't seen Alex's sister, the vampire princess and third vampire council member, here. The council had been summoned when Luna and I had escaped prison, so she had to be within the walls somewhere.

"She went to the largest vampire condominium building, where some of the displaced wolf shifters are staying, to instruct everyone to remain indoors unless we call on them. She wanted to go in person, thinking it would keep them calm." Alex rubbed a hand down his face. "Once she reassures them that we're working on a solution, she'll check in with the vampire businesses."

Ronnie's presence had changed Alex for the better, but Gwen had recently become more grounded as well. I wasn't sure if the changes I saw in Gwen were from Ronnie's influence or the elimination of Matthew, Alex and Gwen's eldest brother and the former vampire king. He'd been corrupt and had believed that vampires should be able to feed as they saw fit, even if it cost them their humanity. When he'd realized that Alex had found his soulmate, he'd allied with Azbogah to kill Ronnie.

Sterlyn added, "Griffin linked with all the Shadow City wolf shifters to keep them informed and as calm as possible. The wolves on the police force are informing Kira"—she named her fox shifter contact, who happened to be the head of the police and in charge of the artifact building—"and the police are coordinating efforts to inform the rest of the shifters about what's going on. Killian will get the shifters to evacuate the humans. Maybe if they can get those who haven't witnessed anything out quickly, we won't have to worry too much about exposing our existence," Sterlyn continued hopefully.

I wasn't so hopeful, not if some humans had fled after seeing others attacked. However, right now, we had to focus on the demons and worry about the repercussions later...if we even got the opportunity.

"Call me if you need us." I paused. *Unless you want to stay here?* I asked Levi. If all the angels were gathered together, maybe Levi and the other demons would be safer here.

There's no way I'm separating from you. Besides, Azbogah could be hoping for that. Levi flickered back into his shadow form, making it clear he'd be staying with me.

He was right. It was safest if we remained together, but I was still worried that I was leading the three demons into a trap.

Bune and Zagan followed suit, and I fought the urge to

tell them to remain behind. Bune knew the history with which I wasn't familiar. If Azbogah said something untrue, I didn't have enough knowledge to rebuke it, so having Bune present would be best.

I took to the sky but couldn't enjoy the breeze. It was still midday, but it might as well have been night with the darkness that shrouded the city. The fact that the demons hadn't started their screeching again caused me greater unease.

As I flew over the streets toward the capitol building and the angel neighborhood, the people below seemed on edge, glancing over their shoulders and up toward the dome. They couldn't see the demons watching them, but they didn't feel safe. They sensed they were prey and the enemy was hunting.

I shivered at the creepiness of that revelation.

We flew over the capitol and past the building where I'd been locked in a cell. Ezra was still in there, and I wasn't sure if that put him at an advantage or a disadvantage. He was locked away and remote, but I had a feeling his negative aura would call to the demons.

As we flew over the artifact building, I almost sputtered. There was Azbogah, marching in.

I'd expected him to be with the other angels back at the condominiums, trying to persuade them to side with him.

Of *course* Azbogah would go after the artifacts.

He'd been after them all along.

I changed direction and flew toward the entrance. I wouldn't allow him to use the situation to his benefit anymore. "I have to make a detour. That's where the artifacts are stored."

"He wouldn't be that stupid, surely," Bune rasped.

Confusion flitted through our connection as Levi asked, "What are you talking about?"

Realization settled over me. "He thinks Azbogah is getting the other four demon swords to barter."

Not today.

Not on my watch.

I dove toward the door, ready to do whatever it took to keep Azbogah from selling our souls.

CHAPTER FIVE

WITH EACH FLAP of my wings, anger and disbelief coursed through my blood. I truly believed Azbogah would give up the swords to the princes of Hell to save *his* life.

Though I didn't want him dead, that didn't mean we should hand over the swords to the princes and give them more power. The archangels were already so strong in their own right that if they re-bonded with their weapons, they'd extend their power. To anyone else, including Azbogah, the swords were just normal weapons. But if Asmodeus, Belaphor, and Lucifer got their weapons back and re-bonded with them, there would be Hell on Earth.

Stomach hardening, I realized that Wrath would be with them, too. To get his dagger back, he'd have to kill Ronnie because she'd bonded with it. The weapons' bonding power was why the demons had tried to kill Levi. Instead of bringing them his mother's sword in its case, he'd removed it and bonded with it since he was of the same bloodline. They'd wanted to use the sword that contained his mother's archangel power, which could neutralize a spell or magic. The plan had been to destroy the sword with a spell to neutralize the one that Azbogah's original witch had cast on them to alert the angels if one of the princes of Hell returned to Earth. However, they couldn't use Eliza to destroy the sword until Levi was dead...not that she would have done that, anyway.

But the princes of Hell would ensure that the angels and the artifact building were the first targets. We needed to get back to the angels and handle that. After the angels were settled, I'd meet with Sterlyn, Ronnie, and the others to brainstorm solutions. We couldn't keep reacting; we needed time to strategize, or we wouldn't get out of this alive.

I landed in front of the warehouse where Azbogah had entered. His honeysuckle scent was still strong.

I paused at the door. "It would be best if you three changed into your human form." I didn't want Azbogah to use the demons' shadow form to get the shifters to side with him. I wouldn't put anything past the devious angel.

The three of them changed back, and Levi reached around me to open the door.

My heart skipped a beat at his old-fashioned manners. Though I was a strong, independent woman, I still liked to be treated like a lady at times. Not only that, but his gesture revealed that he cared. I linked, *I love you.* Thank you just didn't seem like *enough.*

I love you, too. He winked, and for a moment, things felt almost normal.

That was, until Azbogah's booming voice demanded, "Roman—" He cut off as he spun toward the door, and his gray eyes lightened to silver as Levi appeared behind me.

The lobby was big enough for the five of us to stand inside with a few feet between us. I strolled closer to Azbogah, who stood at the wooden door that led to the rest of the warehouse. I leaned against one beige wall, wanting to give the perception of confidence, though it was the last thing I felt.

Levi moved beside me and placed a hand on the wall behind my head, his side brushing mine as he relaxed and said, "Fancy meeting you here. I mean...what *are* the odds?"

"Are you surprised, son?" Bune asked, making it clear where Levi got his sense of humor. He stood across the room from us, next to the sole window. "Once a snake, always a snake."

The only one of us not pretending to be comfortable was Zagan, who had stayed close to the door, ready to escape at any time.

"None of you knows *anything*." Azbogah pounded on the door to the inner warehouse again.

"We won't allow you to take the demon swords," I said. There was no reason not to be blunt. Time was not in our favor.

Azbogah blew out his cheeks. "That's *not* what I'm doing."

I crossed my arms and narrowed my eyes. "I don't believe you." He didn't smell of a lie, which meant he was somehow bending the truth. I guessed when you had two millennia of practice, half-truths were quick on the tongue.

"Little one—" he started.

"Do *not* call me that." That nickname had always bothered me, and now that I knew why he'd been using it, I wanted to puke. This angel had targeted my mother—his *preordained*—for the past thousand years. "You don't have the right."

He exhaled nosily. "You're right. I don't."

My legs weakened, but somehow, I managed not to fall.

Don't let him manipulate you, Levi linked, and leaned against me more. *He'll try to influence your emotions.*

Good point, but I wouldn't make that mistake. There'd been too much damage for me to ever fall for his sensitive act.

Azbogah glanced at Levi and then back at me, clearly uncomfortable with the demon's presence, which made me want to smile.

No, Rosemary, I chastised myself. I was letting my bitterness rule me, which was as much of a weakness as yearning. I had to channel my pragmatic side.

"I do want you to know that when I told your mother I didn't want anything to do with"—he cleared his throat and pulled at his ear—"you, it was for your and her own good."

"Really?" I laughed, that damn spasm taking control. However, in this instance, the laughter emphasized my point. "How so?"

"Because I'd lost myself, and there was something strange settling inside me like I could no longer access a part of myself." Azbogah rubbed his chest just above his heart.

I couldn't believe what he was doing. "It's because your mate bond—which is located within your heart—disconnected, and you were losing your emotions. All of which *you* caused." He wouldn't make himself into a martyr. He'd done *all* of this. Every damn thing was because of the decisions he'd made on our behalf.

"You think I don't know that?" he snapped.

Levi growled, "Watch how you speak to *my* preordained. You gave her up and neglected her, and that's something I would never do."

"Can we talk *alone*?" Azbogah asked me as the inner door opened.

Roman appeared on the threshold, his lime green jaguar-shifter eyes focusing first on Azbogah before flicking to me, Levi, Bune, and Zagan. He seemed to have aged rapidly since the last time I'd seen him about four months ago. Despite being in his late twenties, he had deep crow's feet around his eyes, and the dark olive skin of his forehead was lined with worry. "No one alerted us that you would be visiting, and we're a little preoccupied with a few witches ensuring the artifacts are securely sealed."

That must have been why it had taken him so long to come to the door. In my short time knowing Roman, I'd learned he was a man who did what he thought was right, and I held no ill will toward him. I tended not to like other people much, but Roman had been kind to Ronnie back when she'd been human and Matthew and Azbogah had held her captive here for a short while. He'd allowed Alex to help Ronnie when she'd been dying, even though allowing Alex into the warehouse had been against the rules. Later, Roman had given Griffin and Sterlyn helpful information regarding the shifter turmoil.

"I'm pretty sure none of us should be here right now, but I was passing by when Azbogah came barreling through," I interjected.

Azbogah puffed out his chest, reminding me of the angel I'd always known. "I'm a council member, and—"

"A council member who caused the attack on the city." I wouldn't let him bully Roman or downplay his part in this situation.

"What do you mean, *caused the attack*?" Roman pushed his shaggy toffee-colored hair behind his ears.

Azbogah opened his mouth, but I spoke over him. "He forced the angels to fall, which created demons, and now they're here for vengeance."

Zagan snorted. "They're out for blood. Remember, there's always a cost for turning on your own."

He had a point, but I'd rather avoid any more deaths.

Both sides had lost enough. Still, the princes of Hell probably wouldn't rest until Azbogah had paid for his sins.

An idea popped into my mind. Would the princes of Hell be satisfied if Azbogah were thrown into Hell to live out the rest of his existence?

For some reason, that didn't sit well with me, either, even if some might consider it just. Though I didn't like the angel, he was my father.

No matter how hard I racked my brain, I couldn't determine a solution.

"I've paid for it. Believe me," Azbogah murmured, his voice breaking at the end.

He sounded as if he'd experienced pain, but how could he if his emotions had dissipated? This had to be a tactic to get us to believe whatever story he was concocting to explain all his misguided decisions.

Rolling his shoulders, Roman stood straight. "Being a council member has no bearing on access. You know that. To grant anyone access, the whole council has to approve and send word to Kira, who then contacts me about who should be allowed inside *this* door. Besides, the door is spelled."

"You can take down the spell," Azbogah growled. "You did it for the vampire king when his mate was injured."

Roman was part of the reason Ronnie was still alive. Alex had reached her in time to turn her before her heart stopped beating.

"That was under extenuating circumstances," Roman said gruffly, his jaw clenching.

"And so is *this*." Azbogah waved toward the three demons and at the door. "Demons are surrounding us."

Levi laughed, sounding carefree, but he couldn't fool the bond. His fear and tension coiled inside me. "Though

I've never lived in this city, even I realize you're taking an opportunity to abuse the little bit of power and influence you have left."

Irises turning greener, Roman focused his attention on my mate. His forehead creased. "You aren't from this city. Are you here to attack us?" He glanced over his shoulder, back toward the hallway that led into the warehouse where, I assumed, witches were reinforcing spells and other shifter cops were on guard.

"They aren't part of the attack," I hurriedly reassured him. "He's my pre—" I cut myself off. I needed to use the vernacular they were most familiar with. "Levi's my *mate*." I laid my head on his shoulder to physically reinforce my words and nodded toward Bune and Zagan. "That's his father and friend. They came here to help us to lessen the loss of life on both sides." And I was in full support of that. Whether Azbogah wanted to admit it or not, the people attacking the gates were our people, too. They had as much of a right to be in this city as the rest of us, but the choice had been stolen from them.

Nodding, Roman crossed his arms. "There are never winners when it comes to war."

His words sat heavily on my shoulders. Angels were always so focused on *winning* that I hadn't contemplated any other outcome. I didn't want more demons to die than necessary, but I still thought of this war as something we would *win*. Either way, however, our people would suffer.

On both sides.

We'd already lost. We were just mitigating the destruction...or trying to.

"That's how the weak-minded think," Azbogah scoffed.

Even after everything, he was still arrogant. "If that's what you think, it's time to head back to the high-rise," I said. That was what the older angels called our home. "There's a meeting happening as we speak, which is how I realized you were planning something when I flew by."

"I need access—" Azbogah snarled.

Roman placed his hand on the handle of the gun holstered on his waistband. "Until I hear from Kira, that won't happen. You don't have permission."

"Do you think your little gun will do anything to *me*?" Azbogah boasted.

"If I pin down your wings and Levi and Zagan hold your arms and legs, then his gun will work just fine," Bune countered, moving closer to Azbogah.

The two of them stood almost eye to eye, but Bune was more muscular. After seeing Azbogah's subpar fighting skills earlier, I had no doubt Bune could hold him down.

Azbogah's shoulders deflated marginally as if he'd realized the same thing. "Since Rosemary has informed me that the angels are meeting, I agree that I should be there to explain my decisions. *That* is why I'm leaving, not because I couldn't find a way inside."

"Whatever makes you sleep easier, old man." Zagan chuckled and placed his hands in his pockets.

Nostrils flaring, Azbogah sneered. "Don't get too confident. You are in the city, after all, and only one angel cares about your well-being. The rest of us don't care whether you live or die."

Get Zagan to stop, I linked with Levi. *The angrier Azbogah becomes, the more desperate he'll get. Let's not nudge him more.*

He kissed my forehead and unraveled his arm from around my waist as he replied, *I'm only doing this for you.* "Come on, let's get some air." Levi walked past Zagan to the front door and waved his friend outside.

Zagan paused, but then he stood straight once more. Scowling, he didn't say anything as he followed Levi.

When they were out of the building, Azbogah turned his attention to Bune and asked, "Did you purposely teach the young ones to disrespect their elders?"

"No." Bune rocked on his heels. "We teach them to respect only those who are worthy." His insinuation rang clear.

We had enough wars going on without another one breaking out inside. "Thanks, Roman," I said. "We're sorry we bothered you."

He nodded. "It wasn't you. And no one needs to worry about coming back unless Kira is with them or has called ahead. There will be *no* exceptions to the rules, especially now." He stepped back into the hallway and shut the door behind him.

Azbogah's irises darkened to slate gray. He didn't like anyone going against his wishes.

With an overdramatic swoop of his arm, Bune again gestured for us to leave.

When Azbogah moved first to exit the lobby, my mouth almost dropped open. However, I had enough sense to make sure it remained tightly closed. Speaking would only further irritate the angel, and I'd just gotten Levi to get Zagan to stop doing that very thing.

Eerie silence still engulfed the city as the demons watched us through the dome. I'd have been more worried if they hadn't been because at least we could keep tabs on a portion of the demons this way. Maybe they'd stopped scratching at the dome with their weapons because they'd realized it was impenetrable.

I'd expected Azbogah to fly off immediately, but he

stood there, arms crossed, waiting for the rest of us to come outside.

His black suit had wrinkles. I'd never seen him look so disheveled, not even during the fire at the Elite Wolves' Den when he'd helped me save Griffin's mother, Ulva, from the collapsing building. He'd indicated I shouldn't tell anyone that he'd helped, and I never had.

"Aren't you going to the high-rise?" I asked. The fact that he wasn't rushing there disturbed me. Was he trying to get us to leave so he could force his way back inside? I hoped he wasn't self-serving enough to pull Erin or any other witches away from the gates to get them to take the spell down so he could get inside the building, as he was desperate to do.

He smiled, but it didn't reach his eyes. "You didn't trust me and made sure I didn't get inside the artifact building. I'm returning the favor. After all, *you're* the one who got caught with three artifacts and thrown into jail. You could be trying to recreate the crime."

My disdain for the man increased every time I interacted with him. He'd moved beyond arrogant to entitled. "I didn't steal those artifacts, and you *know* it. You kept visiting me in jail"—I gestured toward the building, which wasn't far from here—"begging me to admit it, and now that I have, you don't seem relieved."

"Because we have more pressing matters." He flapped his wings, rising into the air. "Like meeting with the angels."

The conversation was futile. We were only sparring.

I turned to my friends. "He's right. Let's go."

The demons flickered into shadow form, and the five of us hurried toward the high-rise.

As we flew over the sizable forest between the downtown area and the angel homes, the lack of animals alarmed me. There were usually a few wolves running or birds flying at this time, but the oaks, cedars, and redbuds were deserted, with only the slight breeze made by the witches ruffling their leaves.

The glass high-rise the angels called home soon towered into view. It was fifty stories high, enough for all the angels to live in one location. The entire building was made of angel glass so the iridescent swirls of the heavenly lights could filter to us whenever we desired them.

My heart flipped in my chest. Usually, the sight of my home gave me comfort, but not this time, with all five hundred angels standing cramped together on the grassy knoll outside the building, turning on one another, throwing punches...and the demons above getting to see it all.

The demons might not even need to get inside the city—the angels were already imploding.

Maybe that was their plan.

I scanned the massive group for Mother and Father. I found the two of them in front, their attention on a man standing with his sword drawn.

Raziel—Azbogah's best friend.

Only an inch or so shorter than Azbogah, he towered over my mother. His caramel wings, fluffed for intimidation, spread from his back. Even from here, I could see his flinty eyes narrow, making his fair golden skin stretch over his jutted jaw.

With all the yelling, I couldn't make out anything being said, but out of the corner of my eye, I saw Azbogah smirk.

Why would he be happy about this? I had to be missing something. I scanned the crowd again and noted something that each situation had in common. Every argument involved one of Azbogah's followers. Had he planned to have them instigate this conflict?

Azbogah increased his speed, pulling down his suit jacket to ensure he was presentable.

He was going to get the situation under control, and I couldn't let him. Without thinking, I soared past him, placed two fingers into my mouth, and blew hard.

CHAPTER SIX

MY PIERCING WHISTLE froze everyone in their tracks. One of the men closest to me pulled back, his blow narrowly missing Ingram.

Now I wished I'd waited another second. Ingram was what Annie would call a twatwaffle. I wasn't sure what that meant, but it suited him.

All eyes turned to me, and I tensed. I wasn't a leader, but Azbogah couldn't be seen as one anymore.

Levi pushed comfort toward me, but it didn't help. I linked, *I didn't think this through. I believe Azbogah set this up so he could show up and control the situation, and I don't know what to do.* Having emotions was flipping hard.

Just speak from the heart, Levi responded.

I need you beside me. Whenever he was next to me, the situation didn't seem as horrid.

He replied, *Always and forever,* as he slowly inched toward me.

Azbogah hovered in the background, watching my every move. I'd expected him to come up here and challenge me for control, but he was allowing me to...fail.

Little did he know that failure wasn't in my DNA. "We've got to stop fighting each other." I gestured toward the dome. "The demons are *watching* us. Have you lost your minds?"

Eleanor rolled her eyes as she flew over and landed a few feet from me. "Are you the one to be asking that question? After all, your *preordained* is a demon."

Murmurs from a group in the back were like the demons' screeching—not because of the volume but because of the dissent. Azbogah and his followers intended to use my relationship with Levi and my confession about taking the artifacts to discredit me. That was why he wasn't worried about me taking the lead. He probably found my attempt humorous.

Mother shook her head slightly, telling me to stand down. Her lack of belief in me that I could rally the angels hurt, but in fairness, I wasn't sure I could, either.

Trust me, Levi connected as he reached my side. *Be honest with them. Let your sincerity speak for itself. That's the quality I love most about you—your sense of right and wrong.*

It couldn't go much worse than this, so I relinquished some of my control to my emotions. Maybe there was a balance to it all.

"Yes, Levi is my *mate*," I said, emphasizing the term that shifters, witches, and vampires used for their other halves, and took Levi's shadow hand. "And he wouldn't be a demon if Azbogah hadn't caused the angels to fall."

His worry slammed through our connection. *That wasn't what I meant, but that works, too.*

If Eleanor was attempting to shame me over my relationship with Levi, it wouldn't work. And I needed Levi to realize the same thing. For most of our time together, I'd doubted him and insulted him, and now I'd made him feel unworthy of my support. That ended now. "Not only did Azbogah make our people fall, but my mate, Bune, Zagan, and so many others *still* didn't choose to turn evil."

"Yeah, right," Ingram spat. "You know they're demons, yes? They have a way of bending the truth, and they even smell faintly of a lie so you can't tell as easily."

"I know all that, but there's one *simple* way to tell, and a second that's a little more extensive." These angels wanted to pretend they knew everything about demons, but we only knew what Azbogah had taught us.

"Really?" Raziel chuckled menacingly. "And what's that, *demon* lover?"

Levi's anger flashed through our bond, making the temperature sizzle. His body lurched, but I held his hand firmly.

Don't. He wants you to get angry. This was one reason I had never been interested in joining the council and attended the meetings only out of duty. I hated political games. "Fallen demons have red eyes." I gestured to the dome, where hundreds of red eyes watched us. "Demons who have retained their humanity have normal colored eyes, both in solid and shadow form." I gestured to Levi, then Bune, and then Zagan, who had locked eyes again with Eleanor. "And the less obvious tell is that a demon who has embraced evil has blue blood. The..." I paused. I'd almost said *undecided* because that was the term Levi and the others used, but they weren't undecided. They had chosen to be *good*, or at least decent. "The ones who haven't forgotten their angelic roots bleed crimson, just like us and mortals."

Munkar tilted his head toward the demons overhead, then looked at my preordained.

I was getting through to *one* angel, but I had to reach at least half, and preferably more. "My mate, Zagan, and Bune risked their lives to come here to help us gain an advantage. They understood the risk they were taking by walking into a place of hatred, but they learned that none of us knew what Azbogah had done. Bune came back to save his brothers and sisters when he didn't have to."

A few of the angels closest to me hung their heads in shame.

"Don't listen to her!" Azbogah shouted. "She's trying to win you over, but I'm the only person who can stop the demons from attacking. I can help defeat the demons. No one else. Not Rosemary, Bune, or Yelahiah. Me and me alone."

The truth washed over me, and nausea roiled inside. "That's what *all* of this is about."

Levi's curiosity filled our bond. *Rosey, what did you figure out?*

"Which is what?" Azbogah flew beside me and placed his hand under his chin.

His motivations. Everything Bune had told me helped me connect Azbogah's actions. "You think that because you were the first non-archangel created that you're entitled to rule them all," I said to Azbogah. "You think Fate *owes* you."

His face turned red, and his smug expression disappeared. For the first time, he appeared unguarded.

Mother plucker. I'd hit a nerve.

"There was no reason I shouldn't have been an archangel." Azbogah's chest heaved, and he snarled, "I was worthy enough to be given the power of judgment but wasn't special enough to have my own weapon as an extension of my power?"

Ishim's head jerked back, and a feather fell from his wings.

Hearing Azbogah confirm my assumption didn't sit well with me. I hated that I was right. I'd hoped he would tell me I was wrong and then share a valid reason for his action that wasn't pure jealousy.

Bune rubbed a hand down his face. "You don't get to make that call!"

"Says who?" Azbogah pounded his chest. "I *am* judgment, and I rule that I should be the leader of our people and the strongest of this world!"

"Azzy," Mother said, sounding bewildered, "you allowed over two-thirds of our people to fall because you were *jealous*?"

Azzy. That was a horrible nickname and one I hoped to *never* hear again.

That really fits him. Levi's arm shook, indicating he was laughing. At least he was in shadow form, and no one could tell.

"I wasn't jealous of you, Yelahiah." Azbogah's tone softened. "You were deserving, but I was as strong as Marissa and as intelligent as Lucifer. Why were they chosen and not me?"

This is one of the worst temper tantrums I've ever witnessed. I wasn't sure what else to call it. He was acting like a temperamental child and didn't see how unreasonable he was.

Phul closed his eyes and massaged his temples.

Murmurs came from the angels, and Raziel sharply shook his head, but the warning was too late. The damage had been done.

Azbogah pulled at the collar of his black button-down shirt and scanned our people. Perspiration beaded on his forehead, indicating he realized he'd messed up. The very situation he'd planned on using to regain control had slipped through his hands.

To ensure he buried himself, I knew there would be no better time than to ask, "Did *you* get a witch to steal the artifacts from the building?"

His head jerked toward me. "That's a preposterous question."

"Then you won't have a problem answering it," Mother said as she flew toward us.

Thank gods she was finally moving to take control of the situation. I wasn't cut out for this, not like she was.

"I won't dignify you with a response." His breathing quickened, and his fingers trembled at his sides.

That arrogant angel I'd always known was crumbling before my eyes. But the truth had a way of bringing us to our knees—like it had done to me when I'd learned he was my biological father.

Father stayed beside Raziel but spread his white wings as if he might take off at any moment. He said, "Yes, you will, Azbogah, because your failure to do so will confirm you were behind the theft."

My parents were the only two archangels still on Earth. They should have been leading our people, not Azbogah, who desired to become a *dictator*.

Jaw twitching, Azbogah showed more cracks in his composure. He didn't have anyone to blame but himself.

"I did *not* take the artifacts." His voice sounded hoarse with anger.

Chuckling, Levi moved so he could stare down the indignant angel. "That's not what she asked. She asked if you were the one who asked a *witch* to steal the artifacts."

The angels quieted, everyone desiring to hear what Azbogah said next.

Azbogah focused on the sides as if he expected his followers to cause a distraction, but even they remained silent. After all, who wanted to align themselves with an angel who was about to lose everything?

"We're waiting." Ingram pulled in his wings, bracing for the answer.

Slate gray eyes locking on Ingram, Azbogah exhaled as his face twisted in fury. For once, people were betraying him instead of the other way around.

"That's what happens when you deal with less than forthright people," I murmured, only loudly enough for those closest to me to hear. "Their loyalties waver at the first sign of trouble."

"Love, I'm sure he knows how that is," Levi interjected, unable to resist.

Under normal circumstances, I'd have chastised him, but Azbogah was devolving. I was certain there was no way he could redeem himself.

Ishim shook his head as his nose wrinkled. "How could you?"

"Everything I did has been for us," Azbogah barked. "Don't you *dare* try to turn this around like I'm the bad guy."

"That's *exactly* what you are," Phul shouted from the other side of the clearing. The warrior shook a fist. "You had us arrest Rosemary for something she didn't even do!"

Azbogah laughed. "She admitted to taking the artifacts."

"Yes, I *took* the artifacts that had been planted under Mother's side of her mattress." I was tired of him continually repeating that, so it was time to tell the full story now that the truth was out. "*You* planted the golden ring, the skeleton key to Hell, and the ruby in an attempt to damage her reputation."

"Is that where you got them?" Mother's emerald eyes widened.

Of course she didn't focus on the artifacts, but rather on where the items had been hidden. She must have realized I'd also found the picture she'd kept of her and Azbogah from when they'd been together. It was hand drawn, seeing as cameras hadn't been invented then, making it more intimate. They'd been in each other's arms, and I hoped my memory of the image would fade with time. "Yes."

"The key to Hell?" an angel named Kafziel asked from his spot just outside the glass condominium. A slight breeze ruffled his curly ginger hair, which emphasized his flawless porcelain skin. He stroked his long, bronze-colored beard. It made him appear far older than the actual fifty years he had on me. Of all the angels in Shadow City, he was the one I'd found the most attractive, but not anymore. My connection with Levi caused his appeal to be lost on me.

Breezing past Levi and me, Bune landed where the trees gave way to the grassy knoll. He flickered back into human form, the version of himself the angels knew. "When the witch created Hell, a key was made to stay on Earth to retain balance. The key forces a portal to always be open between Hell and Earth. If that key were to be damaged, then Hell and Earth would merge. At least that's what the witches who live in Hell explained to us."

"That's enough." Munkar waved a hand. "We don't need to hear any more. It's clear that Azbogah has set us on a path to annihilation. Now, all we can do is try to find a way to survive, and we're wasting time listening to all of this."

Father nodded. "Right now, the demons aren't actively trying to break into the city. Munkar, Ishim, and Phul, why don't you get a group of angels together to assess the problems? Maybe Bune and Zagan would be willing to accompany you to provide insight."

I tensed. "No, they need to stay with Levi and me." Levi had risked his life for his father—I couldn't just hand him over to a risky situation.

"I promise that Bune and Zagan are in no danger with us." Munkar steepled his fingers. "Bune is a former warrior who once completed our group, and now that I know he had no choice in his decision, we hold no ill will against him."

Phul nodded. "I will protect them with my life, just as I would any of my people."

Though I trusted those warriors, I'd feel happier if the two of them remained by my side.

"It's fine, Rosemary," Bune interjected. "They are men of their word, and maybe Zagan and I can glean something the others can't. Though the demons are fallen angels, our experiences in Hell changed us in ways that no one who hasn't been there can understand. To determine the best solution, we'll need to work as partners."

Still concerned, Levi squeezed my hand and linked, *My father wants to do this. Let him. He wants to work with his brethren again.*

Okay. Though I still felt uncertain, if I were Bune, I would feel the same way. He'd been a fighter here before he'd been forced to fall. Of course he'd want to help because helping was inherent to him. I did trust those three men, and they'd ensure the other angels fell in line.

"One thing that everyone should note." Zagan inched forward in his shadow form. He must have felt comfortable now that he knew the angels weren't actively working to kill him. "The demons won't be in a rush to end this. They enjoy tormenting others mentally, maybe more so than physically. They'll ensure they cause as much havoc as possible before they try to slaughter everyone."

Hardness coiled in my stomach. I hadn't thought of it that way. Demons had been waiting for over one thousand years to exert their revenge. They wouldn't rush to strike us down hard and fast, but rather try to drive us to insanity.

"Until a plan has been determined between the warriors and the council, we should have at least ten angels on either side of the city helping the vampires and shifters ensure the gates don't fall," said Mother. "Eleanor"—she nodded at the angel who hated me—"coordinate a schedule and make sure there is round-the-clock assistance." She looked at everyone else. "If you aren't working, you need to be training or resting. Until we attack or the gates fall, we need to be at our best."

I stared at my mother. Why had she asked Eleanor, of all people?

She's doing it to keep her preoccupied and make her feel important, Levi explained.

For a second, I wondered if I'd asked him outright, but then I realized he'd felt the change in my emotions and intuited my thoughts. The sting of betrayal eased just a little.

"Ingram, I need you to check in at both gates to see if they need anything right now." Mother pointed at him and Eleanor. "Can I trust you two to perform these jobs?"

They nodded eagerly. No doubt, they wanted to prove themselves to her since their lifeboat—Azbogah—was sinking.

"Raziel, you should go with Munkar, Ishim, and Phul to see if you can provide any insight as well, since you've been the closest to Azbogah these past hundred years," Father said kindly.

But every angel knew the truth. Father wanted the warriors to keep track of him.

"Time is of the essence." Father waved his hand. "Everyone, figure out your next steps while Yelahiah, Rosemary, Levi, and I talk with Azbogah alone."

The others obeyed, and most of the angels flew toward the hovering training facility above our section of the dome.

I turned my attention to Azbogah, uncertain about what the angel would do.

His gray eyes flickered as if he were seeking a way out of this situation. But there was no way out. He was no longer thinking strategically, but rather desperately.

"Will you come willingly, or will we have to force you?" Levi asked almost hopefully.

Azbogah jerked, and that's when I knew he was going to run.

CHAPTER SEVEN

I READIED myself to chase after him. I couldn't fathom how he thought he could get away, but desperate people rarely acted rationally.

Azbogah groaned. "I'm not going to run, Rosemary. It's not like I could get out of the city even if I wanted to."

He headed toward the high-rise, but I didn't drop my guard. Sometimes, the best strategy was to catch your enemy off guard.

Enemy.

But he wasn't. He was an angel...and, devastatingly, one of my creators. I wasn't sure I could ever accept that piece of information.

What's wrong? Levi's hand tensed in mine. *Beyond what's already wrong. You grew more upset.*

In some ways, our relationship had always existed, but I still wasn't acclimated to my emotions, let alone having someone feel them and recognize them before I did. Sometimes, like now, it unsettled me. *I'm still coming to terms with that angel being my father.* Using that word with someone else for the first time made my skin crawl.

He's not your father. Not in the ways that matter. He made it sound so simple. *Pahaliah has always been there for you, right? There to support you and stand by you?*

Yes. Which was one reason the news unsettled me so much. Heart hammering, I confessed my fear. *What if that changes?* I kept my eyes locked on Azbogah as we flew to the balcony of my parents' condo on the top floor.

Do you really think he never knew? Levi challenged. *It sounds like your mother knew who your father was, so do you think she would hide that from him? Also, he didn't seem shocked when the news dropped back at the gate. I have a feeling, Rosey, that your father—the angel who raised you— has the same concerns as you do.*

Despite my anger with Mother, his words resonated with me. Mother had withheld information from me, but could I blame her? If Azbogah had wanted nothing to do with me, why share that horrible piece of information with me? I could see the logic in it. It was similar to the reason why I hadn't told them about the portals the witches had closed—to avoid subjecting my parents to something that could affect their position in Shadow City. It wasn't exactly the same, but I had a sinking suspicion she'd hidden the truth out of protective instinct and not to deceive me.

I couldn't imagine the type of person I'd have become if Azbogah had been a parental figure in my life, especially with what he'd done in the name of vanity. *I hope you're right.*

Love, you really should start listening to me more. You don't give me nearly enough credit, he teased, and for once, there wasn't any seriousness behind his words.

Heart swelling, I took a moment to enjoy just being with *him*. Who knew how much more time we had together? *I do...now.*

It's about damn time, he shot back.

We reached our glass balcony, which was frosted so we couldn't see our neighbors below, and breezed past the four wicker lounge chairs, each large enough for an angel to sit with their wings spread out around them. When Mother reached for the handle of the sliding glass door, I couldn't shake my unease. Why hadn't Azbogah attempted to escape? I'd expected him to take off and try to find a witch to cloak him.

Mother flew into the house as Father paused and motioned for Azbogah to enter in front of him. Father had always seemed so even-tempered, like things rarely affected him, but not this time. His body was rigid, and his irises turned a shade darker as he focused on me.

If this was hard for me, I didn't want to consider how hard it was for him. The woman with whom he'd spent a millennium and helped raise a child had her former lover in our living room. Not only was Azbogah her former lover, but worse, her preordained.

I hovered near the edge of the balcony, ready for Azbogah's change in strategy. It had to be coming, or he had some other plan brewing.

When Azbogah entered my childhood home, my breathing relaxed. I'd expected a chase.

Father stayed at the door and asked Levi, "Do you mind if I have a moment with Rosemary?"

"Of course not." Levi paused, still standing close to me.

A corner of Father's mouth tipped upward. "Alone."

"Oh, *right*," Levi said, his voice rising on the last word. "Alone. That makes sense." He loosened his hold on me, and the urge to clutch him nearly overtook me.

At one point, I would have hated to admit that I felt better when he was beside me. However, I was done pretending that our bond didn't make us stronger. The only reason I didn't cling to Levi was because Pahaliah was my father, and we needed to talk. *Don't go far, please.*

I'll be right on the other side of the glass. His shadow face inched toward my cheek. His lips touched mine, and my skin sparked with electricity. *All you have to do is ask, and if you become distressed, I'll be here in seconds.*

Pretty sure I'm already panicking. I exhaled, my hands shaking slightly. I'd never felt anything like this before, but for the first time in my life, I was unsure—unsure of what Father wanted to say—but avoiding it was pointless. He deserved a chance to talk with me, especially if he'd taken me when he'd never *had* to.

Levi ran a hand down my arm and linked, *I promise you, Rosey. You have nothing to worry about. I wouldn't step through those doors if I thought he might hurt you.*

I wasn't thinking clearly, and that wasn't a good look on me. Father was important to me. Even before I'd begun to feel all these emotions, in some ways, he'd been my rock, more so than Mother. Mother and I were too similar at times and clashed despite caring for each other, but Father had always been there for both of us. I dipped my chin, and Levi floated to the frosted balcony floor and changed into his human form.

High heels clacked on the glass floor inside, drawing closer to the door, and Mother appeared at the doorway. "Are you three coming in?"

"I need a minute." Father lifted a brow.

Mother exhaled and fluttered her wings. "We don't have time—"

Father crossed his arms, but his tone softened lovingly. "Understood, but I'm making time to talk to my *daughter*. We won't be long."

He rarely stood his ground with her, and that was when the truth slammed into me. He was in love with her and truly thought of me as his child. Moisture burned my eyes, and I blinked, holding back the tears. I didn't want to cry, especially with demons watching overhead.

"Come on, Mom," Levi said as he looped his arm through my mother's. "Let's keep an eye on Assy."

Mother's mouth dropped, but she was too stunned to move away. Rather, she stuttered, "It's *Azzy*."

"Sounds the same to me." He pulled her inside and shut the door.

I couldn't help but chuckle.

"It's nice to see you smile." Father sighed.

I pulled my attention to him. "Meeting Levi changed everything."

His forehead wrinkled, and he kept his hands at his sides. "I'm glad. I always worried you wouldn't find someone to love. That no angel ever would again. But it sounds as if times may be changing, and they need to. I hated that Azbogah, Yelahiah, and I were the only ones who could still feel...at least, your mother felt more than the others."

"What do you mean?" If she'd lost her capacity to feel, she wouldn't have held such maliciousness toward Azbogah, and she wouldn't have kept that picture of the two of them. I'd wondered why she'd kept it. However, I didn't want to bring it up and risk hurting my father with that knowledge.

"She did change a lot, but I think Azbogah's betrayal prevented her from letting go of all her emotions." Father blew out a breath. "I'm less certain now that I know spells were involved. Maybe her unique level of feelings had to do with Azbogah being her preordained. Either way, she didn't completely lose her humanity. I was both relieved and upset at the same time because the emotions she held on to were mostly negative."

That I could see. "It might have been more about her guilt over her brother's death." I could only imagine what feeling responsible for that would do to a person, angel or not.

"Maybe. I believe I kept most of my emotions because of my closeness to humanity. And Azbogah, well...he was too miserable to look at..." He frowned. "Anyway, it doesn't matter."

Somehow, his reticence hurt even more. "If Azbogah didn't lose his emotions, why wouldn't he want me?"

Father hung his head, and my chest constricted. I'd hurt him, and that was one of the last things I'd ever want to do. "I didn't mean that the way it sounded," I hastily added. "You have done and given up so much for me. More than I've ever realized. But I know how much angels covet having a child."

He straightened and focused back on me. "You said nothing wrong, and I can't answer that for him, but Rosemary, I need you to know you will always be my daughter. This changes *nothing* on my side, and I can only pray to Fate you feel the same way."

We'd both been terrified of the same thing. "I do feel the same way. *You* are the one who raised me, and you were there for me every time I needed you." I treasured the memories of us playing chase when I was a young featherling and the way he had looked so proud at my warrior graduation. "Nothing will ever change what you are to me."

His shoulders relaxed. "I'm so glad to hear you say that. I was afraid—" He waved off the sentiment. "That doesn't matter. The fact that we will always have each other means more than Heaven to me."

He was a true father, unlike Azbogah, who'd given me up, which I still didn't understand.

Without thinking my actions through, I landed in front of Father and hugged him. I'd never instigated a gesture like this...at least, not in the past seven hundred years.

His body stiffened. Maybe this was too much, even for him. But as I readied myself to pull away, he returned my embrace with vigor. His arms wrapped around me so tightly that if I'd been any other sort of supernatural, I'd have been crushed in an instant. However, the gesture felt nice instead of awkward, and warmth exploded within me.

I told you everything would be okay, Levi linked. *Listen to your baby. He always knows.*

There's no way in Heaven I'm calling you 'baby.' That was a term used for infants, and that was *not* how I wanted to think about him. *I could call you 'sweet bottom.'* I did enjoy staring at his butt.

Please don't. Humor wafted through the bond. *How about 'beast'?*

You don't get to choose your nickname. After all, I told you I didn't like Rosey. Granted, it had grown on me. *And your bottom is one of my favorite parts about you.*

Then I guess I can't complain, though I'd rather you used 'buns of steel' or something like that. His happiness wafted through the bond, and I enjoyed the moment of tranquility.

Father released me and pursed his lips. "We should probably get inside. I just wanted you to know..."

"I love you, too." The words came naturally. It had just taken Levi and demons breaking free from Hell to make me realize it, and I wanted him to *know* in case I didn't have another chance to say those words.

His irises lightened back to the sky blue I was most familiar with. "And I love you, little featherling."

A month ago, that term would've bothered me. I was a skilled warrior and a thousand years old. But he didn't mean it as an insult, and a smile sneaked across my face.

Not wanting to ruin the moment, I hurried to the door and opened it. As we entered the living room, I found Mother standing between the two dark charcoal couches that almost matched my wings, facing Azbogah, who sat on the right side. She placed a hand on her chest. "The three items you took from the artifact building were my ring of justice, the key to Hell, and a ruby."

Levi stepped away from the wall, moving to stand beside me.

"In fairness, *I* didn't take them." Azbogah leaned back in the seat with a smug expression. He enjoyed the control he had over the situation, even though he was on the losing end.

"We don't have time for your games." I despised the way he was acting. "We get it. You're a great con artist, but your time has run out. You need to stop pretending we're at a council meeting and tell the truth, or your arrogance will get every last one of us killed."

Levi tilted his head as he examined the dark angel. *Please don't get mad at me.*

Before I could ask what he meant, he said, "Or maybe you don't care that Rosemary will be one of the first angels they seek to kill, especially since most suspect she's your spawn."

I clenched my hands, ready to punch him, when Azbogah's expression fell.

No. There was no way *that* could've gotten through to Azbogah.

The dark angel stiffened and glanced at Mother. "My goal was to make it look as if you wanted to merge the worlds."

Bile inched up my throat.

"You were going to set me up for taking the items *and* attempting to free the demons, too?" Mother blinked. "Why would you do that to me?"

Azbogah's feathers ruffled. "It wasn't personal. It was business." However, his voice had lost its gusto. "You were the only reason the rest of the angels weren't falling in line. I needed to eliminate the barrier."

"Like you needed to kill *my brother*?" she spat, the pain sounding fresh.

This was another huge betrayal. Though he hadn't attempted to kill her like he'd killed Ophaniel, he had set her up for a life spent in prison alone. However, that wasn't what we needed to address now, and I needed to keep my mother as grounded as possible.

"How were you going to make that information common knowledge?" I asked. There was a piece missing— something just out of my mind's reach.

Then it hit me like a bolt of lightning.

Jegudiel—Azbogah's former best friend who was put into solitary confinement five hundred years ago for attempting to break into the artifact building.

"Did you jail Jegudiel because he learned the truth?" Maybe Azbogah had set him up the way he'd planned to frame Mother.

Pride reflected in Azbogah's eyes. "I always knew you were smarter than the other angels."

I hated the way his words made me feel special. I wanted to fluff my feathers at his praise, but I pushed the uncomfortable sensation away.

Not now.

Not ever.

Levi held my hand, anchoring me the way only he could.

Azbogah shrugged as if it were no big deal. "One of the witches was quite smitten with him and shared the truth about what had happened to the fallen archangels. He threatened to expose me, so I handled the threat."

I hadn't thought of that. Even higher-ranking witches alive today would know about the spell from over one thousand years ago that had created the demons, caused the loss of preordained mates, and eventually trapped the demons in Hell. Though the demons had seen only one witch, a spell that powerful would have required a large coven. They must have used some sort of charm or runes to channel the power to the one witch so they wouldn't all be in view. "He was going to tell everyone the truth," I murmured.

"And I couldn't risk that." Azbogah frowned. "I did what was necessary to keep my plan in place."

"But after everything that happened, how could you remain convinced that you had done what was right?" That was the part I didn't understand. He had to see that the more he schemed, the more Fate intervened.

His eyes glistened as he answered quietly, "Because losing everything had to be worth something. I couldn't just throw away my plan after sacrificing so much."

A faint pain throbbed in my temples. Every time he spoke, he created another riddle that needed to be solved.

"Stop it," Mother rasped as she rubbed her head in the same spot that ailed me. "For Heaven's sake, and for once in your life, speak the truth. Or have you forgotten how to do that?"

"Yelahiah," Father murmured as he walked to her, each

step louder than the last. When he reached her, he pulled her into his arms. "This won't accomplish anything."

"Why don't you stay out of it?" Azbogah stood. "This doesn't involve you."

It reminded me of how Killian and Levi had acted around me at first, which Sierra had insisted was because both men were interested in me. Did Azbogah still have feelings for my mother?

"Like feathers it doesn't!" Father exclaimed as he moved Mother behind him. "You can't just come in here and expect forgiveness. *You* made all of those decisions."

"I didn't know the *price* until it was too late." Azbogah's face reddened. "The witch told me there would be a cost, but I thought *I* would be the one to pay it. Perhaps I wouldn't remain immortal, or I'd lose my feathers. I didn't know the cost would be the woman I loved and the one person who balanced me and kept the darkness inside me in check. When our bond was severed, I could still feel love for her, but the connection was gone. It consumed me."

Levi shook his head. "You've got some nerve. You caused all of this and had innocent people thrown into Hell where their anger controlled them. Then children were born and raised in that toxic environment where being selfish was celebrated and cruelty was encouraged. I won't feel sorry for you."

He never spoke of his life in Hell, and I'd never asked, mainly for this reason. I could only imagine the things he'd seen, especially seeing as he, Bune, and Zagan never flinched when the innocent were killed in front of them. Yet they were still choosing the best path they could.

"Don't you *dare* tell me about the darkness consuming you and that you had no barrier. Don't pretend you're the only person who experienced hardships." Levi held out his arms. "We all have because of you."

Heart fracturing, I realized Hell was worse than I could comprehend. All I could do now was make Levi's life as joyful as I could in the time we had. "Azbogah, you made horrible decisions, and you spiraled. No one is to blame but you." Arguing was futile and a waste of energy. "But none of that matters. You mentioned the ring and the ruby. Why did you choose those two?" We all understood why he'd taken the key.

"Because your mother's ring of justice sparks flames against the unjust, and the ruby amplifies the energy," Azbogah answered robotically. "She was going to use the ring to fight for the demons and amplify her power to rule over all."

"No one would've believed that. That's *you*, not her," I said. He had to see that his plan was asinine.

"Not if the evidence couldn't be disputed." He stretched his wings.

And that had been his plan all along: Make it so the angels would have no choice but to believe him.

"I've heard enough." Mother spun on her heels and marched toward the door. "I'm going to check on things and make sure Eleanor and Ingram are following through on their word."

Father kept his gaze on Azbogah.

There was no way I was leaving these two alone.

I wondered if I could get something out of Azbogah if they left me alone with him. *Will you ask Father to go with you to the kitchen to get something to eat or drink to give me time with Azbogah?*

Are you sure? Levi asked.

I nodded and followed Levi's lead from earlier. *You*

brought up that I'm his child, and his demeanor changed. I was thinking that maybe... I trailed off. Either I was being foolish, or it was wishful thinking.

It's a good idea, but I won't be gone long. Levi released my hand and walked to Father. "Will you help me figure out how a glass kitchen works?"

Father shook his head, but when he glanced at me, I mouthed the word *please*.

"It's not much different from what I assume Hell's is like," Father said as he clapped Levi's shoulder.

I watched them go into the kitchen on the left. Then I turned to Azbogah.

The dark angel tilted his head but remained quiet like he was waiting for the question.

My heart pounded. It shouldn't matter, but for some reason, I needed to know. I just wasn't sure if the answer would give me peace or hurt me further.

"Why didn't you want me?"

CHAPTER EIGHT

EVERY SECOND HE waited to answer, my heart raced faster. I was foolish to allow him to have any influence over me, but I needed to understand why. With the demons set on killing him, this might be my only chance to find out.

"It's not a good answer." His voice had grown deeper than normal.

"I don't expect it to be." I grimaced. Being blunt was ingrained in me, and it would take more than a month for me to change a lifelong habit.

He smirked. "I've always appreciated that about you."

"That's not an answer." I didn't want compliments or any other tactic to delay him from ending the mystery. "I want the truth. Please spare me the theatrics, and tell me... while you still can."

"That's fair, especially with Eleanor dropping the information like she did. She wanted to see you hurt, and though you didn't fall into her trap, I realize it must have unsettled you. It unsettles us all."

Unsettled. That was the word he'd chosen to describe this situation? I bit my bottom lip, hoping to prevent myself from saying something that would keep him from continuing.

A squeak sounded from the kitchen, reminding us that we wouldn't be alone for long.

"I've made mistakes, Rosemary." Azbogah sat on the couch and ran his hands through his hair, ruining the perfect spikes. "Heaven only knows I have. If I'd known the cost, I wouldn't have made the same decisions."

If he was seeking absolution from me, he'd be sorely disappointed. "Everyone has to face the consequences of their decisions, both good and bad."

A sad smile slipped onto his face. "You sound just like your mother."

I wasn't sure what the appropriate response was, and for a moment, I felt like the awkward Rosemary from not too long ago.

"And that's why I decided not to raise you, even though you were the very thing I coveted most in this world." He held out a hand as if that explained everything.

My brain churned, trying to decipher what had happened. I prided myself on my intelligence, and I could normally pull out the hidden message in anyone's story, but in this instance—possibly because I was so emotionally invested—I couldn't glean what he meant. "I'm not following. You wish you'd made different decisions...and that's why you chose not to raise me?"

"Exactly." He steepled his fingers. "I made such horrible decisions and betrayed your mother and my people in the worst way imaginable. I couldn't do that to you as well."

"*Betray* me?" I snorted, the sensation more peculiar than laughter. "Some might call giving me up before I was born exactly that."

"Is that the word people use for individuals who decide to give up their infant for adoption because they can't provide adequate support, whether it be emotional or physical?" Azbogah swooped out a hand as he leaned toward me once again.

My breath caught. He had a point. "But this is different..." I wasn't sure it was.

"Because we're angels?" He arched his brow. "Haven't you said that just because we're angels doesn't mean we're superior to anyone else?"

I didn't like him tossing my words back at me. It was hard to swallow. "But you're selfish. If you'd wanted me, you wouldn't have given me up."

"Giving you up was my *only* selfless act." He ran a hand down his face. "Rosemary, didn't you notice that even though I try to keep my distance, I still single you out at times? When you were a featherling, I'd come to watch you train, sometimes under the ruse that I was there to ensure the warriors were doing a fine job. I had no doubt Munkar, Phul, and Ishim were the best and wouldn't fail me."

He had. I remembered hating it when he came because I'd always felt his gaze on me.

"And at your warrior graduation, I told you I was proud of you." His eyes turned back to their normal stormy gray. "Then I wanted you to observe the council meetings because I wanted you to see everything I'd done."

That sounded more like the Azbogah we all knew. "To see how you set up Ezra and Dick Harding to do your dirty work? How you were trying to undermine Sterlyn because she's a blasphemous silver wolf? And how you tried to have Ronnie *killed* by finding the demon Andras to be her *father*?"

"I didn't realize he was her father at the time, but she

was siding with Sterlyn to open the gates more. And I wanted Sterlyn gone because her presence reminded Yelahiah of what I'd done to her and her brother all those years ago." He rubbed his hands together. "I didn't want the angels to leave the city for fear it would start *this*. And that was why Ezra was taking Annie back to the demon wolves —I didn't want an angel to leave and cause a war we weren't prepared to fight. She was promised to a prince of Hell, and I didn't want them finding her here with us."

"Don't act as if you did all that for good reasons. All you did was try to keep what you'd done hidden. It all comes back to *you* wanting the angels to rule over everything with you as their leader." He didn't get to skew the truth.

He sneered. "Then little one, what should I have done?"

"Admitted your mistake as soon as you realized the cost. Maybe *all* this"—I spread out my arms—"could have been prevented."

"And lose everyone's respect? How does that make sense?" His voice rose. "How would that have fixed anything?"

That was what made him different from Mother, Father, Sterlyn, me, and all my friends and allies. He was too proud. Maybe Lucifer wasn't the one with that fatal flaw. "Because, most often, doing the right thing is the harder path. That's why those who take it are some of the strongest people in the world. You wanted everyone to see how strong you were, but all you've done is prove how weak and pathetic you are."

A strange expression flitted across his face. He glanced around the room as if searching for something, and for once, my words might have made an impact on him. I'd been honest, brutally so, but Azbogah had *needed* to hear this. He had a vision of himself, but his perception had been distorted by his own insecurities.

There was no point in continuing to talk now that we understood where the other person stood. However, there was one last thing I wanted him to know. "For what it's worth, I do believe you," I murmured.

His head snapped up, likely due to my tone, and he narrowed his eyes. "About what?"

"That you distanced yourself from me to save me from your darkness." I needed to let him know that I understood.

Scratching the back of his neck, he averted his gaze to the frosted glass floor. "And you forgive me?"

I wished he hadn't asked that. I was trying to have one nice moment with him where we weren't at odds. Clearly, he wouldn't allow that. "No, I don't. I believe you, but the problem is you should've owned up to your mistakes. If you had, then you wouldn't be here, seeking my forgiveness."

He pursed his lips. "That's what I figured you'd say. You *are* just like her."

Father and Levi reentered the room. Levi held two glasses of water and handed one to me.

"If by *that* you mean they're both strong women who always make the right decision, then I agree with you." Father crossed his arms as he stood at the end of the couch across from Azbogah. "They have an uncanny way of seeing right and wrong, not only in others but in themselves. They both strive to be a better version of themselves, especially when they make mistakes. The one thing Rosemary can do better than her mother and me is to see the bigger picture and not hesitate to align with those who share her vision, even when our own people don't understand."

My hand tightened on my glass. I took a deep breath, moved by what Father had said. I'd always felt inadequate compared to him and Mother in different ways, and his words meant more to me than he'd ever know.

Levi's love wafted through our bond. "Rosemary is loyal and will put her life at risk to save anyone she loves. I've never met anyone so willing to sacrifice themselves without a moment's hesitation to do what is right. Most people draw a line when their own health is at risk, but not her."

A lump formed in my throat, and I tried to swallow it. The last thing I wanted to do was cry in front of everyone.

As Azbogah opened his mouth, the sound of approaching angel wings infiltrated the room.

I spun to see Munkar, Bune, and Zagan flying toward us. Though I couldn't make out the expressions on the two in demon form, Munkar's tight mouth spoke volumes.

There was nothing good about our predicament.

Munkar reached the door and slid it open as the two demons changed back into their human form. The three of them entered, but Zagan paused. "Is everything in here glass?" His head turned toward the kitchen with its round glass table, the legs in the shape of angel wings, and all-glass cabinets and fixtures. "It's a little insane."

After getting to know other supernatural races, I'd realized they were more attuned to the styles of the mortal outside world with wooden tables and chairs and carpet or wood floors. Angels were the anomaly. "It's because we're partial to the lights of Heaven." I gestured outside, but demons hovering over the dome were blocking the usual iridescent swirls. "We frost our doors, floors, and walls for privacy or clear them so the lights can wash over us."

That was how angels recharged the quickest and most naturally, and one reason, I suspected, that we'd closed the city—so the lights could dance around us at all times. Even at night, their colors swirled, though not as vibrantly as they did in daylight.

"I hate to interrupt the history lesson, but we need to discuss a concerning matter," Munkar interjected. He glanced uncomfortably at Azbogah. "Whenever we're able."

"Let me text Yelahiah," Father said as he removed his phone from his back pocket and typed out a message.

Since we had a moment, I asked, "How are the vampires, wolves, and witches?"

"They're okay—which is part of the problem," Bune answered.

Do you have any idea what he means? I didn't want to keep questioning them since they were waiting on Mother... and because Azbogah was sitting here. But at least I knew our friends were safe.

Levi wrapped an arm around my waist and answered, *No clue, love. Sorry. But you need to stay hydrated.* He tapped the glass he'd handed me.

He was right. During a battle, we would exert a lot of energy. Not only did we need to drink, but we needed to eat as well. Although considering how my stomach was feeling, drinking was currently the best bet. I took a sip of water, and the cool liquid brushed past my sore throat. I hadn't realized how thirsty I was. Though angels couldn't die of starvation or lack of fluids, we still operated best if we had enough of both.

We stood in silence for a few minutes, and just as Zagan began to bounce on the balls of his feet, Mother came back into the house. The woman who returned was the mother I'd always known. She was put together, and her emerald eyes sparkled with determination. "What's going on?"

"Do we want to speak with *him* here?" Munkar asked, pointing at Azbogah. "He's the traitor who started all this."

"Unfortunately, he might have details that no one else knows." Mother's jaw muscle twitched. "There's no point in withholding information from anyone in this city. We should never have done it to begin with. In fact, we should be more like Rosemary and her friends."

I held my head high, trying to remain humble but not wanting to take away from my or the others' accomplishments. Instead of harsh criticism, our camaraderie might finally be getting the attention it deserved.

"Very well." Munkar moved a few steps to the left, standing between Bune and Pahaliah. The warrior rubbed his fingertips together. "We expected the demons to continue their assault, but that hasn't happened, despite the deaths of the two humans. The demons are still surrounding the city, but they aren't attacking as we'd hoped."

"Hoped?" Azbogah laughed. "Why would we want that? They clearly realized they can't win against us." He straightened his shoulders.

"That's not even close to what he means." Bune rolled his eyes. "I'd hoped they'd let their rage take over. They expected to attack and get inside before we could prepare. Even though we"—he motioned to Levi, me, Zagan, and himself—"got here only a few minutes before the demons, it was enough to get people moving."

I hadn't considered that. Breena had reinforced the city's protective spell faster than she might have otherwise.

Munkar pulled his wings close to his body. "Erin spoke to us for a moment on the vampire side. The first round of demons were under a spell that, if our witches hadn't begun their spells quickly, could have allowed the demons to stampede through our barrier."

"So they're conserving their energy," That wasn't ideal. I'd wanted them to expend their energy so that when we finally attacked, they'd be tired and their greater numbers wouldn't have such an impact.

"Exactly." Munkar frowned. "We believe they're making a new plan to get inside or will wait until we get tired of them watching us and confront them."

A shiver ran down my spine. I didn't like the sound of that. "Or until the vampires run out of food."

If the vampires didn't get blood, they would become desperate. Though that had never happened, and they didn't enjoy drinking from other supernaturals, food was food.

We were running out of time. The other supernaturals just didn't realize it yet.

"What do we do?" Zagan asked worriedly.

That was the question. "We've discovered a way for the other supernaturals to see the demons, but the people who know the spell are outside the city," I replied.

"What do you mean?" Mother stopped pacing between the two couches and stared at me.

Levi interjected, "When I went back to Hell to retrieve my mother's sword, we also saved a witch who was trapped down there."

"Yes, I heard that the witches who were trying to prevent Rosemary from escaping the city saw the demon sword," Azbogah snarled. "I wonder why it wasn't listed as missing in the fox shifter's inventory list."

Of course he'd hone in on Kira. I could understand being angry that the sword had been stolen and taken to Hell. "It's back in the city, so it's no longer missing. Levi bonded with it so the princes of Hell can't use it."

"Though that *never* should have happened, that's beside the point," Mother said, redirecting the conversation.

"Tell us about this spell. Is it something Erin and her coven can cast?"

I didn't want to answer that, but we might not have a choice. The question was whether Eliza would be willing to pass it on. "I think they could, but I have to make sure our friends will share it with them."

"Why wouldn't they?" Father walked across the room to face Azbogah and placed his hands on the back of the couch.

Here was yet another thing that Azbogah had impacted. "Because the witches who are our friends were supposed to be the witches *inside* the city. Instead, Erin's coven performed the spell for Azbogah and was let inside in their place."

Azbogah cringed. At least he had the decency to be ashamed over everything he'd caused. The arrogant angel who had been there moments ago vanished.

I removed my phone from my back pocket and texted Ronnie, Annie, and Sterlyn: Do you think Eliza would share the demon-vision spell with the Nightshadow coven?

I wouldn't blame Eliza and Circe if they wouldn't— Erin's coven had done horrible things to them.

My phone buzzed, and a message from Annie flashed across: Cyrus will talk to Circe and Eliza. He's with them and Killian, assisting in getting the humans out of the city. I'll let you know.

"Someone is going to ask the witches." I purposely left out who. The less Azbogah knew, the better. We might be including him in our plans, but that didn't mean I'd hand him every detail so he could take the credit. "I'll let you know when a decision is made, but right now, the witches are helping Killian and the others evacuate the humans."

"I'm not happy with that decision, but several humans

have already escaped." Munkar pursed his lips. "So I guess it doesn't really matter."

My phone buzzed again, startling me. I hadn't expected anyone to text me back so quickly.

Annie's message flashed: They will. Balance is more important than personal grudges.

I smiled and exhaled. That was one reason I respected their coven so much.

They sent the words to the chant, and I glanced at Levi. "We need to find Erin. They gave us the spell."

"You two go to the shifter side. That's where she is. We'll stay here and keep an eye on *him*," Bune said as he glared at Azbogah.

Levi flashed into demon form, and the two of us hurried away.

Soon, we were in the sky, heading toward the witch priestess. I realized I hadn't even asked if he was okay with the plan, so I linked to him, *If you aren't comfortable giving blood to them—*

I'm not, but we don't have a choice. We need every capable fighter to be able to see the demons, and if Eliza is stuck outside, that means they can't help anyone in here.

Things progressively continued to worsen. *I'm sorry.*

You have nothing to apologize for. Right now, we focus on what we can control and deal with the consequences later. He groaned. *If we don't give the Nightshadow Sisters our blood and the demons get in and kill everyone, we'll have to live with that choice. Let's do our best with the information on hand and hope that Fate will protect us.*

I wasn't so sure I trusted the Divine Plan. At least, not lately.

As long as we're together and you're by my side, I can deal with whatever shit gets thrown our way. He took my hand and squeezed. *I love you and want to have a family with you. I'll do whatever it takes to make sure that reality comes true.*

My chest warmed, and my love for him multiplied.

When we reached the shifter gate, Griffin and Ronnie were already talking with Erin. The priestess's smile was wide, her blood-red lips contrasting against her stark white teeth.

She turned to me and ran a hand through her black and scarlet hair. "I hear you have a spell for me."

I hovered in the air, not wanting to get close. "We'll need to go somewhere private to provide one of your ingredients."

"Oh." She arched a brow and glanced at Breena. "I'll be right back. Are you okay here alone?"

"We'll be fine." Breena kept her attention on the gate.

With eagerness, Erin spun and sashayed toward the rest of the coven. We followed her toward the woods. The witches lived on the other side of the forest, across from the angels.

We'll be there soon. I've been told it's through the woods, I linked. I'd never visited the witches' section and had no desire to do so now.

When we reached the woods, two witches stood waiting. They had black bowls like Eliza and Circe, but the maliciousness emanating from their souls attacked me. My knees shook.

"So, from what Griffin and Ronnie told me, we need your blood." Erin motioned to the bowls, and the man and woman stepped forward eagerly.

A warning siren rang in my head. I didn't want to do this.

But we didn't have a choice...did we?

CHAPTER NINE

ALARM SWIRLED THROUGH ME, making my hair
stand on end. Everything inside me screamed not to do this,
but I wasn't sure what other option we had. Either Levi and
I offered up our blood to give most of the residents in the
city a chance at protecting themselves, or we lived with the
knowledge that we might have been able to save hundreds,
if not thousands, of lives and didn't.

When put that way, there wasn't a choice...not for me.
But I refused to force Levi into something he didn't want to
do. That could destroy not only our relationship but maybe
the entire spell as well. Being around Eliza's coven, I'd
learned that for a spell to be performed as intended, all
parties had to be willing. *If you don't want to do this—*

Levi interjected, *What I want is irrelevant. This has to
be done. You can't tell me you're comfortable with it.*

No. I'd be forthright with him. Always. *I do not trust
these witches.*

*But like you, there's no way I can stand by and let your
friends and family die...no, our friends and family. My father
and Zagan are at as much risk.* He edged in front of me,

flickering back into his human form, as if he could prevent something horrible from happening to me. *I'd rather take my chances and deal with the consequences because that would mean we're both alive.*

"Ahh, there he is," the female witch cooed.

The two witches stepped closer. The female stood in front of me, wearing a smug smile across her nude lips. Pieces of her wavy penny-colored hair fell in front of her shoulders, the tips reaching midway down her arm. She was about Annie's height, so around five and a half feet, with her olive eyes locked on me. If she hadn't smelled of herbs, I could have easily mistaken her for a vampire because of her very pale skin.

The male witch nodded toward the bowl, and his sand-colored irises narrowed. His creamy skin was stretched over his cheekbones, making him look unhealthy, and dark circles lined his eyes. He was a few inches shorter than me and very thin.

"Here, you can use my knife." Erin's misty gray eyes lightened as she handed me the implement. The black handle matched the color of her fingernails.

There was no telling what she'd used that knife on. That blade would *definitely* not be pricking my body, even though I was immune to diseases. "No, we're good." You'd think with how close her coven was to Azbogah, she'd realize I would use my feathers. Unless he paid attention to her only when he needed her, which sounded in character for him.

"Suit yourself," Erin huffed. She flipped her wrist and chanted, "*Absconde nos ab intuitu.*"

I stiffened, unsure what she'd done.

She rolled her eyes, her heavy mascara making the gesture seem more dramatic than when Sierra did it.

Though Erin was at least nine hundred fifty years younger than me, the faint crow's feet that lined the corners of her eyes made her appear older. But she was a mortal, after all.

Erin snickered condescendingly. "I hid us so the demons can't see what we're doing."

Her words struck a chord, but I could address that later. Right now, Levi and I needed to get this task accomplished so we could get back to the others.

"Do you vow to use the blood only for this spell?" Levi interjected, and his trepidation would have been palpable even without our connection.

Erin scoffed. "Absolutely not. We might be able to determine other effective spells that we can cast with your blood. I will not limit what we can do if it can further protect the city."

She had a point, but I believed there was more to why she didn't want to make that vow. However, our hands were tied. *We don't—*

Let's just get this over with, Levi replied.

I wrapped my wing around Levi and flipped my feathers to the razor-sharp side. With my other wing, I cut my wrist, and Levi followed suit.

"Pour your blood in this one." The girl smiled at me. "And he can use the other bowl. That way, we can ensure we mix equal amounts."

Wanting to get this over with, I held my wrist over the bowl. The metallic scent of Levi's blood and mine thickened as we worked to fill the two large bowls. I wasn't sure if this spell would be enough to impact everyone in the city, but the dome would limit the space so the spell could stretch. Outside, Eliza's coven had to account for wind, weather, and whatever natural ailments would affect the reach of the spell, making it weaker and not as long-lasting. I didn't want to give them too much blood and have them use it for other spells.

I'd expected Erin to leave now that we were with the other two witches, but the priestess stayed, likely to keep up her cloaking spell.

The three witches didn't talk. When the bowls were halfway full, my patience began to run thin, so I cut my other inner arm, increasing the flow. I could heal Levi and myself, so we weren't at risk of bleeding to death.

The longer we stayed close to the witches' homes, the more sludge coated my skin. Though these witches didn't feel as malicious as demons, they weren't good people.

Just as my head started to spin, the female witch pulled the full bowl away. "There. We're good."

Fatigue hit me, and I quickly tapped into my core to heal myself. I didn't need to lose any extra blood and allow myself to become vulnerable.

Once my injuries had healed, I turned toward Levi, my hands glowing white. I covered his wrist and poured magic into him. Though he required more energy to heal, our bond provided me with extra power from him when needed. As my warm power poured into him, his cool essence responded. The two sensations complemented each other, and my soul felt complete.

Once the skin on his wound had closed, I looked at Erin. Her eyes were locked on me. A chill slipped down my spine, but I refused to move. I didn't want her to realize she'd gotten a reaction. "Is something wrong?"

She shook her head. "I've just never seen an angel heal before."

The fact that my people could heal wasn't a secret in the city, but the way Erin had watched indicated more than curiosity. My head still spun slightly, though it wasn't anything I couldn't handle.

"Is there anything else you need from us? Won't that blood congeal if you don't store it properly?" Levi asked as he took my hand. "Because if we're done here, Rosemary and I have plenty to do."

Erin kept her hand turned upright. "Witches cast a spell on the blood to prevent it from congealing, so no worries, and I'll keep them cloaked until we get the blood into the compound house so we can go over the spell. I don't want the demons to realize we have something more strategic in our midst than what they know."

Despite not liking the priestess, I admitted she was cunning. I'd always suspected that Erin had something to do with the death of her sister, the priestess before her. She'd perished suddenly a few months prior to the death of Atticus, Griffin's father, the former alpha shifter of Shadow City. Erin's sister had been one of the few from their coven to have a good soul, and she'd aligned with Atticus in opening the city gates to integrate into the world. Erin had taken her position as priestess on the day of her sister's death and had never seemed to mourn.

Sometimes, mortals forgot that angels lived forever, and we'd been around to watch Erin and her sister grow up together. They'd never gotten along, similar to how Diana and Breena were at sisterly odds. And it didn't help that both sisters had been left to their aunt, Erin, to raise, adding to their turmoil. History tended to repeat itself.

But none of that mattered. It might later...if we survived.

Come on. Levi tugged my hand as he flickered into his demon form. *Let's go back to your parents' place.*

The two of us took to the sky, racing toward the high-rise. I feared what Azbogah had done while I was gone, and I could only pray he hadn't tried to pit the angels against one another again. We didn't have time to be split into factions—the entire city needed to be united.

When the edge of the angel section came into view, Levi said, *I'm glad to get away from the witches. They're almost worse than the ones in Hell.*

That wasn't surprising, seeing as these witches were descended from the ones who had created Hell.

The high-rise came into view. To the right, a few angels were training with Munkar, Phul, and Ishim. Red demon eyes watched from above, taking in everything they were working on.

When we landed on the balcony, Levi flickered back into human form. We entered the house and found Mother and Father sitting on one couch with Azbogah on the other, flanked by Zagan and Bune. They weren't leaving him unattended, which was good. Azbogah had an uncanny ability to find redemption in the eyes of angels, and we didn't need his influence to cause more problems than it already did.

Standing, Mother crossed her arms as she acknowledged us. "Is everything settled?"

I nodded. "The witches have everything they need to perform the spell."

Rubbing a hand down his face, Bune groaned. "Are you sure giving your blood to the coven was the right call?"

"What?" Mother's face went slack and turned a shade paler.

"You gave *Erin* your *blood*?" Azbogah croaked, his composure slipping into horror.

The world rotated faster. Out of everyone here, Azbogah's reaction unsettled me the most. I'd seen the dark angel proud, manipulative, and angry, but never terrified.

Levi's arm brushed mine, and he said, "I'm pretty sure Rosemary left that part of the spell out of the conversation for a reason."

"Oh, I'm sure she *did*," Mother gasped, and marched toward me.

"Yelahiah," Father said as he grabbed her hand. "Calm down."

"Do *not* tell me to *calm down*," Mother spat, and jerked her hand away.

I'm not nearly as old as him, and I know better than that. Levi laughed but covered it up with a cough. He pounded his chest as if that would make his action more believable.

This entire situation was horrible, yet I found myself on the verge of laughter. *Clearly, since your acting skills are subpar.*

But my bedroom skills aren't, he flirted.

I had to calm my hormones and head and keep the conversation on track. "Mother, what choice did Levi and I have? The spell requires our blood. It was either give it to Erin so when the city inevitably has to open the gates, everyone has a fighting chance against the demons, or let everyone die."

She stilled, though her breathing remained ragged.

"Believe me, it was hard to allow—" Levi's eyes widened, and he cleared his throat. "I mean, it was hard not to argue with her about giving the N—er—coven our blood."

I glared at him. Eliza had told us that knowing a coven's name held some sort of power. We needed to keep that knowledge to ourselves. *You almost made a worse mistake than Father.* He'd managed to save himself...barely. In fairness, he was trying, and that counted for something. "And I wasn't thrilled about either of us having to do it. There are no right choices, just the horrible ones that we can live with."

But see, I self-corrected. His pride filled our bond.

For some reason, I found it endearing. He was working at making our relationship healthy—we both were.

Azbogah clenched his hands. "This is how you get into trouble—thinking about *other* people."

"No." I wouldn't allow him to manipulate this situation. "I wouldn't be in *this* situation if someone hadn't been determined to prove he was as strong as an archangel."

His shoulders sagged as if I'd knocked the air out of his lungs.

I *almost* felt bad for calling him out on it.

"Little one," Azbogah rasped, "angel blood was used in the original spell that severed preordained bonds. I'd hate—"

The sad truth was that he hadn't realized he was twisting the truth to benefit himself. "This conversation is a waste of energy. The Night—Erin's coven already has our blood. The decision was made, and there's no going back. We need to focus on the active threat, which involves the demons watching us train as we speak."

"So you know the coven's name." Zagan pumped a fist.

Father's brows furrowed. "How did you learn Erin's coven's name?"

"From Eliza." I realized I didn't know Eliza's coven's name. Not that I needed to, but I found that interesting. From what I could tell, a coven's name was a personal and sacred matter, and here we were, throwing Erin's coven name around as if it were nothing. "She knew the coven that had ousted them from the city."

However, Azbogah definitely didn't need that knowledge.

"So what is it?" Azbogah glanced down at his hands nonchalantly.

"Nothing you'll ever learn." I wouldn't play games with him. "But we could use your influence on Erin."

"How so?" He climbed to his feet and moved toward me.

I could see his mind spinning, determining all the various ways he could get something in return. I hated that I had to bargain with him, but he had influence over Erin when no one else did. "I want you to ask her to cloak the city, or at least the angel area, so the demons can't watch us train everyone."

Father turned to me. "What do you mean, train *everyone*?"

I filled them in on the integration of the silver wolves with Killian's pack and the vampires and how we'd trained everyone to defeat the demon wolves. We hadn't had much time, but we'd made our army stronger. "That's what we need to do now. We need to take the few weeks' worth of blood storage we have and work hard to train everyone in this city. If we can cloak the angel section and bring as many people here as possible, the demons might not realize what's going on."

"Are you insane?" Azbogah scoffed. "You want us to train the other supernaturals on how to fight against us and win?"

"They won against us once." Mother jerked her head in his direction. "Remember? The council was formed because the silver wolves took us down after your decisions led to *all* of this."

His nostrils flared, but he didn't respond. There wasn't anything he *could* say. The silver and demon wolves were created after the angels had fallen.

I forced my tone to remain indifferent. "Can you help us?"

"And what do I get out of it?" he asked.

I'm going to kick his ass, Levi growled, and shifted his weight.

Securing Levi's arm, I held him beside me and said, "My appreciation."

Azbogah snorted, but Bune interjected, "This might be your only chance to get it. I'd think wisely, my brother."

Sobering, Azbogah bit his bottom lip. "Fine. If you promise to spend some time with me."

My stomach swooped. I hadn't expected him to counter with *that*. I would have guessed he'd ask for freedom to train the angels, to remain on the council, or something that would keep him in a leadership position.

"Little one, you gave your blood to *Erin*." He held his hands out at his sides. "Is my request *that* horrible? My days are limited because the demons won't be satisfied until I'm dead."

He was right. I took a deep breath, thinking through the situation. I didn't cherish the thought of his death, and I hoped I could prevent it. I didn't want anyone to die, but there was a real probability that *he* would.

You should do it, Rosey. Levi's concern washed over me. *But I want to be with you the entire time.*

Maybe I could do it with Levi beside me. "But it can't deter us from getting ready for the war. We need to get everyone ready to fight, including training the prisoners as well. Everyone should be battle-ready—even Ezra." He couldn't be trusted. Knowing him, he'd make a deal with the demons to save his own ass, but we needed numbers. I wasn't worried about the witches or Azbogah betraying us; the demons were after them, and there was no denying they were the main traitors. The angels would also be targets since they'd followed their lead. The demons wouldn't care if we didn't know anything because we hadn't taken the time to ask the questions. Yet another way we'd betrayed them.

"Prisoners?" Zagan scratched the back of his neck. "Is that smart?"

Bune stretched his legs out in front of him. "I'm sure it'll be fine. My guess is, since Azbogah was involved, most of the people in prison are there because they did something the council didn't approve of. They could have been imprisoned for simply talking about their leader in a negative light."

That was true. The handful of residents who had done horrible things had been executed, but centuries had passed since something like that had occurred. Those with minor infractions were thrown into jail to send a message, which was usually due to an abuse of power because they weren't even true crimes.

"That's a good point." Mother moved to the side of the couch and placed her hand on Father's shoulder. "I can handle training them, and they will receive a second chance to be acting residents of the city when it's all done."

"Right now, we need rest," Though it was early evening, both Levi and I were exhausted. The day had been demanding from the start, and between the loss of blood—twice—and healing, we needed to recharge.

"Where should Rosemary and I sleep?" Levi asked as he pulled me to his side.

My skin buzzed, and our connection sprang to life. "We should go to the vampire mansion to be close to the others."

"No, stay here. Your father and I are going into the city to check on things." Mother rubbed her hands together and glanced at Bune. "Do you mind keeping an eye on Azbogah?"

Azbogah gestured toward the sliding door. "I can stay in my own condo."

"You won't." Father stood and shifted his wings. "We won't let you go to your condo—there's no telling what's there to help you. You can either stay here so we can keep an eye on you, or you can join Ezra."

The dark angel scowled. "I'll stay here and message Erin. It would be best if she didn't understand the severity of my situation."

He realized that my parents had the most say. However, I knew he would try to find a way to be on top again.

"We'll keep an eye on him." Bune smirked as he tapped his foot on the glass floor. "It would be my honor." At least Bune would get some justice from the situation.

Now that it was settled, I was ready for some alone time with Levi. "Let us know if you need us," I said, taking his hand. Then I led him toward the back of the living room and into the hallway that ran behind the kitchen to my room on the left.

As usual, my glass wall was frosted over. I'd always enjoyed privacy more than the swirls of light in my room.

Levi chuckled. *Why am I not surprised that your comforter is burnt orange?*

My focus landed on the king-size bed in the center of the exterior wall. *Because you know it's my favorite color and reminds me of sunset, my favorite time to fly.*

And your charcoal dresser and end table match your wings perfectly. His attention flicked between my feathers and the furniture.

My cheeks burned. *That was Father's doing. When I was younger, I always admired his white feathers. He asked me one day if I wanted him to paint my furniture his favorite wing color of all time. I'd assumed it would be white like his, but I came home to find this.* I'd forgotten that until now, likely because his actions had meant so much to me. I'd *felt* something, which I'd been unable to do for so long. Maybe that was why I hadn't remembered those small moments—because I couldn't relate to them after losing a piece of my soul.

He's a good angel. My father respects him very much. Levi slowly turned around, taking in the room, and his forehead creased. *No pictures of anyone? No stuffed animals? No mementos of your days in training? Just no...stuff? I figured this would be a shrine to your friends.*

You have to remember that I didn't feel much before I met you. There's no impulse to collect mementos when you don't experience emotions. Glancing at my room now made my heart constrict. It seemed so lonely and sad, and nothing like the angel I'd become.

Well, then, it's a good thing I'm here. He winked and closed the frosted glass door, locking it in place. *Now we can create some memories.*

My body warmed at his suggestion. Though I was tired, I had enough energy to spare for him. After all, there was no guarantee of how much time we'd have together.

He stepped toward me and pressed me against the glass wall next to the bed. I'd thought he would push me onto the mattress, but instead, he kissed me eagerly.

Warmth and desire flooded me. I opened my mouth, allowing his tongue entrance. His spearmint taste consumed me, and my body heated.

Normally, we took things slow with his bittersweet torture, but today, we were desperate. Whether we liked to admit it or not, it felt like a clock was ticking and our time was running out.

Forever had felt like a certainty for so long, but now the time seemed fleeting. Even eternity with him wouldn't be long enough.

His fingers tangled in my hair, and he gently pulled, causing a sting. The pain hurt but felt amazing at the same time. Pain and pleasure were at times equal, especially with angels who lived for such a long time.

Sliding my hands under his shirt, I scratched Levi's back hard enough to break the skin. He groaned as he deepened our kiss and untangled one hand to cup my breast. His finger rolled over my nipple, and I arched my back.

I unfastened his jeans, needing to feel him. I loved him and needed to connect with him in the most primal way two mates could. After pushing down his underwear, I stroked him and reveled as he groaned.

Gods, I love you, he linked as he removed my clothes.

When I was undressed, the coolness of the glass and air couldn't quench the desire flaming inside me. He leaned over, taking my nipple into his mouth as his hands slid between my legs. He rubbed, and my body tensed.

We stroked each other, moving at the same pace, and just before I could climax, I removed his hand from between my legs. I pushed him away, and he stumbled back a few steps in surprise.

"Together," I rasped.

I moved to the edge of the bed and lay on my back. He walked over, removing his shirt as he moved, and stood between my legs, lifting them so they wrapped around his back as he thrust inside me. Like before, his finger rubbed the sensitive spot between my legs as he increased the pace.

My body quivered, and I rocked against him, desperate

for all of him to fit inside me. His fingers increased the pressure, and I tipped over the edge. As my body convulsed, Levi followed closely behind, our ecstasy mixing together in a rush through our bond.

Once our breathing calmed and our shudders quieted, he crawled into bed next to me, and I fell asleep in his arms.

THE NEXT WEEK flew by in a blur. When we weren't sleeping, we were training with the entire city. The bears even opened their massive underground training facilities for use, so all we had to do was cloak the city during shift changes. Munkar, Phul, Ishim, Bune, Zagan, Levi, and I trained the angels, while Ronnie and Alex trained the vampires, and Sterlyn, Griffin, Kira, and Roman helped trained the shifters. While we trained, the witches worked on spells. We all had three four-hour sessions every day. During that time, we still had a few angels training in our area so the demons wouldn't think something unusual was going on; they only saw a handful of us preparing for war.

Every day, the demons brought a sacrifice—usually a human—to each gate. Though we didn't give them an audience, they still went through with the murders on both sides. They left the bodies there to ensure we could see the growing pile. I hated that there was so much needless loss of life, but if we opened the gates, more people would die. Every night, when I closed my eyes, I saw the image of the corpses. They were seared into my mind.

Killian and his pack were working hard to get the humans out of Shadow Ridge and Shadow Terrace, but more humans kept coming to the towns to verify the things they'd heard from the people vacating. Thankfully, the demons were still focused on getting inside the dome and not on torturing as many people as possible.

The demons' witches hadn't used any more magic since that first day, but I figured that was because they all knew we had limited resources. We had only a few days' worth of blood left before we'd have to open the gate for supplies.

Levi and I had just gotten out of a shower after a long day of training when my phone buzzed on the end table.

I glanced at the message from Sterlyn, and my heart turned cold. We need you at the vampire mansion now.

CHAPTER TEN

LEVI'S ARMS slipped under my towel and around my waist. He kissed the side of my neck as one hand cupped my breast. *You're tense, and I need to calm you.*

Every night, despite how exhausted we were, we'd ravage each other multiple times. Then we'd wake up to have sex again before starting the day. I'd always been sexually charged, but I'd never been like *this*. It was more than just the ecstasy he gave me multiple times a day—it was the connection we achieved. From the buzz of our skin to the surge of sensations, our emotions and senses were heightened in ways we couldn't replicate as intensely any other way.

As much as I want to toss this phone down and focus on all your deliciousness, we have to get dressed. Something's wrong. I turned to him and sucked his full lower lip into my mouth. His taste caused my body to respond in ways that would cause us both frustration. *We have to go.* I pulled back and stared at his rugged features. His scruff was longer, but that only added to his masculinity. He was the most attractive man I'd ever laid eyes on, and he was all *mine*.

How wrong? he asked as his hands grabbed my butt.

His fingers dug in just enough to make me want him more. He *knew* what he was doing. *Not sure, but we're needed at the vampire mansion. We can't ignore them.* If we did and something happened, I couldn't live with myself.

He exhaled loudly and released his hold on me. *Fine*, he growled as he kissed me once more. *But only because I love you and don't want you the least bit distracted when I make you orgasm. I want your mind solely on me.*

I grinned as his words charged my body. *Deal.*

He tugged the towel away and ogled me.

This was the complete opposite of getting dressed. "You just said—" I started.

He gestured to me. "I'm just admiring my mate's naked body since I'd planned on giving it *much*-needed attention. I need something to get me by until I can get underneath you."

I rolled my eyes, but I was thrilled.

He winked at me, feeling my approval. Now that I had him beside me, I couldn't fathom how I'd lived so long without him. He brought so much joy to my life, and I realized I'd been merely surviving before. I couldn't even consider what I'd been doing as living until I'd met Sterlyn and the others, but even then, I hadn't been fulfilled—I just hadn't known it.

My phone buzzed as another message from Sterlyn flashed: Are you on your way?

Reality crashed back over me. I picked up the phone and typed, Yes, we'll be there soon.

Tossing the phone onto the mattress, I hurried to my closet. I grabbed a pair of jeans, and as I went for a burnt orange shirt, I paused. If we were going to fight, black would be ideal instead of a color that would give me away in the darkness.

Levi brushed past me and snatched his jeans and a navy shirt. The new clothes we'd obtained for him took up half the closet.

The two of us quickly dressed and headed into the living room. Azbogah stood at the glass door, while Bune and Zagan sat across from each other, playing chess. Head turning in our direction, Zagan blinked. "Uh...what's wrong? If it's Eleanor, we were *only* training together, even if it looked strange."

I had no clue what he meant, but I hated that we were easy to read. I'd always prided myself on being able to maintain my composure. I didn't want to worry anyone until I confirmed there was something to worry about.

"Why would you ask that and bring up training?" Bune moved a knight, keeping his attention on the game.

Zagan shook his head. "Seriously? As soon as they get here, they always run to their room and take a shower, and they're gone for at least an hour before they come out for dinner, all lovey-dovey. This is usually their first-round-of-sex time. I figured someone texted them or something."

Turning away from the door, Azbogah glowered. "I understand that they're preordained, but I'd rather not hear about my daughter's sexual acts."

My chest constricted. "And I'd rather you not call me your daughter."

Though he'd been agreeable during his week here, I'd spent as little time with him as possible. I'd agreed to see him, and I made sure to talk with him for a few minutes every night to keep my end of the bargain. The last thing I needed to do was encourage him to work against us. When we spoke, it was strictly about what was going on with training and how things were proceeding, including with the recently released "criminals."

Luckily, Mother and Father weren't here. Azbogah called me his daughter more and more, and it infuriated her every time. Surprisingly, it didn't seem to faze Father.

"We have to go check on something." Levi looped his arm through mine. "Sterlyn asked us to come over for a visit."

His craftiness helped in situations like these. The way he'd worded it wasn't wrong and would mitigate questions.

Wrinkling his nose, Azbogah remained silent.

At one point, I would've taken his actions as hatred for a silver wolf, but now, I wasn't so sure. Seeing him watch Mother—especially when it came to her interactions with Pahaliah—had made me see him in a different light. I used to think he held nothing but disdain for her, but now I wondered if it was actual pain.

Could he still be in love with her, but his guilt over everything he'd done had eaten up his soul and allowed his greed for power to take over? The pain I'd felt whenever I'd been separated from Levi had been worse than anything physical I'd ever endured, and that alone softened me toward the dark angel—which meant I had to keep my distance. Me warming to him could be his plan.

Levi and I made our way to the door. My parents were still at the training grounds, meeting with the warriors.

"What about dinner?" Azbogah *tsk*ed. "You haven't eaten and were training all day."

I'd never imagined that he would worry about me eating. "Sterlyn and Griffin eat food, too. I'm sure we can find something over there. Griffin is usually cooking hamburgers or steaks." Here, we all grazed with no formal meals. Angels saw food purely as sustenance; we didn't cook elaborate dinners or make grand gestures. We just grabbed whatever was in the refrigerator, which was usually some sort of cooked meat and veggies.

Levi opened the door and waved at me to exit first. The longer we took to reach the mansion, the more on edge I became. Sterlyn's short message had made it clear that *something* was wrong, and my mind was getting away from me. If the demons had broken down the gate, she wouldn't have messaged me like that; she'd be too busy fighting.

I called over my shoulder, "Call or text me if you need me."

As Levi shut the glass door, Azbogah grumbled, "Call or text. We should never have opened those damn gates."

At one time, I would have agreed. Sometimes, the convenience of technology made people lose their sense of community and at times spew misinformation like loose feathers in the wind. However, since I'd started handling one horrible situation after another, phones had made communicating when there were pressing threats more convenient. Like now.

Levi flickered into his shadow form, and we took to the sky. The closer we flew to the top of the dome, the more the demons' red eyes unsettled me. Our observers switched out every couple of hours and usually inched around the top of the dome. I'd worried at first that after some time, people would overlook the threat surrounding us since they couldn't see it. However, with the witches constantly rein-forcing the boundaries, Lucifer's daily killings, and the severe rationing of food, people didn't congregate outside like before.

My skin crawled from the unwanted attention, and I shuddered as an equally unpleasant thought took over my mind—the coven had our blood. Nothing worrisome had happened yet, but that didn't mean it wouldn't. The witches had been rotating for training just like the rest of us, working with their magic for endurance. They trained with Zagan, Bune, and Levi in demon form, locating them and forcing them to the ground. I'd been worried at first, but so far, the witches had not harmed them. Still, that didn't mean that they wouldn't hurt them at the first opportunity.

Soon, we were flying over the deserted capitol building. All meetings were now taking place underground in the bears' hidden lair, none of us wanting to chance a witch from Hell using magic to overhear our plans. Though the malicious witches on the outside weren't trying to get into the city, that didn't mean they weren't trying to get an idea of what we were doing. Despite Erin and the others spelling the barriers, we didn't want to take any chances.

When the four-story Neo-Renaissance-style mansion came into view, some of the weight fell off my shoulders. This section of Shadow City wasn't crawling with demons. Though I'd hoped to find it just like this, I hadn't been certain.

Gwen, Alex, Ronnie, Griffin, Sterlyn, and Ulva were living here for the moment, though none of them were in sight. We headed to the front door, and when I moved to ring the doorbell, the wooden door swung open, revealing a stoic vampire in a black suit similar to Azbogah's. His ever-green eyes scanned the area behind me as if to ensure there were no imminent threats. When he was appeased, he jerked his head toward the foyer, but his slicked-back cedar-colored hair didn't budge a millimeter.

In an attempt to seem more mortal-like, I forced a smile. "Thank you, Sergio."

He took a hesitant step back and yanked on the bottom of his suit coat. "You're welcome?"

Since I was certain he hadn't meant it as a question, I didn't respond but rather walked past him into the enormous foyer.

I'd never been inside the mansion—I'd spent the majority of my time with my friends outside of Shadow City. My gaze swept the marble floors, which gleamed as if newly polished. The canary yellow walls surprised me. Once again, my biases were apparent—I'd figured Alex's brother Matthew would have painted all the walls crimson like blood. The one thing that delivered on my expectations was the oversized chandelier hanging in the center of the room.

Levi chuckled as he changed back into his human form.

Sergio had been uncomfortable with me before, but now his face twisted in horror, and he clutched his chest. "I'll never get used to that."

I mashed my lips together, trying not to laugh. He was one of the worst fighters in Shadow City, probably due to his butler duties. Though he worked hard, most of his labor wasn't physical, and it showed.

A large staircase dominated the other side of the foyer, and I wasn't surprised when Sterlyn and Griffin hurried down the stairs, their faces lined with strain.

"You're here," Sterlyn said with relief.

"What's wrong?" I tried not to snap at her, but I hated not knowing. I wished she would've told me something in the text.

Griffin touched Sterlyn's arm, and his eyes glowed faintly, indicating he was using their mate bond to speak telepathically. He then smiled at Sergio, but the warmth didn't meet his eyes as he said, "Do you mind giving us some privacy? Or should we take them to our floor upstairs?"

"No, sir," Sergio responded eagerly. "I can check on things in the kitchen to ensure the royals' blood is being prepared."

A grimace flickered across Griffin's face, and Sterlyn assured the butler, "That would be perfect."

Though Sergio appeared more comfortable around Sterlyn and Griffin, he still wasn't at ease with Levi and me. I couldn't blame him. Though Levi was on our side, even training us on how to fight his kind, he still resembled the enemy. Not only that, but Sergio had just recently acclimated to the wolf shifters staying here.

He blurred as he rushed to get away from us. When we heard the kitchen door shut, I murmured, "What is going on?"

Breathe, Levi linked as he placed his hands on my shoulders and massaged them, trying to calm me. His touch buzzed, but not even that could subdue my inner turmoil.

Sterlyn sniffed and surveyed the area. "There's been an issue."

"Clearly," Levi deadpanned. "You've got Rosey upset and concerned with all the buildup."

"Hey, back off, man." Griffin crossed his arms, stepping in front of Sterlyn. "We didn't want to send any details where your *guest* might see."

"We weren't trying to worry you, Rosemary," Sterlyn said as she stepped around Griffin. "Knowing how much you care, I should've handled it better. I just didn't want to risk—"

"I understand." I hadn't considered that. Azbogah was sneaky; of course they were worried he'd find a way to read my texts. "We're all stressed and don't need to fight one another." I glanced at Levi and Griffin. "We have enough enemies."

Griffin blew air out of his cheeks and averted his gaze.

"As usual, you're right, love." Levi beamed. "How'd I get so damn lucky?"

My cheeks caught fire. I still wasn't used to that kind of affection.

"I hate to ruin the moment." Sterlyn placed a hand over her heart. "I love seeing Rosemary so happy, but Alex, Ronnie, and Gwen are handling an issue."

She'd named only the vampires, and Griffin had looked unsettled when Sergio had mentioned checking on their blood. "Are you telling me the blood is gone? I thought we had a few more days."

The adoration that had filled our bond from Levi's end morphed into fear. "Is that what the problem is?" He then linked, *How did you know?*

Just a gut feeling, though I hope I'm wrong. Let it be almost *anything* else—a vampire riot opposed to fighting the demons or something we could rectify. A food shortage... well, that would force us to go to war imminently. We'd been planning on fighting in a week, so there would still be a few days' worth of blood on hand to get the vampires through the war. Any injury that caused significant blood loss was life-threatening to them.

"You know how the vampires were rationing since the demons appeared?" Sterlyn bit her bottom lip and leaned toward us, lowering her voice more. "Apparently, a few of the vampires objected, and they invaded the blood storage area while we were in training today. They handed blood out to the vampires in the condominiums, and now we're critically low."

This was only slightly better than the demons finding a way inside. "How bad is it?"

Levi's hands stilled on my shoulders.

"Two days at best." Griffin laughed humorlessly.

That was the amount we'd planned to have on hand while fighting the war. "We're out of time." There was no way around it. We couldn't wait until the blood was depleted because then the vampires would be more focused on finding food than fighting.

"Why the *hell* did they do that?" Levi dropped his arms to his sides. "Didn't they realize this would force our hand?"

Sterlyn lifted her palms. "They were younger vampires, and they were hungry. Between the rigorous training and reduction in blood, even by a small amount, they were feeling hunger pains they've never experienced before."

In other words, the residents were spoiled. Most of the city had never been outside these walls. They didn't understand the concept of making a temporary sacrifice for a greater purpose. "So they threw a temper tantrum," I said.

"A lot of people do that here." Levi shook his head.

He wasn't wrong. The war was upon us. I tried to keep my voice level despite the dread pitting within me. "Where are Alex, Ronnie, and Gwen?"

"They're on their way back from the prison with Kira." Sterlyn turned toward the door across the room. "They should be here any second. For the moment, the guilty vampires are locked up until we're ready to declare war. We don't want panic to spread among the rest of the vampires, so we tried to contain the message. Gwen figured out what happened while we were in training, so she and Kira rounded everyone up before we got back. Good thing, because we didn't get their messages while we were underground."

And Levi and I had raced back to the condo, so they'd had to handle it while we were enjoying each other. My heart constricted. At least we'd had one last moment alone before we'd learned of this.

"We need to alert the council," I said. This couldn't remain hidden. "They might as well meet us at the capitol building."

"You're right." Sterlyn removed her phone. "I'll call Ronnie. Griffin, why don't you call Erin? And Rosemary, contact your parents. Let's resolve this."

We stepped apart to make the phone calls. Time was of the essence.

TEN MINUTES LATER, we were walking through the hunter green doorway that led into the capitol building. The entryway was huge and bare, and at this time of evening, the coffee shop in the corner was closed.

This is disgusting, Levi complained as he observed the yellow-stained walls in desperate need of repainting.

Azbogah advised the council to keep it like this to remind everyone of how long they've been around. Another manipulative move to intimidate others with the importance of the council's role.

I led the way to the doors in the middle of the far wall, and we all entered the council meeting room. The U-shaped table awaited, its inner curve facing the door, but no one sat at the table. Instead, Ronnie, Alex, Gwen, and Kira stood in the center, with Erin, Diana, and Breena leaning against the wall on the right.

I hadn't seen Kira since I'd learned she had given Levi the demon sword. She'd been training at the artifact building with Roman and the other guards, ensuring the building wasn't breached again. Her emerald eyes focused on Levi and stilled as she twirled a strand of her poppy-red hair around one finger. She was short, about the same size as Annie, indicative of her fox-shifter stature.

"Hey, Kira," Levi said formally, and nodded.

She arched a brow but didn't respond. Instead, she leaned back on her heels, her demeanor clear. She wasn't happy with Levi.

You can call her Red. I was fairly certain he hadn't used the nickname because of me, but I no longer felt threatened by it. I had no question in my mind about who owned Levi's heart, and it wasn't her.

Nah, I kind of like only calling you by a nickname. He wrapped his arms around my waist and pulled me against his chest.

As usual, our connection sprang to life.

The door opened, and I glanced over my shoulder to find Mother, Father, Azbogah, Bune, Phul, Ishim, and Munkar entering with Sterlyn and Griffin close behind. Though I wasn't thrilled about Azbogah being at the council meeting, we didn't have much of a choice, especially with Bune and the warriors coming. We'd told them it was time for war.

Erin pushed off the wall. "What's going on? We have a week, and this meeting is cutting into our time—"

Before she could finish, Alex interrupted her and informed them of the blood supply issue.

When he finished, the room was quiet. It was clear that everyone was in agreement.

Erin's face had paled, and she straightened. "What does this mean?"

Munkar rasped as his wings expanded, "There is no time to waste. War begins now."

The words hung in the air, suffocating us. We'd known war was coming, but now that it was here, I would have done anything to wind back the clock. I should've trained harder and spent more time with Levi.

Bune stepped forward. "We should attack now, like we've been planning. Once the residents go home, the witches can cloak the city again. Since the night creatures have been waking to train with us during the day, the city hasn't been active at night, anyway. Nothing will seem odd at this time as long as we move quickly."

He was right. We'd implemented a strict six-hour time when everyone had to sleep or rest since we all had to train in our allotted slots. As we wanted everyone to rest, the witches provided a concoction to make sure the nocturnal residents could sleep, and the added benefit was that the demons wouldn't find it odd that the entire city was indoors. We'd wanted set times when the city was inactive so we might surprise the demons with an attack during that window. However, that meant Levi and I wouldn't have another chance to be alone before we fought.

"Then there isn't a real decision to make." Mother waved her hand. "Everyone, go home and prepare for war."

Erin and the witch coven were the first to leave, with the angel warriors following close behind. When Bune and Azbogah had walked through the door and my parents moved to follow, Kira said urgently, "Wait! I...I have something for Yelahiah and Pahaliah."

I froze in place, pulse racing.

My gods. What had she done?

CHAPTER ELEVEN

AZBOGAH CAUGHT the door before it shut and turned around, his gray irises lightening with interest.

Kira stiffened.

"Come on," Bune said as he stepped next to Azbogah in the doorway, but Azbogah shook his head.

"What is it?" Mother asked as she pivoted toward the fox shifter.

Rubbing her arms, Kira didn't seem like her normal, confident self. "I was hoping to speak to you two alone."

Her words implied secrets, and I gritted my teeth in an attempt not to chastise her. Though I'd never been fond of her, even before she and Levi had connected, she *had* proven to be a reliable ally. My coldness toward her was due to her sneakiness. She had an uncanny way of learning information she should have never obtained, but that ability had benefited us of late due to her loyalty to Sterlyn and Griffin. Still, that attribute had also caused us some problems—such as when she'd provided Levi with his mother's demon sword.

"We don't have time for this," Azbogah rasped. "And if

you can't share it with everyone, that makes me *very* suspicious."

I hated the fact that Azbogah and I had similar thoughts, but I'd bet that most people here understood Kira's implication.

Kira lifted her chin. "I don't give a damn if you're suspicious."

"Didn't we just address how we all needed to work together? We need to at least pretend to get along," I said. If we fought amongst ourselves, we'd give the demons more of an advantage over us. "If we don't, we're going to *lose* this war."

Nodding, Levi stood tall. "I can go with my Father and take Azbogah back to the high-rise."

"That won't be necessary." My father lifted a hand. "Azbogah and Rosemary are right. We are supposed to be working together. Not doing so would be like flying in the rain while attempting to prevent our feathers from getting wet—impossible. If we start bickering now, we might as well open the gates and let them kill us."

Alex lifted a finger. "Just to be clear, I'm against that plan. I want as much time with my wife as Fate will allow."

"We all do, man," Griffin said as he stepped closer to Sterlyn.

"Get on with it," Mother commanded. "We need to hurry."

With a shrug, Kira reached into her back pocket. She opened her hand, revealing the golden ring and a black-gold pendant in the shape of angel wings on a corded necklace.

Father inhaled sharply as he jerked forward before stopping. "My necklace. But how—"

"Did you not *learn* the first time?" Azbogah marched back into the room. A vein between his eyes bulged as he got in Kira's face. "Giving a demon a demonic sword we can't take back from him wasn't bad enough?"

Closing her hand, Kira covered the artifacts like she thought that would prevent Azbogah from grabbing them.

Sterlyn shoved Azbogah, pushing the angel back as she commanded, "That's *enough*."

He laughed coldly, sounding more like himself. "You may be part angel, but I'm no wolf. You aren't *my* alpha, and I don't have to obey."

Things were escalating again, and I wished Annie were present. She had a way of diffusing tense situations even better than Sterlyn could.

With a long hiss, Gwen rubbed a hand down the front of her black sequin dress. Her messy ivory hair hung slightly past her shoulders, and her chestnut-brown eyes narrowed to slits. "Why don't we ask her why she did it instead of threatening her?"

"Very well." Azbogah retreated a few feet. "Please, enlighten us."

"I wasn't trying to cause more problems. From what you told us, the ring is Yelahiah's ring of justice." Kira glanced at her palm where her fingers still clutched the artifacts. "And I figured the necklace with angel wings might be valuable and took it as well."

This was when my narrow-mindedness became an issue. I hadn't considered retrieving the artifacts we had on hand to aid us in battle. We needed as much help on our side as possible. This was one reason Levi had taken to Kira. They both saw that sometimes, doing the very thing some might consider wrong was actually *right*.

Ronnie flanked Kira's other side and stared Azbogah down. "That was a smart decision. Do *you* take issue with it?"

He placed his hands behind his back. "She should have discussed it with the council."

"Because we have so much time on our hands." Levi fisted his own hands and sneered. "And it's not like your vote has weight any longer."

"Listen here, *demon*..." Azbogah cracked his knuckles.

I wouldn't allow this to escalate. "That *demon* is my preordained, and you will treat him, Bune, and Zagan with respect." If Mother wouldn't handle this imploding time bomb of a dark angel, I would. "And he didn't say anything wrong. Your *vote* doesn't count. You don't get to vote when you're the one who created this mess. And your jealousy of my *parents'* powers ends now." I marched to Kira and took the items from her.

Before Azbogah could intercept me, I placed the ring on Mother's hand and gave Father his necklace. I'd heard rumors of the sparks the ring could create when Mother was serving justice, but I didn't know what the necklace could do.

"And why do they get to keep those items?" Azbogah asked with less maliciousness.

I'd expected him to challenge me. "Because we need every advantage on our side."

Bune jumped in, explaining the horrible past of the angels and making it clear that Azbogah had brought us to this point. Everything led back to him.

As if Azbogah could hear my thoughts, his lips mashed into a line. The more information that was shared, the worse things were for him. I might feel bad for him if he would show a shred of remorse. However, he appeared to be growing angrier.

Munkar steepled his fingers. "There is no reason any of us shouldn't have weapons that can aid in this war. I concur that Pahaliah and Yelahiah should have their jewelry of power."

Jewelry of power. That was an interesting term. "Wait. Do the demons have similar things?"

"They're in the artifact building," Azbogah reassured us. "As are their swords."

Of course that would be the case. "Then maybe Erin should put extra witches on guard duty at the building." I hated to give Erin yet another powerful tool, but if the demons obtained their jewelry and swords, more lives would be lost.

Mother grimaced. "That is the last thing I want to do."

"Dear, I think Rosemary has a point," Father said. "Erin is relentless, but *if* the demons—"

"I *know* what you're going to say." Mother waved a hand and closed her eyes. "But I agree that the risk the demons pose outweighs my discomfort."

Eyes glowing, Sterlyn gripped the edge of the table. "We'll figure a way out of this, but things are growing more intense on the other side. Killian reported that the demons are surrounding the university as we speak."

They were escalating the threat, wanting to terrorize not only humans but the supernaturals outside our city, too. If students were injured, there was no telling what the repercussions would be, especially since we'd opened the university to introduce select Shadow City residents into society.

"At least the numbers that can immediately attack the city are reduced." Bune's body slackened.

We could theorize all night and never account for every possibility. "As we discussed—everyone, go to your people. Let's meet in front of the capitol building once it's confirmed that the witches have cloaked our city. Kira, can you inform Erin to send us a text when the deed is done?"

Kira nodded.

"In the meantime, I'll have Killian and some of the silver wolves run the perimeter of both towns so we know where the demons are stationed before we open the Shadow Ridge side gate. We don't want them attacking from both entrances, and I'm worried that blood-crazed vampires could add to our issues." Sterlyn used the black hair tie around her wrist to pull her hair into a low ponytail. "Griffin, Ulva, and I will head over to the shifter side of the city to gather everyone while Ronnie, Gwen, and Alex go to the vampire side, since they can't link like we can. Griffin has coordinated efforts with his mother to bridge the gap between the other shifter races, so it would be great for those two to gather the shifters while I strategize with all the residents who reach the gate prepared for war. When Erin notifies us that the artifact building is reinforced, our group can meet back here in front of the building."

That was one thing about Sterlyn—despite being an alpha in her own right, she respected that her mate was the alpha of the city. The fated mates supported each other despite both being alphas, which I admired greatly. Even when it was difficult, they never felt threatened by each other's position within the other's pack.

Griffin pursed his lips. "Fine, but I hate being separated from you."

All mates despised it, but sometimes, it was inevitable. Levi had left me twice to visit Hell. I shuddered slightly at the memory but then took Levi's hand and tugged him toward the door.

The three warriors pivoted as Phul muttered, "About time."

When we reached the lobby, I paused until Bune, Azbogah, and my parents exited. I wanted to keep Azbogah in my sights. He'd use any sort of distraction to his benefit, though I wasn't sure what he could accomplish now. Even his supporters had turned against him...or so we thought. On the other hand, we'd thought his supporters had turned before when he'd killed Ophaniel and the rest of the supernaturals had fought together to beat the angels.

The demons flickered into their shadow form, and our group raced toward the angel high-rise once again. Adrenaline pumped through me.

Levi must have felt the change because he squeezed my hand tighter and linked, *During the battle, we need to stay together as much as possible. I need to make sure you're always safe.*

That didn't sit well with me. *Though I'm all about us staying close, I'm a warrior and will do what is required in battle. We can't let our emotions affect our focus, or we will get hurt. Besides, if I get injured, you'll feel it through our bond.* A fact that I detested. If Levi was sparring with someone, the last thing I wanted was his attention diverted to me. However, that was the price of our bond.

And here I thought you'd feel the same way. A little bit of hurt wafted through us.

I almost snapped but took a deep breath instead. This was a time when being emotionless would have been beneficial. Stress was making me irritable, and it was making him worried. The two didn't mesh well. Going into battle upset with each other wasn't what I wanted. I had to calm down and not let my emotions control me. I still struggled with that because these days, they hit me like a torrential wind when I needed to keep my wings steady. Not impossible, but it required much concentration.

I do feel the same way, but I don't want us to get hurt because we're focused on remaining close. His fear came from a place of unconditional love. Forcing myself to remember that eased some of my frustration.

He sighed loudly. *Sometimes, I wish I could remain logical when it comes to you. I envy that it comes so naturally to you.*

I laughed, causing Mother to start in front of me, which made me laugh even harder.

Mother plucker. I'd gone from slightly unbalanced to sounding like Sierra—unhinged.

Are you okay? His humor rolled through the connection. *What's so funny?*

I'm fine, I assured him. *I just find it humorous that you called me logical. It's hard for me to be that way around you, and I have to force myself to think beyond my emotions when it never used to be that way. All I want to do is hide you somewhere so nothing bad will happen to you. I know what it feels like to think I'll have to live without you...* I stopped, unable to continue.

Our connection warmed, thawing the chill running through my body.

I love you, he connected. *And I regret every day what I put you through.*

That wasn't what I'd been getting at. *You don't need to apologize. I understand now why you felt you had to do it, and I wasn't bringing it up for that reason. However, that pain haunts me whenever we're about to enter a risky situation.* When I thought I'd lost him, it had felt like I couldn't breathe or function.

He intertwined our fingers and linked, *I know. You're a forgiving person. It's one of the many attributes I love about you.*

I wasn't sure if *forgiving* was the word I'd used to describe me. I'd consider my attitude more like...learning how to tolerate a person.

The green trees of the Shadow City forest appeared underneath us. Since it was past curfew, no animals were roaming the area, but that would change in the next few minutes. The smell of oak swirled into my nose, and I yearned for the fall foliage outside this city since the witches ensured Shadow City remained at a moderate temperature year-round. In here, you'd never realize it was the end of November.

Pushing away the negative thoughts, I forced myself to concentrate. I hated to consider that this would be my last moment of peace with Levi for some time, but I couldn't be a buffoon. I wanted to enjoy the wind in my face with my mate by my side.

As we approached the high-rise, a few angels stood on their balconies. They watched with questioning gazes as we rushed toward our homes. No one was supposed to be out at this hour, and our group was generating interest, which would help when Erin notified us that we could move into position.

We reached the balcony, and our moment of peace ended. Our group hurried into the living room to wait for the call.

Heart pumping, I breathed deeply. Our combined floral scents made me sick to my stomach. Levi stepped behind me and wrapped his arms around my waist, and I tried to focus on the gentle buzz of our connection, but not even that could ease my turmoil. Leaning against his chest, I inhaled his sweet peony scent, which was similar yet different from Father's. Levi's scent and touch were the best defenses I had for my sanity.

"Is anyone running low on their magic?" Father stood at the balcony door, staring outside as he clutched the necklace in his hands.

Mother played with the ring on her right ring finger. "Everyone should be all right. Since the demons have been blocking the sunlight, we advised all the angels not to do anything that would require a lengthy recharge."

Though angels used their magic mainly for healing, we sometimes tapped into it to get a sense of the area around us and search for hidden enemies. None of that was needed within the city, but it was best that Mother had put that stipulation since we had no idea what tactics the demons would employ. The heavenly light that the dome captured mirrored our magic and helped recharge us. With the demons blocking it, it could take days for a depleted angel to get back to functioning levels.

"What are your plans for me?" Azbogah asked from his place on the couch. He was the only one sitting. The warriors stood on the other side of Father, ready to walk out the door at first notice.

Ishim glanced over his shoulder. "You'll be fighting with the rest of us."

Zagan entered from the direction of my parents' room. His hair was wet, and water dripped down his face and neck. His black shirt clung to him like skin, and his jeans showed splotches of water.

"Do you not know how to dry off?" Levi shook his head. "I swear, you don't use a towel."

His friend shrugged. "Don't need one. I'll air-dry."

As Levi opened his mouth to retort, Mother's phone dinged.

My breath caught. This had to be it.

She glanced at her screen. "It's time."

"Time?" Zagan scratched his head, splattering water droplets on the glass floor. "For what?"

"War." The one word was all I needed to say.

His mouth dropped. "But I just *showered*."

"Well, at least you'll smell good for the demons. I'm sure Lucifer, Wrath, Asmodeus, and Belaphor will appreciate the effort." Levi chuckled, but the joke fell flat.

Zagan rolled his eyes. "I was hoping we would have more time, though I knew it was wishful thinking."

"The situation has changed." Mother opened the door and flew outside just as the horn from the training grounds blew, alerting us that the hour had come.

The rest of us followed suit, with the demons changing into their shadow form.

We dropped twenty-five stories to hover in the middle of the building. Levi was on one side of me and Azbogah on my other. Bune was between Zagan and Levi while the warriors lined up on the other side of Azbogah.

Door after door opened, and soon, angels were hovering in front of their balconies, facing our group. Mother and Father flew in front of our group in the leadership position toward the condo, and I watched as Azbogah began to move forward, too, but stopped himself.

"War is imminent!" Mother yelled as the horn blew from the training grounds. "Though we expected to have another week, circumstances force us to begin the attack now."

Every face was lined with worry, and Eleanor spoke first. "Maybe we should hand Azbogah over to them so they won't try to kill us all."

Azbogah sucked in a breath.

My parents didn't respond, and I realized they wanted Azbogah to see how far he had fallen.

"No." Chest constricting, I brought everyone's attention to myself. The thought of Azbogah dying bothered me. His death would be wrong, though I didn't want to dwell on my relief that I could justify keeping him alive. "He's one of us, and we don't turn on our kind." The truth was that simple, and I refused to stoop to Azbogah's level.

Ingram's brows furrowed. "You *have* to be joking. He caused this problem."

"Yes, but do you really think handing him over will stop the demons from attacking anyone else?" I resisted pointing out the fact that Ingram had been shoved under Azbogah's wing weeks ago.

Inching forward, Levi spoke up. "She's right. Yes, they hate Azbogah, but they hate all of you, too. They believe you all *knew* about what he did and still stood behind him."

"Then we explain the situation," Cael suggested, his gunmetal-blue eyes bright in the darkness.

Bune snorted. "They won't take the time to listen. They'll kill you without concern over what you wanted to say. All you would be doing is handing them Azbogah and whoever escorts the betrayer to them. There's no way of avoiding this war."

Telling them they were wrong wouldn't get them to listen. I needed to employ a tactic Sterlyn would use—appealing to their vanity. "The demons want to *kill* us, but they've forgotten who we really are."

"And what's that?" Eleanor smirked as she fluttered her wings faster.

That was the question I'd been hoping for. "Warriors and survivors. We will fight because we have no choice, but we will do it with grace and dignity the way that Fate intended. We won't turn on one another, nor hurt our brethren without due cause. If the undecided demons don't attack us, we give them grace. After all, they are *our people*, and they didn't choose evil or the life they were given."

A few angels nodded, shocking me.

You're getting through to them. Levi's pride filled my chest.

I hadn't expected it to work, but I wouldn't stop until every single angel was with us. "The witches have a spell that will allow everyone to see the demons. My parents now have their archangel jewelry, so their powers will be magnified. Between that and several witches spelling the artifact building so the demons can't get in, I believe Fate is on our side. Let's free our brethren who have been tormented and find a way to forge a bridge between us. I suspect Bune, Levi, and Zagan will be the key to that."

The energy surged between the angels as my words had the desired effect.

"Let's do as Rosemary suggested!" Munkar pumped his arm.

We turned and flew toward the capitol building, and Azbogah appeared at my side. "Thank you for saving me," he murmured, his voice cracking with emotion.

See. Forgiveness, Levi said, his love warming me inside.

I wasn't sure that word was accurate. "I didn't do it for you. We can't continue to turn on one another. Not anymore. The cost is too great."

The dark angel nodded. "Still...thank you. You don't know how much that meant to me."

Unfortunately, I did. I didn't want him to die, and it wasn't only because he was an angel. Over the past few days, I'd grown...tolerant of him, even if I couldn't ignore everything he'd done.

As we approached the capitol building, it seemed the entire city had gathered. People were going into the nearby bear shifter restaurant to grab the weapons we'd stored there days before.

"I'll bring you a weapon," Azbogah said as he flew toward the restaurant, leaving me with my parents and Levi. I looked around and went to speak with Sterlyn, Ronnie, Alex, Griffin, Erin, Breena, and Diana, who all stood on the lawn in front of the building.

As we approached, the sparkling colorful spell fueled by Levi's blood and mine surged around us. I looked at Erin, who had several coven members standing close by with the black bowls. The magic swirled and enveloped everyone in the area.

When we landed, Griffin blinked. "The spell worked. I can see a murky shadow next to Rosemary."

A nearby shifter stumbled back as Levi breezed by. The tension between the shifters became more overwhelming now that they could see the threat above.

"Are we ready?" Erin asked through gritted teeth. "About a quarter of our people are staying in the artifact building to spell it during the fight, which has weakened the spell on the dome. The longer the rest of us witches hold the spell to keep the demons out, the faster we'll drain. We need to start the fight."

Munkar, Phul, and Ishim flew toward us with their weapons. The angels were moving quickly and efficiently, as we were trained to do.

"We'll only open one gate," Mother said as she landed beside Erin. Her forehead creased with worry. "That way, they can't attack us from both sides."

"Then it should be the Shadow Ridge gate," Alex suggested. "Most of the demons are there, targeting the university. Also, some of the vampires in Shadow Terrace have gone rogue."

Yet another problem for after we'd settled this. We didn't need rabid vampires causing issues along with the demons.

"Sounds like a plan. Now go." Erin gritted out, her voice rough with strain.

"Killian and the others are in place." Sterlyn nodded. "Eliza is close by and will perform the visibility spell from the blood they got from you at the secret silver wolf neighborhood when the gate begins to open."

Griffin's eyes glowed. "I'm telling the wolf shifters at the gate to open it when they see us."

"Everyone, stay safe, and shout if you need help." Ronnie glanced at our friends and hugged Gwen. "Remember, we're always here for each other."

Sweat beaded on Erin's lip, indicating the witches were using more power to cloak the city than we'd realized.

"It's time!" Father yelled. "Everyone, move toward the Shadow Ridge gate!"

I'd turned to fly when Mother's scent filled my nose, and her strong arms wrapped around me. "No matter what, I love you, and I'm proud of you. You've always done what you feel is right, even when I thought it was wrong."

Tears burned my eyes. "We are *not* saying goodbye." I couldn't, not to anyone here, but as I pushed ahead, regret slammed into me. What if she never heard me say the same words in return? "I love you, too," I called over my shoulder.

Our group headed toward the gate, reminding me of the war movies I'd watched from time to time. I could almost hear our steps beating in unison.

The sound of war.

The gate came into view, and it began to rise. I'd expected a handful of demons to be standing on guard since the demons had spread to other targets. However, with every inch, more and more red eyes appeared. The crowd was as thick as the one that had covered the dome night after night.

Loud screeches rang out, and the overwhelming urge to cover my ears surged through me.

One thing was certain: they'd responded to our declaration of war.

Then they surged toward us.

CHAPTER TWELVE

WE SHOULD HAVE KNOWN. We'd cloaked the city to move undetected—the Hell witches could have hidden their own numbers just as easily. Eliza and our witch allies hadn't wanted to use their magic to search for the witches outside because that would have alerted Hell's witches to a pending attack. Erin and her coven had been so busy channeling all their magic into securing the gates, cloaking the city, charging the crystals that kept the city hidden from human eyes, and adding extra layers of protection to the artifact building that they didn't have any magic or time left to search for additional threats.

It didn't matter. There was no preventing this. I just hoped we could kill a few demons right away to thin out their numbers.

The demons swarmed, their attention focused on the angels. They didn't bother with the shifters and vampires who charged them. After all, they thought only people of angel descent could see them.

Azbogah tossed me a sword, and I clutched it firmly in my hand. Heart pounding, I readied myself for a fight. I'd trained harder in the last days than I had in centuries, and I felt even more confident in my abilities. However, so many of our residents had merely had a short stretch of training this past week, and I could only hope that I could do enough to save as many lives as possible.

I glanced at Azbogah and said, "You need to stay behind the pack. As soon as they realize who you are, they'll be desperate to kill you."

A tender smile crossed his face, and his eyes glistened. "That may be true, but when they realize who *you* are to *him*"—Azbogah gestured to Levi and then himself—"and *me,* they'll be just as desperate to kill you."

My heart skipped a beat. Though logically I realized who Azbogah was to me, he didn't feel like my father. Only one angel had ever been that to me, but that didn't change biology. Although most of these demons wouldn't know who I was to Azbogah, they would all know I was Levi's preordained and try to kill me.

He's right. Levi's desperation swelled between us.

There was no time to panic. *It doesn't matter.* I was ready to fight. After all, I was a warrior and a protector of this city. I wouldn't hide because things got complicated. *I can't sit idly by.*

I know that, but that doesn't mean I have to be happy about it, Levi countered as he flew next to me.

As a demon passed a wolf shifter in front of me, the shifter swung his sword, severing the demon's head. The demons behind hesitated, blinking and processing what they'd seen.

A dark-haired vampire next to the wolf shifter swung his weapon at a demon close to him, slicing through its neck. The ones that had been watching screamed. "The shifters

and vampires can *see* us!" one of them yelled. I couldn't tell
which because the swarm was so massive.

Our surprise advantage wouldn't last long, and I
barreled past the others, ready for action.

Since only a few demons had gotten all the way
through, I hurried toward the horde. The smaller number
would be easier for the rest to fight, and I flipped my
feathers over, ready to attack with my wings as well as my
sword.

A snarl from below had me glancing downward to find
Sterlyn, Griffin, Ronnie, and Alex rushing below me. The
strongest fighters were pushing forward to protect the
weaker ones for as long as possible. I wanted to tell them to
stand back, but that wouldn't do any good. The horde
would be in here momentarily, and we'd all fight together.

A demon soared in my direction, its eyes locked on me,
and hissed. "The day has finally come to kill my betrayers,"
she said. Her red eyes glowed brighter, revealing that her
rage or excitement had increased. In fairness, it could have
been both.

If she wanted witty dialogue, she'd found the wrong angel.
I swung my sword, killing her on the spot. Blue blood splattered
my shirt. The sludge from the maliciousness that wafted off the
demons and their blood weighed me down. The overly sweet
floral scents of decaying magnolia, lilac, and violet churned my
upset stomach. A breeze intensified the stench, but I couldn't
see outside the gate due to all the demons flooding through.

As I turned to battle yet another demon, something cold
clutched my arm, yanking me backward. I shifted my wings,
but before I could behead anyone, the grip went slack. I
glanced to the side in time to see the demon fall to the
ground.

We need to cover each other's back, Levi linked as he moved beside me. Blue blood dripped down the blade of his sword, the sterling silver handle revealing it had belonged to the princess of Hell—Levi's mother. Nearly the entire handle was decorated with the engraving of a double-barred cross and an infinity symbol that connected at the bottom.

I'd hoped he would use another sword, but this one was his now. I hated that it would make him more of a target. If Levi died, the sword could only bond with an heir of his bloodline, and since we had no children, no one else could access the power it contained. But they'd try to stop him from using it.

Following his suggestion, I placed my back to his. The demons were descending, and their focus was locked on whoever was closest.

Pained groans echoed, and the metallic stench of blood thickened all around.

Swarming, the demons continued to infiltrate the city. They flew over our heads and ran under our feet, attacking everyone in their wake.

With each breath, I swung my sword and twirled my wings, cutting and slicing through every shadow that came near me. Though I couldn't see every demon I struck, I had to hope I was injuring them enough that they wouldn't pose as great a threat. However, the panicked frenzy with which the demons moved told me everything I needed to know— we'd caught them off guard. *At least they're doing what you, Bune, and Zagan expected.*

These are the weakest demons who served the princes of Hell. The princes will let them eliminate our weakest fighters before they come inside with the witches. Despite Levi not having wings, he was moving as efficiently as any angel.

At least everyone had an idea of what to expect. We'd guessed the first fighters would be the easiest to decimate. We needed to kill as many as possible before the princes and the stronger demons made their way inside.

I took a moment to glance at my friends below and focused on Ronnie. She hadn't yet changed into her demon form, and I breathed a short sigh of relief. We needed to keep her identity secret—we didn't need Wrath targeting her to get his dagger back.

Part of our training for the shifters had been to pay attention to eye color before attacking. If a demon had human-colored irises, that meant they hadn't chosen evil. But so far, all the demons had red eyes.

Similar to Levi and me, the group below had formed a tight circle, keeping their backs to one another and an eye overhead. At least on the ground, they didn't have to worry about an attack from below, unlike those of us who were flying.

I sliced through the neck of another demon as I looked at the open gate. The flow of demons was thinning now that the majority of the first wave was inside the city. For now, the fight was equally balanced.

In my peripheral vision, I saw a dagger swinging toward my chest. I'd been distracted too long.

Rosemary, Levi linked, and his panic swirled between us. The clanging of metal on metal informed me he was engaged in his own battle.

His warning caused the blood to pound in my ears, adding to my alarm until I almost froze.

I'm fine, I replied as I jerked my wings away, breaking the paralyzing fear inside me. I barely blocked the blow. The blade bounced off the edge of my flight feather, nipping the end.

Mother plucker! That would throw off my aerodynamics. But it could've been worse—I could have lost the whole damn thing.

Frustration and anger boiled inside me, and I clenched my jaw. I couldn't believe I'd been foolish enough to allow a demon to nick me.

Are you injured? Levi asked as the sound of his battle continued. These demons were slightly better fighters than the ones that had first surged inside.

Despite the demon being in shadow form, I could see its chest heaving. I wasn't the only one feeling annoyed. It hadn't landed the kill shot, and I wasn't sure how it had missed.

The word *feeling* flashed like a neon light. I was allowing my emotions to get the better of me, and they were driving my erratic decisions. I needed to channel my former self if I wanted everyone I loved to make it out of this alive.

I'm fine, I assured him. *Please focus on your own enemies.* If he died because he was worried about me, I couldn't survive it.

Another demon raced over to the one that had failed to eliminate me. Both sets of eyes focused on me, and the demons spoke in hushed tones. I soared toward them, but I couldn't make out what they were saying over the deafening sounds of war. There were screams of pain, begging on both sides, the clanking of weapons, and worst of all, laughter from the sick scoundrels who enjoyed inflicting torture. However, I didn't need to hear the pair of demons to know what their plan was: simultaneously attack and kill me. I'd just have to watch for signs of how they decided to attack.

Failed Attempt Demon and Pity Demon inched toward me, taking their sweet time. They wanted to control the situation.

A demon hurried past them as if to fly by me, but a warning chill ran down my spine. They had a third attacker.

The corners of my lips lifted, and I didn't attempt to hide my smile. They needed to understand that though the angels of Shadow City might have been blocked off from the world, we weren't fools. Not like them.

Making a point of not looking at me was the demon's fatal flaw. As expected, when it came within ten feet of me, its eyes fixated on the location of my heart.

Not bothering to humor it, I flew forward, closing the distance. I dropped a little more than I'd intended because of the blasted feather, but I quickly corrected my elevation. Clueless Demon's eyes widened a moment before the blade sliced through its neck. Like all the others, its head fell to the ground while its body stayed elevated for a few seconds before tumbling after.

When I lifted my head to find Failed Attempt and Pity, they had paused in their progression. I'd taken away their control for the moment.

A low hiss came from Pity. Whoever I'd killed meant something to it. That was fine; they wouldn't be far behind.

I lowered my sword, wiping off the sticky blood on the leg of my jeans. The urge to soar across the distance suffocated me, but I'd told Levi I'd protect his back. I couldn't do that if I moved farther away from him, so I'd wait for their attack. I wanted to check on Levi, but I could hear him breathing behind me. The absence of pain also told me just as much as if I were to glance his way. No more distractions.

Pity Demon removed something from his pocket and placed it on his middle finger. It looked as if it were made of iron with three spikes on top that were clearly meant to injure me. If he stabbed an artery, I'd bleed out, and if he hit anything else, it'd hurt like hell.

Failed Attempt Demon waved its knife again as if that would terrify me. I glanced around them to ensure there wasn't another party attempting to attack. Though there was no one right there, five demons were breezing in behind them, their attention either on me or Levi.

I breathed, trying to remain *rational*. Apparently, that would be my mantra for this entire war or until I died. Whichever came first.

Pushing that troublesome thought away, I linked with Levi, *How are you on the battlefront?*

Let's see. Levi's frustration bled through. *Every time I kill one, another one pops up and takes its place. But your heart is beating, and I'm breathing, so I'll take it.*

I held in my smile. Even during a war and while covered in blood, he had a way of warming my heart. *I hate to tell you this, but five more are about to attack.*

When the demons had flooded in, they'd rushed to get *in*, attacking whoever was near with no evidence of strategy. That was changing, and the demons entering were searching for particular targets. I had a feeling that our three demon-defector allies were just as wanted as Azbogah and the angels. They were viewed the same way—as traitors.

We need to pull inward so more angels surround us, Levi responded. *We're still in the front because of the chaos. Now that the battle is settling, we need to form larger groups with our people.*

Our people.

I liked the sound of that.

Let me kill these two. Then we'll do that. Hopefully, the five demons wouldn't attack immediately.

Pity Demon barked, "Go that way, and I'll get her this way." He moved toward my left.

Were they that stupid, or were they attempting to

disorient me? It didn't matter. As long as I paid attention, I could determine their real strategy.

They approached me from different angles, and I chuckled. They weren't trying to trick me at all. They didn't think I could fight off two demons at once.

Then the five new demons flanked them while ten more headed our way. No, they had something else planned.

The world spun. If I didn't get myself under control, I wouldn't be able to determine their plan in time.

They were attacking us—seventeen to two. *We have to go.* I managed to remain stationary and school my expression into a mask of indifference. If I moved too soon, they'd soar toward us, and we'd be greatly outnumbered.

Let me kill this last one, Levi replied.

I could hear his grunts as his battle intensified.

The seventeen demons moved my way.

We're out of time. I tightened my hold on the sword. There was no way out of this attack.

Eight broke away and headed for Levi as nine made their way toward me. I wasn't sure why I'd gotten the group with one extra, but better me than him.

The sound of slicing skin put me a little at ease...but barely. Levi inched closer to me, and my feathers nearly grazed his back.

Don't get any closer. My wings are set on their sharp side, I warned. He didn't need an injury that could be prevented, especially not from me.

Breathing became easier as his pride wafted into me. *I figured so since they're covered in blue blood. Don't worry. I won't get too close. I just don't want to leave a large enough space for them to exploit.*

That worked.

The five closest demons swarmed me, two on each side,

aiming for a hand and a leg, with the fifth one sailing straight at me with an ax aimed at my neck. The message was clear—*we'll kill you the same way you kill us.*

Dead was dead for an angel, whether it be a severed head or a wound through the heart. The demons behind them would launch a second attack if I got through this. Now that I was in the moment, it seemed asinine that I hadn't trained for this scenario, but training provided only the foundation for what you needed in battle. You couldn't predict every situation.

I prepared to lift my sword as I kicked out my legs and hit the two demons going for my feet in the face. I swiveled, lifting my sword so it blocked the ax. As the sword caught the ax, I swiped it downward, ripping it from the demon's hold, and spun, my wings beheading the demons going for my arms. When I twisted back around, I severed Ax Demon's head. In a matter of seconds, I'd killed three of my nine attackers, but that wasn't enough. Levi didn't have wings to aid him in battle.

Risking everything, I glanced at my preordained, scared of what I'd find. As expected, they were launching a similar attack on him.

My blood ran cold.

We weren't making it out of this unless I did something quickly—something that would skew the odds in our favor.

Something unexpected.

And that was exactly what I would do.

CHAPTER THIRTEEN

I SCANNED THE SURROUNDING AREA, noting everything I could. Once I began spinning, I wouldn't be able to see anything.

I almost wished I hadn't. The scene was tragic. Blue and red blood coated the roads and the residents of Shadow City. Everyone was engaged in battle, and something hard balled up in my stomach as I saw my people lying dead in the streets.

The witches stood in a line about a hundred yards from the entrance, chanting spell after spell. A demon sneaked behind a witch at the end as he was spelling a demon on fire in front of him. The demon reached around the witch and slit his throat. The woman beside him spun in the nick of time to save herself and called the wind to push the demon away.

As my gaze flicked back to Levi, I noticed Raziel. He sat propped up against a building with blood spilling from his chest. Of course, he had been one of the first targets because he'd been Azbogah's close friend. In any other situation, I'd have rushed to help him. He was still an angel, after all, but

I couldn't stop and help every person I came across who was in a similar condition without winding up that way myself.

This was a war.

Glancing through the crowd, I ascertained that Sterlyn, Griffin, Ronnie, Alex, and Gwen were standing strong. They were drenched in blue blood, so none of them were critically injured. Demons were fighting them and the other shifters and vampires on the ground, but the majority remained focused on the angels and the witches.

Excellent. The witches had magic, and the angels were made for battle, even the ones who weren't trained as warriors.

The four demons who had been behind the first five attackers were almost to me, and Left Demon and Right Demon, the ones I'd kicked in the face, had rebounded. It was now or never.

Do you mind if I tap into your magic? I despised doing it, but I didn't have much of a choice.

You never have to ask, Levi replied as the clanging intensified. *Do whatever it takes to stay safe.*

The only way to be safe was to run away, and if he thought I was considering leaving him here, he'd soon realize how wrong he was, but I wouldn't keep distracting him; I just didn't want to catch him off guard by pulling his energy from him unexpectedly.

The seven demons advanced. I tapped into our preordained bond and began to spin. As I moved faster, I wrapped my wings around myself, the speed of my swirling keeping me elevated. Blue blood flicked onto my face from my kills, so I kept my eyes and mouth closed. I couldn't see, anyway, since my wings covered me. Completely sealed in darkness, I heard the sound of weapons hitting my feathers, and I moved toward my enemies. I slammed into something solid, and after a second, nothing struck me.

Yanking more magic from Levi, I moved in my mate's direction much faster than I normally could. *Move out of the way*, I warned him. I wanted to knock down his attackers without harming him.

Done, he told me. *You look like a freaking tornado descending to the ground.*

I hadn't even realized I'd dropped. That damn clipped feather was causing me issues, and I couldn't judge my height. *I need you to direct me.* I moved faster while inclining my body. As long as I kept up my speed, I should be able to maneuver in the air.

Just as I was about to ask if I'd fixed my elevation, I barreled into a demon.

Toward me! Levi exclaimed.

He hadn't provided a direction, right or left, up or down, but I followed the link to him.

"She can see us somehow," a female cried moments before I ran into two more demons.

They've spread out, Levi connected.

In other words, I couldn't easily hit them. I slowed, straightened my wings, and flapped once more.

Five demons were edging away from us and each other. I couldn't hit them effectively, but knowing I could pull that stunt at any time, they might be more wary about attacking us.

A sour taste filled my mouth that I couldn't swallow. *They're circling us.* I had hoped that I could take them out, one by one, but I'd been arrogant. These demons were smarter than I'd given them credit for.

Correction. Levi's dread mixed with mine, and my chest tingled. *They've* formed *a circle around us.*

I glanced over my shoulder. The five demons who had tried to attack me had filled in the gap behind us. I'd hoped to have better luck with that strategy.

The three I'd tossed away inched toward us as the others waited. All thirteen got into position, ready to attack simultaneously. That was fine; I'd take each one of these evildoers down.

What's the plan? Levi asked, his dread turning into determination. He moved so we were again back to back.

Confidence was the only way we would get out of this situation alive. *Kill them*, I replied simply. I was certain of one thing—I didn't want them to make the first move.

Only one of the demons showed his weapon: a silver mace with a spiked ball at the end. My gut said he was the one who'd attack first.

Wanting them to focus on me, I charged Mace Demon. He raised his weapon while the four demons on his left and the three on his right moved toward me. I'd take on all eight because that meant only five would be charging Levi. Though Levi was a strong fighter, he didn't have the added protection of weapon-proof wings.

As I sailed toward Mace Demon, I noted that the demon closest to his right was now wielding a spear. The sharp silver edge formed a small point, but the handle was made of wood, which could work in my favor.

Though the other demons hadn't revealed any weapons yet, I had no doubt that they carried some. They wanted the element of surprise, which, unfortunately, was very strategic. I couldn't counter a weapon until they decided to use it.

Focusing on the mace, I swung my sword at the demon's neck. Mace Demon lifted the weapon. In an effort not to lose my sword, I stopped my ascension, causing Mace Demon to jerk his hands almost over his head.

Spear Demon jabbed the spear at my side, and I moved left, using my wing to block it. However, the demon closest to Mace Demon on the other side jerked out its hand, displaying three sharp edges on the end like claws.

I'd been counting on a spear, a mace, or a sword—something that required distinctive movement for attacks—but Claw Demon had caught me off guard. The claws slashed through my waist. A scream formed in the back of my throat, but I wouldn't allow it to release. That would only encourage the demons more.

A sharp pain surged through my body, and Levi's concern followed a millisecond behind. *Rosey!*

This was one of the less ideal aspects of the bond—his ability to feel my pain.

I'll be fine. I had to be. There was no other option.

Claw Demon gave a distinctly masculine chuckle as his red eyes flicked to my wound. No doubt he enjoyed watching the blood pour from the injury.

Sicko.

I headbutted him. His head jerked back, giving me a perfect target. I sliced through his neck, but the movement caused me so much pain that vomit inched up my throat. My side burned as if it were on fire, but I worked to push the sensation from my mind.

Mace Demon spun, swinging his weapon out to the side. The movement reminded me of one of those sports with a bat I'd seen Killian watch on television a handful of times. However, the demon was aiming for me and not a ball.

The other five demons soared toward me, planning to overtake me. I'd try the move from earlier again. I moved one wing, stopping the mace's impact, then spun through, ready to become a tornado again. However, a moment before I could seal my wings around me, the spear pierced my uninjured side and stuck.

Luckily, my adrenaline was pumping, and the other injury hurt a hell of a feather more. I continued to swirl as I used my free hand to yank the spear from my side, holding the sword and the spear close to my chest.

I hit the five demons who had been inches from toppling me. A loud screech confirmed I'd caught at least one unexpectedly. Clearly, it was one of the dumber ones. They'd all seen me do this before, so they shouldn't have been surprised.

"Keep spinning." Munkar's familiar voice sounded like music to my ears.

My eyes burned. I hadn't expected to make it out of this alive. "Levi! He needs you."

Though I could use help, Levi required it more.

"He's got help, too," Munkar replied.

The clanking weapons calmed my breathing. We weren't alone, and things couldn't be too horrible if people were beginning to help one another.

Since I wasn't slamming into any more demons, I slowed. Now that some of my panic had dissipated, the scorching pain in my side was hard to ignore.

As the world stilled, I found Phul and Ishim fighting alongside Levi and Munkar on my side. Though we were still outnumbered, relief coursed through me.

Munkar fought Mace Demon and another demon armed with a dagger. Another demon hurried toward the angel from behind.

That had to be Claw Demon. Though I couldn't see his weapon, the sneaky movements reminded me of when he'd hurt me. As if Fate wanted to confirm it for me, a drop of red blood fell from wherever he had the claw hidden.

He wouldn't get a cheap shot against another one of us.

Four demons rose toward us from the ground. They must have been the ones I'd hit while I was an angel tornado. We'd kill the three here before they reached us.

I tapped into our bond, borrowing power from Levi. With my injury, I was already moving more slowly, and I worried I couldn't catch Claw Demon in time.

As expected, the claw appeared on the shadow's hand. He'd strike at any second.

Though I wanted to use the spear because of its light weight, that wouldn't kill the demon. I wasn't one for slow, painful deaths, but I might make an exception because of the excruciating pain the demon had caused me.

Gritting my teeth, I raised my sword. Spots danced across my vision, but I wasn't sure if that was from pain or a lack of oxygen. Forcing my lungs to move, I swung the sword as hard as possible. Agony exploded in my side, and my arms wanted to weaken, but failure wasn't an option.

With every ounce of control I had, I pushed through the pain, fearing I couldn't kill Claw Demon in time. Channeling more power from Levi, I drove my arms through my swing and felt the blade hit its mark a split second before it would have been too late. The demon's head tumbled to the ground, and its body stilled. The claw halted its forward progression inches from Munkar's shoulder.

Munkar beheaded Mace Demon and spun around to Spear Demon just as the four other demons reached me.

Even though I couldn't afford to expel the energy, I needed to heal myself soon, but I had to eliminate the incoming threat first. I took a moment to look at my wound, the blood dripping from the bottom of my pants leg. The imbecile had clawed me deep.

No, *I* was the imbecile for allowing it to happen.

"She's bleeding," a demon rasped. "A lot."

I'd hoped they wouldn't figure that out. They would exploit my weakness.

I lifted both the spear and the sword high, concentrating on stabilizing my arms. I needed to give the illusion that I wasn't as hurt as they imagined.

My act didn't fool them. Instead of slowing, they raced toward me faster.

The four of them split apart, reminding me of the first group that had attacked. They would go for my arms and legs, but this time, I couldn't react as steadily.

I braced myself. When they closed in, Munkar and Ishim flanked my right with Levi and Phul on the left. My entire body wanted to shut down now that I had the four of them with me, but even if they each took on one of my attackers, any demon around could take their place, especially if they saw me weakening.

White-hot rage surged from Levi, making my blood boil. He linked, *You said you were fine.*

In fairness, I thought I was, but I ripped the wounds worse while fighting demons afterward. That wouldn't make him feel better since I should've alerted him.

"Levi," Munkar said through clenched teeth. "Take her somewhere. Now!"

"No problem." His irises darkened to coffee-brown as he inched over to me. *We said we'd tell each other.*

I'm sorry. I should have said something, but we were besieged. I didn't mean to not tell you. Needing to get out of the way before the three men attacked, I floated toward the ground. Walking would be less painful than flying.

Let me help you, Levi linked, his frustration melting into concern.

Though I'd love for him to help, that wouldn't be ideal.

If you do anything that shows how hurt I am, anyone looking for an easy kill will attack us. I had to appear strong. *I need to go somewhere to heal, preferably indoors.*

Surveying the area once again, I watched as the witches forced demons to the ground from the sky so the vampires and shifters could deal with them. A few vampires held guns but weren't shooting, likely because the demons were moving so quickly that a bullet could miss them and hit an angel in the sky.

That was the problem with firearms. At least with swords and daggers, the impact range was much smaller.

I hoped Eliza's coven knew how to cast the same spell to force the demons to the ground. She was strong and knowledgeable, so they should be able to do it as well.

"Rosemary!" Sterlyn exclaimed from below.

Adrenaline coursed through my body at the horror in her cry. They needed my assistance.

My head snapped in her direction, and I saw all five of my friends standing tall. Ronnie, Alex, and Gwen were engaged in a battle with three demons, but Sterlyn and Griffin were staring at my side.

My head grew lighter, and I hoped it was from the realization that they were all safe. But I'd lost a decent amount of blood.

We landed beside them, close to where the shifters and demons were fighting. Although winning should have provided relief, the demons had more numbers than what was within the city. Something wasn't right.

Levi nodded toward a tall golden building near us. "If you need us..."

He didn't say more, but with Sterlyn, you didn't have to.

"Holler if you need anything," she said as she lifted her sword. She rushed past us, re-engaging in battle.

Griffin growled, "She's going to be the death of me," and raced after her.

Not too long ago, I would've rolled my eyes, but now I understood all too well how seeing your mate in battle felt.

Keeping my back straight, I moved steadily on my feet. Luckily, the golden building—a restaurant—was only a few feet away. Levi rushed to the glass door and opened it. It was vacant, but the round wooden tables were set as if the restaurant would open at any second. I hurried to the far side, away from the windows, hoping to hide the glow of my hand. "Levi, stand in front of me."

He obliged me, and I placed the weapons against the wall. Crossing my arms over my body, I placed one palm on top of each wound. As my magic funneled through my hands, the area around me lit up, but there wasn't much I could do other than hope I didn't catch the attention of a demon. The demons wouldn't check the buildings for survivors until they had locked down the risk outside, so as long as we didn't draw attention, we should be safe.

When the pain eased, I almost whimpered in relief. It had been excruciating, but I had to be careful I didn't deplete my magic too much. The battle had only just begun, and others might need healing.

As soon as the wounds had scabbed over, I released the tug on my core.

Levi pulled me into his arms and whispered, "You scared me."

I exhaled and leaned into his embrace. "I'm sorry." That hadn't been my intent.

The front door to the restaurant opened, and I stepped away, reaching for my sword and spear. Levi stood protectively in front of me, his sword extended outward as a musky freesia scent filled the space.

It's Sterlyn, I linked as she appeared in front of us.

Her iridescent silver irises glowed as she locked gazes with me. "We've got to get to Shadow Ridge. The princes of Hell have taken over Killian's pack neighborhood, and they're holding everyone captive, including Annie and the other silver wolf mates. They'll exchange them for Levi, Ronnie, Yelahiah, Pahaliah, and Azbogah. And if they don't come soon, the princes will kill them all, starting with Annie."

CHAPTER FOURTEEN

I FELL BACK against the wall, needing the extra support. My legs were wobbly, and it wasn't purely from the blood loss and the depletion of my magic.

Levi moved beside me, wrapping his free arm around my waist. Under normal circumstances, I'd have pulled away. To most people, especially angels, this would make me appear weak. But it was just him and Sterlyn, and the weight of the world had crashed down over me.

"Everyone is beside themselves, and Cyrus is about to lose it," Sterlyn murmured hoarsely.

However, something still wasn't clear. "How did they find Annie and the other women in the hidden silver wolf pack neighborhood?"

"Asmodeus spent time searching for her, finally tracked her down, and brought her to Shadow Ridge. That's as much as I know."

Asmodeus. The prince of Lust.

"The prince of Hell she was promised to." My hands clenched as my breathing quickened. "We should have anticipated this."

"Do *not* blame yourself," Levi rasped as his mocha eyes found mine. "We all thought the demons who knew about that secondary silver wolf pack location were dead. No one could have foreseen this, but either someone we left behind knew or they got the information from someone."

Sterlyn rubbed her forehead. "A wolf from Killian's pack vanished, and they found him dead not too long ago. That could be how they got the information."

"What's our plan?" Levi's hand tightened around his sword.

We didn't have a choice, and the princes of Hell knew that. We wouldn't risk the people we loved. I assumed they'd realized Annie's connection to the silver wolves since Annie's musky floral scent tied her to her silver wolf mate. And when we'd attacked the demon wolf pack, the demons who had escaped back to Hell through the portal had seen Ronnie fighting alongside Annie. Add in Levi staying with us during his time on Earth, and they no doubt had realized that taking Annie would force the hand of almost every person they hated. As for those who weren't directly connected to her, like my parents and Azbogah, they were hoping that Levi being preordained to an angel would bring them in, too. This was one reason supernaturals thought that remaining separate made us stronger, but I had to believe that by fighting together, we had a better chance of making it out with minimal lives lost.

Everything in my body screamed not to take Levi anywhere near the princes, but keeping him away would only extend the torment and chaos, especially since his sword might come in handy when dealing with the witches from Hell. The better decision was to save as many lives as we could, which meant we had to give the illusion of handing people over. "We can't allow them to hurt Annie or anyone else, and maybe we can use this to our advantage. I knew there weren't enough demons attacking us here, and things are already calming." The battle turning in our favor so quickly meant the stronger demons were with the princes of Hell.

"You're right. With your injury, you should stay here." Levi released his hold quickly, as if he thought that would appease me.

Sterlyn snorted, but her eyes were still tense with worry. "I'm not your mate, and even *I* know that won't work."

I stood and filled my lungs to keep my head clear. "He does, too. He's just hoping."

"Rosey, you were just severely injured." He waved a hand at my side, where crimson blood coated my skin. "And you used a decent amount of your magic."

Though he was right on all accounts, there was one thing about which he wasn't thinking clearly . "And if you're going to face four princes of Hell who want you dead, there's no way in Heaven I'm staying behind. If you were in my situation, what would *you* do?"

He scowled, but his lips remained sealed. He didn't have a good response.

"Then we're wasting time and energy." And I didn't have much to spare. The intense fighting, especially while in pain, coupled with my magic being about a quarter depleted, made moving more challenging. Even the lights of the dome in full force hadn't given me much of a boost, but at least I'd gotten something out of it.

I took a step and cringed, waiting for the intense agony to swarm over me. When I only felt a twinge of discomfort, tears of relief burned my eyes.

What's wrong? Levi asked as he turned to me. He had felt my dread.

I forced a smile, wanting him to see I wasn't hurting. *Nothing. I expected it to hurt when I moved, but I healed myself enough that it no longer does.*

I moved to the window and glanced outside. There were still intense battles taking place. Motionless shadow forms covered the ground, as did the corpses of residents of the city, with pieces of buildings falling from the impact of bodies and weapons. The death and destruction fractured my heart. Our world was crumbling, but we wouldn't be around to rebuild if we didn't fight. Our lives depended on it.

"I'm linking with Griffin." Sterlyn hurried to the door, eager to get back to her mate. "He's going to get Kira and Ulva to lead the shifters, and then he'll look for Ronnie and Alex so they can turn things over to Gwen. Then we can all head out."

Even though Alex would be adamant that Ronnie should remain here, I knew she wouldn't allow her foster sister to die. Ronnie and Annie had been thrown into this crazy world together and would do anything to protect each other. There was no way Ronnie would stay behind.

"We'll get my parents and Azbogah and meet you outside the gate," I said as I headed for the door.

As we made our way outside, Sterlyn split to the left, while Levi and I turned right.

The flickering lights of Heaven washed over me, recharging my magic. I glanced skyward to see that the top of the dome was clear of demons, but I frowned as I took in the surrounding chaos. With all the bodies battling in the sky, it would be difficult to find my parents and Azbogah.

Flames licked the purple-domed building that was my

favorite in the city. For a second, I thought the building was on fire, but the flames disappeared as quickly as they'd come. Something familiar jolted through me as if the flames contained magic similar to mine.

My heart jumped. Someone had said mother's ring shot flames of justice. That had to be what I was seeing. *This way*, I linked with Levi.

I could feel him following me, and I took to the sky. The witches were pushing the demons down and lighting a few on fire. But even on fire, the demons pushed through their agony to attack anyone close to them. Their screams added more urgency, and they trampled over nearby fighters, using their ignited bodies to inflict casualties on our side.

A flame flashed near the purple-domed building again, calling to my soul. Through the smoke and the crowd, I glimpsed Mother and Father fighting side by side. Mother slashed the head from a demon's body as another charged at her. She held up her hand with the ring, and flames engulfed the demon. The demon fell to the ground, lifeless despite its head remaining intact.

How is that possible? I'd learned that the only way to kill a demon was to behead it. Yet here was Mother, killing them with her sword *and* with flames.

Levi surged ahead of me, slicing the head off a demon that rushed him. *My mother talked about Yelahiah and Pahaliah at times. Yelahiah channels the flames of justice, and any person with ill intentions will suffer death upon the judgment of her ring or sword.*

I exhaled and smiled. Anything that tipped the odds in our favor was more than okay with me.

Beside her, Father spun, his wings severing the neck of a demon who had been closing in. Blood spattered his stark-white clothing and coated his pale skin, and he looked like an avenging angel instead of the kindhearted one I knew.

In reality, I didn't know either of my parents now that their emotions were returning. We'd been shells of our former selves, having lost touch with one another and our feelings due to the horrible decisions of one of our own.

With leaden wings and aching muscles, I pushed myself to fly toward my parents. Levi moved equally slowly beside me, but neither of us commented on our pace.

As we approached, I called, "Mother. Father." I didn't want them to attempt to fight us, thinking we were demons attacking from behind.

Mother's head snapped in my direction. Her normally tamed hair was wild, her green eyes bright from battle. Despite the blue blood coating her face, she looked breathtaking, as if this was the role she'd always been meant to embody.

Father's soft blue eyes lightened to almost white. "What's wrong?"

He'd always had an uncanny way of knowing I was upset, sometimes even before I did. "The demons. They captured Annie and many of the silver and Shadow Ridge wolves."

"Where are they?" Mother's voice shook with rage.

"The Shadow Ridge wolf pack neighborhood." I wanted to wince, but I kept my expression indifferent. She was going to give us a hard time about leaving the city, and rightfully so. "From what I understand, all four princes of Hell are there. They say they'll start killing them, beginning with Annie, unless you two, Azbogah, Ronnie, and Levi come to them."

"Of course they would take the demon wolf that Asmodeus has coveted since she was conceived, who is birthing a child she created with a silver wolf." Mother scoffed, her jaw twitching. "And they just expect us to leave our people here and rush to them?"

The answer was obvious, so Father and I remained silent.

"Uh..." Levi's mocha eyes glanced around. "Yes?"

It was rhetorical. A bit of lightness filled my chest, which I desperately needed. Maybe that was why Sierra cracked jokes at inappropriate times—because sometimes, in dark times, a little light was needed.

Mother cut her eyes to him but remained silent.

That was for the best. Before she could change her mind and speak, I refocused the conversation. "We have to be careful, though. The number of demons here isn't anything like it should be. And where are their witches?" Granted, they probably hadn't expected much resistance since most of the city couldn't see the demons.

Four demons surged our way, and we dispersed, taking one each. The one I soared toward lifted a standard dagger. Thank the gods. At least it was something I'd been trained to defend against.

A loud growl came from the demon as if to intimidate me. I felt near normal with the lights swirling around me, and my confidence swelled. The demon shook his head as he tried to focus on me.

I smirked. Demons weren't used to the heavenly lights. Some of them might have never seen them before. I scanned the area and noticed that several more demons seemed disoriented, but that didn't stop them from pushing forward, determined to kill.

As he drew closer, the demon moved his hand in front of him so it blended in with his chest. He didn't want to reveal his plan of attack, so I'd have to go by the direction he moved and the way the blade of the dagger tipped.

When he was only a few feet away, the blade flipped straight toward me. He was going for a front slice straight into the chest. He didn't want to take the extra time to strike at a side.

Efficient.

As he jabbed forward, I spun sideways, and the blade ricocheted off the sharp side of my feathers. He grunted, and then a second, smaller knife aimed for my side.

These demons liked going for the sides and did it when we employed our wings for protection. The princes of Hell had taught them well.

I blocked his thrust with my sword, knocking the knife from his hand only a second before it would have injured me. I finished the twirl, using the tip of the feather that had been snipped to behead him. That feather was jagged and sharper than the others.

I spun, ready to help Levi and my parents, but they were each finishing off their own attacker.

"We need to find Azbogah and meet Sterlyn and the others at the gate," I said with urgency. "They'll do something to Annie if we don't get there soon." I wasn't sure I believed they would kill her, but some alternatives were worse than death. "We have to protect the baby, who's part *silver wolf*, I might add." I needed to remind her that it was her brother's bloodline.

That did the trick because she huffed. "Fine. Azbogah was in front of the capitol building not too long ago."

"I'll get him," Levi said as he raced toward the building.

He wasn't going alone. I didn't trust Azbogah not to kill my mate in the name of confusion. "We'll meet you there," I called over my shoulder to my parents.

We flew high above the road, heading toward the building. Witches lined the road, chanting spell after spell. Though they weren't drenched in blood like the rest of us, blue speckles marred their clothes, skin, and hair. The metallic stench of blood swirled around us, and I wasn't sure I would ever be able to breathe without smelling it again.

Bloodstains.

That was what I'd always been told. Even if we cleaned the city, I might never be able to forget the flood of violet from the mixture of blue and red blood. Unlike the outside world, we didn't have a sewer system because we didn't have rain. So blood continued to puddle under the feet of the shifters, vampires, and witches.

The capitol building was nearly unrecognizable. The once-white complex had red and blue blood streaming down its sides, mixing in some spots to give it the same purple hue. The heavenly lights flickered, adding an almost sinister glow.

Standing in front of the building were Azbogah and Cael, with Erin and Diana flanking them. The two of them barely had any blood on them, and Erin and Diana dealt with any demon who got close.

And here I'd thought he might have changed. I shouldn't have been surprised. Once a coward, always a coward.

As my attention landed behind them, my stomach dropped. Ezra was about ten feet behind them, lifting his sword, his eyes trained on Azbogah.

Of course he'd try to kill him while we were distracted. Ezra held a grudge over being locked up for the past several months. There was no way I could stop him in time, but I had to try.

Just as Ezra swung the sword down, Jegudiel dropped from the air. He moved his wing to block Azbogah's back, and the demon who had been chasing him hurtled past him toward Ezra.

Stumbling back from the impact, the demon stabbed Ezra in the chest before spinning around to fight Jegudiel once again.

I flew down, descending a little too quickly from the blood sticking to my feathers and my clipped flight wing, but I adjusted. I landed behind them, and Erin shot me a scathing look.

"Are you injured?" Azbogah asked with concern as he stepped toward me. His gaze landed on my side caked with blood. His attention flicked first to Ezra, who had a gaping wound in his chest, then to Jegudiel, who was fighting the demon behind him. I had no time or energy to heal Ezra, and I couldn't bring myself to care. Not for him. Unfortunately, the wound was fatal.

I wanted to tell Azbogah to quit pretending to care, but I bit back the words. I didn't need to argue with him. That would only make his job that much easier. "I'm fine, but Jegudiel just saved your life."

Levi landed next to me and linked, *I'll use the sword on him if I have to.*

My heart warmed, and I channeled my feelings of love toward him. *I hope it doesn't come to that.* Either way, my preordained was at my side in all the ways that mattered.

"We have a problem." I winced at my word choice.

Cael rolled his eyes. "We're *all* aware."

"Watch it," Levi warned. "Or you'll have another demon after you."

Don't give them justification to kill you. That would only help their mission. We couldn't let emotions rule us.

But I was learning that was easier said than done. Yet another way I used to judge mortals too harshly. "I meant more trouble than this demon attack."

"How is that possible?" Diana snapped between spells. Her nose wrinkled as if she smelled something horrible.

I had a feeling it had nothing to do with the overwhelming stench of blood but rather what I'd said, as if this was all my fault. I wanted to point fingers at the culprits, but that wouldn't resolve any matters. Instead, it would have us fighting against one another and give Azbogah more of a reason not to come with us.

"They have Annie," I said simply.

"Annie?" Azbogah's brows furrowed.

I wanted to punch him. He didn't even remember the name of the girl he'd sent Ezra to kidnap. "The demon wolf Asmodeus has been desperate to capture. He has her."

Azbogah's jaw dropped. "Why didn't you hide her?"

"We thought she was safe, but she refused to be too far from Cyrus despite being pregnant." He didn't get to act as if we'd done something wrong. We'd done everything we could think of to stop all of this.

"She's *pregnant* with a silver wolf's child?" Azbogah rubbed a hand down his face. "That's problematic, but there's nothing I can do about it."

"Actually, there is," Levi said happily. "He's willing to exchange you and me for her."

The dark angel's shoulders relaxed. "Well, I know Rosemary won't give you up—"

"No, but we're going to pretend we will." I lifted my chin and glared at him. "We're going to pretend we're giving *both* of you up."

"That's asinine." Cael shook his head and lifted a sword that didn't have a speck of blood on it. "Just let the girl die."

When Azbogah didn't counter the remark, disappointment flooded me, and my breath hitched. I should've known better, but I'd hoped he would change. "After having my *uncle* killed, after giving *me* up, and after having the *people you abandoned* attack the home you built, *this* is how you will continue your legacy? Another selfish move made by someone who won't even fight alongside their people to resolve the wrong *they* committed?"

Azbogah's cheeks turned a shade pink, but he stood tall. He would never be selfless, not even to fix his mistakes.

"That's fine," I said. "We'll figure it out without you."

"Rosey," Levi said with concern. *It may not work without him.*

It'll have to. I ascended into the sky, turning my back on the dark angel. *Because we can't make him. But I had to try.*

Levi followed me, and for some stupid reason, I hoped Azbogah would call after me or I'd hear the sound of his wings pounding behind me.

Neither ever came.

Bune and Zagan came into view, slaying their fellow demons and fighting for the city that had betrayed them.

We need to tell them where we're going. Levi soared toward them.

When we approached, Levi filled them in on what Azbogah had said.

"You two go on. We'll keep an eye on things here. We know where to find you," Bune assured us.

Because of how close he'd gotten to the three warriors who'd trained me, I felt comfortable with him staying here, so the two of us nodded.

We darted out of the city, killing a few demons along the way, but I didn't see Mother, Father, Sterlyn, Griffin,

Ronnie, or Alex. We were supposed to meet them outside the gate.

Where are they? My vision darkened at the edges as I searched for my friends.

Levi lifted his sword beside me, ready for a fight.

When I heard a hiss from beside me, I spun around... and faced a demon.

CHAPTER FIFTEEN

HEART HAMMERING, I swung my sword, aiming for the enemy's neck just as the demon's familiar emerald eyes caught my attention.

Ronnie.

I yanked back, causing my side to twinge with pain from the remnants of the injury, but that was a small price to pay for not killing a friend.

Extending her hand, Ronnie knocked my sword downward and said angrily, "What the *fuck*?"

Now that the threat of beheading her was over, annoyance flashed through me. I gritted my teeth. "What did you think would happen when you floated toward me, hissing? I thought you were the enemy!" But now it made sense why I hadn't sensed her. She had no maliciousness wafting from her soul.

Levi appeared at my side, glaring at the demonic vampire. "You better be glad your foolish action didn't get you killed. Rosemary would forever carry around that guilt, though she wouldn't have done anything wrong."

He was right, but now we were ganging up on her. I

didn't want her to feel that way, either. "It doesn't matter. She's fine." Thank the gods.

Irises dimming, Ronnie exhaled. "I'm sorry. I wasn't thinking. I hissed because Azbogah wasn't with you. I wasn't trying to sneak up on you."

Everybody's emotions were heightened, and Ronnie was one of the most affected due to Annie's dire situation. Though I was upset, I wasn't close to Annie in the way she was. "He wouldn't come."

"Then I'll go get him." Ronnie inched toward the gate, not thinking rationally.

"If we take too long, they'll think we're not coming. We need to get there."

"They want him even more than they want Levi and me," Ronnie said, but stopped. Her breathing was so ragged I could see the motion of her chest even in her shadow form.

That was true, and I didn't know how to comfort her. "It's better for the two of you to show up with Mother and Father than for you not to show up at all." I despised the situation we were in.

"It's not like you could force the dickwad to turn himself over, anyway." Levi tensed beside me, disdain dripping from every word. "Besides, getting him out of that city will be damn near impossible with the number of demons still attacking inside."

As if to prove his point, another twenty demons headed down the bridge toward us. They weren't coming into the city in the same numbers as before, but a few were still making their way here.

"You're right." Ronnie's arm moved upward, the outline of her dagger blending with her hand. Unlike most demons, she had a blood-bound weapon, a dagger that had belonged to her grandfather, Wrath, a prince of Hell. This dagger could be blanketed in shadows as well, just as Levi's sword could.

I surveyed the area for my parents, Griffin, Sterlyn, and Alex. "Where are the others?"

"They're in the woods, waiting for us." Ronnie flew upward. "Your parents flew the three of them so we wouldn't run into issues." She tipped her dagger toward the demons charging at us.

That was a good call.

Following her, we soared above the jetting towers of the huge bridge, and the demons didn't even attempt to follow. Perhaps they had an inkling of who we were and where we were going.

Of course, they'd recognize Levi's essence.

Trying to push away my worry, I focused on the fall foliage I hadn't seen in days. The orange, red, and yellow leaves weren't nearly as thick as they had been before, but there was enough to provide some coverage. I breathed in the crushed-tea-leaves scent of fall. The sun was descending, filling the sky with pink, purple, and orange swirls. Sunrise and sunset were my favorite times of day, and I took pleasure in seeing the sun set potentially one last time before I perished.

We're going to make it through this, Levi connected. His determination wafted through our bond as if to empower me.

I'd always prided myself on being realistic. Sierra sometimes called me a pessimist, but that was never my intent. Thinking only positively was foolish, and as a trained warrior, I had to prepare for negative outcomes. Though I wished I could pretend to believe him, we couldn't become overconfident. *I hope you're right.*

Shadow Ridge's quaint downtown was eerily barren.

No vehicles puttered on the two-lane road in the center of the brick shops. The restaurants, banks, and movie theater were all closed. During the last week of November, holiday decorations were normally strung throughout the area, but none of it was in sight. Between that and the missing tourists, I was again reminded that Hell had descended upon Earth.

The woods thickened along the river, and Ronnie floated toward the tree line. Moments before I descended, something tingled down my spine. *We're being watched.* Though I wasn't surprised—demons should be watching us —this felt different.

What do you mean? Levi asked as his focus swung toward downtown, following my gaze. *I don't see any demons.*

This isn't malicious. Something between two brick buildings downtown caught my eye. When I zeroed in, bile crawled up my throat.

"It's one of those machines that takes pictures." I couldn't remember what it was called, but I knew what it wasn't. "Not a camera. One of those other things they use for the news. Someone is down there holding it, though the contraption is almost bigger than he is." I was familiar with cameras because of my phone.

A strangled cry left Ronnie. "It's a video camera."

"I can't go down there." A lump lodged in my throat, making it hard to swallow. At this height, I would still appear like a large bird in the sky, but I'd been careless. With Killian and the witches evacuating the humans, staying out of view hadn't been my priority, and I'd almost divulged our existence.

Ronnie rose higher again. "It's fine. Alex and the others

are moving. We'll meet them closer to Killian's pack neighborhood so we're out of view."

"Someone needs to get that out of here." I glanced over my shoulder as if I could tell whether Shadow City were hidden, which was preposterous. Of course I could see the city; I was a supernatural. I could only hope the veil around it hadn't dropped. The witches were preoccupied with war instead of keeping our existence secret, especially with the gate wide open.

I sighed. It wasn't like I could do anything right now.

We flew toward Killian's pack neighborhood, moving away from downtown and closer to the bend in the river. Killian's and Griffin and Sterlyn's houses were the two closest to that location.

Ronnie said, "We need to land. Alex just told me that they ran into other shifters and witches, including Eliza, in the woods near where you found Sterlyn in her silver wolf form that first day."

I knew the exact day she was talking about, back when Sterlyn had first shown up at Shadow Ridge University and I'd discovered what she was. The woods Ronnie mentioned were flush with the river and downtown. "Eliza isn't being held with the others in the wolf pack neighborhood?" I'd thought that Eliza and Circe's coven would be with Killian and the others. "And shifters beyond wolves?"

"Every supernatural has a vested interest in getting the humans to leave." Ronnie's tone held an edge. "In fact, half of the silver wolves are heading back to Killian's neighborhood, including Cyrus. They were with some bears and foxes, rounding up the humans who kept trying to come back into town. They didn't notice they couldn't talk telepathically to their mates or other pack members in the neighborhood until one of their pack members called them, telling them the demons had taken over and were holding the silver wolves' women captive back at Killian's."

"They could still feel the connections, so nothing alarmed them? They just can't communicate?" Levi laughed humorlessly. "Those Hell witches have been scouring spells for centuries, preparing for this day."

Stomach fluttering, I tried to remain calm. Life had been easier without emotions. I'd worried about things, but not with this sort of intensity. I could easily get sick if I didn't tamp down my feelings, and that took energy I could use elsewhere. "Have they been transferring their knowledge to the next generation before they die?"

"Not necessarily. There are witches down there who came to Hell shortly after it was created. When the demons realized there was a portal and that less powerful demons could terrorize the world without notice, they sent them in search of witches," Levi explained as we slowly descended, now that we were farther away from downtown and the video camera. "Just like demons would grant the demon wolf pack alpha a longer life, they did the same for the witches every few years in exchange for their spells. There are witches who look like they're in their twenties but are older than us."

I hadn't considered that, which was foolish. I'd seen how young the demon wolf pack alpha had looked when we'd rescued Annie from him. The demon prince, Asmodeus, had given the alpha—Annie's father—extra power and an extended life in exchange for...Annie.

Though angels could also extend people's lives, we never shared our powers that way because there was such an inherent risk in allowing someone access to our essence. Others could use it against us, similar to how witches used people's blood. Our essence was the blood of our magic that powered through our souls.

"Of course they did," Ronnie grumbled. "We've got to hurry. Cyrus is about to lose his shit."

"*Alex* said that?" I asked. Though Alex had more of an affinity for cursing than I did, that didn't sound like something the three-hundred-year-old vampire king would say.

Ronnie snorted. "I'm paraphrasing." Then her expression turned somber.

"What's wrong?"

"Demons just captured Chad and a few of Killian's pack members who were helping out in Shadow Terrace. They've been cut off as well." Ronnie pushed herself harder. "We've got to get there."

I kept pace with her and glanced over my shoulder at the downtown area and Shadow Ridge University. From this view, I could still make out both places, and no one was outside, which was as it should be.

No one but those humans with their video cameras.

Why were humans coming back after being evacuated? None of this made sense.

At least the demons were gone.

We flew lower, and below us, a group came into view through the thinning foliage. At least fifty people, including my parents, Sterlyn, Griffin, Alex, Circe, Eliza, and Killian, were circled together.

My stomach dropped. Sierra and Luna were missing, which likely meant they were being held at Killian's pack neighborhood with everyone else.

Five silver wolves stood strategically around the group, facing the woods and watching for danger. Between two of the five was a wolf who had to be from Killian's pack.

Cyrus paced at the edge of the group, his fingers fisted

in his hair. He didn't pause in his movements; rather, they grew more frantic with each passing moment.

I couldn't blame him. If Levi had been captured, even without our child in tow, I wouldn't have been holding it together. The fact that Cyrus was here when he clearly wanted to attack the demons and save his mate proved that he realized it would be a death sentence. Any overreaction would only give the demons more control.

I scanned the rest of the group, and some of the tension in my shoulders eased. There at least fifteen bears, their hairy, bulky presence giving them away even without their grassy smell, five smaller individuals who had to be foxes, and ten taller ones with lime green eyes that screamed jaguar. Most of the Shadow Ridge shifter population was bears and wolves with only a smattering of the rest, but seeing the mixture comforted me. If the vampires, shifters, and witches uniting could take down the angels, then that same mixture, united with the angels, could surely defeat the demons.

I had to hope, because at this point, hope was all I had.

Present Rosemary understood the importance of hope. It wasn't a weakness. It inspired people to win despite the odds. If I hadn't been molded into the angel I was today with Levi by my side, I'd still fight. I'd always been a fighter and protector of those for whom I'd had lukewarm feelings, but this Rosemary had *everything* to fight for: a life with her preordained, a chance to watch a baby be born to two deserving people I now considered family, and all my friends.

What's going on with you? Levi linked as he flickered back into human form.

The bulkiest dark-haired man growled, "There's a

demon." He rushed toward my preordained mate, and I instinctively stepped in front of Levi.

I spread my wings as I crouched, ready to fight. I didn't give a flying feather how big he was—I could still kick his furry butt. "Back away from my mate," I said through gritted teeth. "He's my mate and on our side."

I'm slightly uncomfortable, Levi connected.

Not only had the bear shifter threatened my mate, but he'd caused him discomfort. *Don't worry. He won't touch you.*

No, that's not it. Levi moved closer against my back. *I should be upset that you just stepped in front of a truck, but I've gotta say, your protectiveness really turns me on at very inappropriate times.*

Truck? He had lost it. There was no truck around us.

"He's the *enemy*," the guy rasped as he waved a large hand at Levi, bringing me back to the present. His fingernails transformed into claws as his animal surged forward.

"Leeroy!" His slightly shorter friend grabbed his arm. "Calm down. He's not attacking us, and the others aren't alarmed by his presence."

"If you have a problem with him, then let's get this out of the way," Ronnie said in her shadow form.

That was enough to distract Leeroy as his head jerked in her direction. His dark brown eyes searched for her. "There's another one!"

Alex hissed, "That's my *wife* and the queen of the vampires. If you dare touch a hair on her head, I will *kill* you."

"Everyone, calm down." Sterlyn placed a hand on Leeroy's chest. "We told you about them. These are two of the demons the princes of Hell want us to hand over."

A tall woman hurried over and looped her arm through

Leeroy's. The moment she touched him, his breathing calmed. She had to be his mate. His racing heart slowed, and his claws transformed back into fingernails. "I know you told us about them, but how he just revealed himself..."

"You have *nothing* to apologize for." Mother lifted her head and extended her wings. "We're all getting used to having demons around. You can tell that Ronnie and Levi are not evil. Their eyes aren't red."

Ronnie changed back into her human form.

"That will be very important to remember when we perform the spell so you all can see demons in their shadow form." Eliza nodded. "I hope that prevents them from fighting against us so hard, but that could be an old woman's wishful thinking."

Marching over to me, Cyrus frantically looked around and asked, "Where is the demon angel?"

For a second, I wasn't sure who he meant, until the panicked look on his face registered.

Azbogah.

This would cause some discomfort. I'd never dreaded sharing facts...until now. "He's not coming."

Father lifted a hand. "Are you serious?"

I wasn't certain why he was surprised.

"Of *course* that bastard isn't coming." Cyrus's irises glowed as his wolf rose inside him. "Somebody needs to bring him here *now*."

Levi brushed past me, heading toward Cyrus. I wanted to grab his arm, but I didn't need the other shifters to think I didn't trust him. Instead, I linked, *Be careful. He's not stable.*

He shouldn't be, Levi said, brushing off the concern. He stopped in front of Cyrus with both hands held high. "I can only imagine what you're going through. If that was Rosemary—" He cut off.

"You wouldn't be standing here. You'd be going to get the angel prick who caused all of this." Silver fur sprouted down Cyrus's arms.

"I'd want to, but there's a war going on in the city." Levi placed his hands on the shifter's shoulders and murmured, "And Rosemary tried, but with everything going on in there, there's no way we can force Azbogah out in time to save your *mate* and unborn baby. That's why we left—because at least most of the people they're focused on are here. They'd rather have most everyone than no one at all. It'll buy us enough time to strategize a way to save her."

My heart swelled with pride. Not only was Levi one of the strongest supernaturals I knew to have survived Hell untainted, but he was growing as a leader. The unsure and devious demon was becoming strong and confident, and I got to witness it.

"He's right, man." Killian ran a hand through his dark brown hair. His milk chocolate eyes focused on me for a second before he looked back at Cyrus. "If we want to save Annie and the others, we have to use what we have, or we'll wind up with nothing."

Cyrus's face twisted in torment as he wrapped his arms around himself. "If something happens to her—"

Stomach roiling, I stepped toward him, but I wasn't sure what to say. There was no way to make this better, and I would be foolish to think my words could make a difference.

"We're going to save Annie and *all* of them." Sterlyn placed a hand over her heart, the iridescence of her eyes shining through. "They won't take a damn thing away from us as long as we don't fall apart."

Her words washed over me. Before I'd connected with Levi, her words hadn't moved me. But I was no longer immune to their power.

Clarity shocked me. "That's it. They *knew* he wouldn't come."

Mother's brows furrowed. "That's impossible. They want to hurt him more than anyone."

"I don't think that's true." To win, we had to outsmart them. We couldn't allow them to control the game more than they already were. They'd had over a *millennium* to plan this. "They blame all of us, especially the other two archangels who stayed behind, and Levi has his mother's sword, which they want. Ronnie has Wrath's dagger. They knew Azbogah wouldn't come, and they hoped we'd implode."

"That's why Lucifer was watching us." Levi scoffed and turned to me. "He wanted to see our dynamics. He was probably one of the demons watching the angel section of Shadow City. He saw our interactions. They had to *know* most of us would come."

Mother hung her head. "We should've cloaked the entire city."

"But that would've worn out the coven, and the demons would've stormed the city instead," Circe interjected.

"They're right, dear." Father closed his eyes. "Lucifer is cunning. I guarantee they had a strategy for every way we could have handled the situation."

A jaguar shifter placed his hands in his jeans pockets, his warm-brown complexion making his lime eyes appear bright. "The longer we take, the more control they think they have, yes?"

"With how they're acting, I would agree, Cato." Killian rolled his shoulders. "We should split up so they don't know our numbers."

"The problem is, until we cast the spell, none of you will know they're there." Eliza exhaled. "And we can't cast it until we have more coven members with us. We left them with Killian's pack in the neighborhood in case of an attack. We didn't foresee the demons finding Annie and using her and the other women as leverage."

Our group had split up, and the demons had taken advantage. "Then Mother, Father, Levi, Griffin, Ronnie, Alex, the silver wolves in human form, and I will go while the rest stay behind," I said.

"How will we know when you need help?" a girl who was only an inch or two shorter than Annie asked. Her warm ginger hair framed her face, making her features seem sharp and foxlike.

Sterlyn smirked, her silver hair seeming brighter. "Because we'll howl. They'll think we're alerting the other pack members within the neighborhood."

The shifters nervously glanced at one another but nodded.

"Listen, we save everyone, and we *do not* allow them to take anyone else." Alex's jaw twitched as his nostrils flared. "I will not be losing my wife tonight."

"That's the thing, Alex." Mother *tsk*ed. "They don't plan for any of us to make it out alive."

I despised that she was right, but the demons wanted vengeance. To them, the worst offenders were part of this group, and they'd found a weakness to exploit for almost every one of us. Once they were done here, they'd move on to Shadow City and finish the job. "Which means we have to kill them all."

"Easy enough for me." Cyrus clapped his hands and took off toward the neighborhood. "Let's go."

Under normal circumstances, I'd argue that we needed to come up with a real plan, but we had no clue what we were walking into, and I couldn't do a flyover because the demons would be expecting that. We'd have to trust our guts.

We all moved, realizing Cyrus wouldn't slow down. Now that we knew Azbogah wasn't coming, he was desperate to get to his mate. Levi took my hand, and we hurried in silence. His presence allowed some essence of peace to flow through me before we got there. I wished I could pass it on to Cyrus.

The other shifters peeled off, staying back now that the neighborhood was less than half a mile away. The five silver wolves and six wolves from Killian's pack also stayed behind to alert the others when the time came for them to appear.

Our group grew more jittery the closer we got to our destination, and when we stepped through the last bit of trees onto the road that led into the pack neighborhood, it was clear our nerves weren't unwarranted.

Forty demons stood there, waiting. Five of them were in human form, which was almost more terrifying because their eyes were still crimson red.

A cruel smirk spread across the face of the demon in front, whose golden-fair skin and ash-blond hair made her appear as evil as her soul. "Kill them all. They didn't bring him."

My breath caught. I couldn't believe they'd do this.

Cyrus's clothes ripped from his body as his wolf surged forward.

Then the demon cackled.

CHAPTER SIXTEEN

I'D LIFTED MY SWORD, ready for battle, when the demon rolled her eyes and spoke through broken laughter, "Did you see their faces?"

"Allaya, angels don't have a sense of humor." A hefty male demon laughed, causing his belly to jiggle. "Why are you so surprised by their reaction?"

She placed a hand on her stomach, which was exposed where her green crop top ended. "Well, I expected the angels to react like that, but all of them did, even the mortals."

Something hard settled in the pit of my stomach as I tried to understand their intention. "That wasn't funny."

Placing her hands on her hips, Allaya took a deep breath to regain control. "It really was."

Throat constricting, I somehow managed to hide my gag. They loved emotional torment as much as inflicting physical pain. Though I wasn't shocked, I hadn't expected *this*, whatever the heavens *this* even was. *They're giving the illusion that they aren't worried.*

They aren't. Levi moved so we were close together, his

shoulder now touching mine. *They think they have this entire situation skewed in their favor. They know their numbers exceed ours.*

That's angels alone. They weren't including all the supernatural races. *Together, we have just as many, if not more.*

Levi lifted his chin, holding his head high as he stared Allaya down while continuing our telepathic conversation. *First off, they don't expect the supernaturals to work together. They saw the hatred the other supernaturals had for the angels before they were locked in Hell. They've also caused mass chaos on the Shadow Terrace side, convincing a rather large chunk of the vampire population to lose their humanity.*

I'd heard that information in passing, but I hadn't discussed it with Ronnie and Alex. I'd been preoccupied with training city residents in the art of combat for fifteen hours a day. It hadn't left many opportunities to keep up with the others. *How do you know this?* Clearly, Levi had spent more time with our vampire friends than I had.

That last day Alex and I were training together, he gave me an update. "I didn't find that lousy joke funny either, and I'm a demon." Levi sneered.

The hefty demon stopped laughing, his golden complexion turning a shade of red. "Well, you're a traitor and preordained to an angel. Besides, you've never been anything special. The only reason you were tolerated was because you were Marissa's child. The princes of Hell felt some loyalty to you, gods know why, but any special treatment was revoked after your betrayal."

Now Levi was the one who laughed, but it was sinister. "I can see why you thought the princes of Hell were loyal to me, seeing as they killed my mother, a princess of Hell in her *own* right, in front of Father and me."

Every time I heard that, my blood boiled. Even back when I hadn't felt strong emotions, if one of my parents had died, I would've been upset. Not like I would be if it happened now, but it would've caused me what we called *discomfort*. Now I understood that was a very light version of turbulent emotions.

"None of that matters. The princes of Hell make the rules." The guy rubbed a hand across his buzzed head. "I don't know why you're determined to hold on to that."

"Because she was my *mother*," Levi said through clenched teeth.

"We don't have time for this, Frikik." Allaya waved a hand, dismissing Levi. "He's always been a little too intense over things that shouldn't matter."

"Where's my *mate*?" Cyrus exploded, his fur sprouting across his arms once again. "You said you'd hand her over if they came here, and they're here. So I want her."

"Not everyone we asked for is here." Allaya arched one ashy-blond eyebrow. "Which means you didn't keep up your end of the deal."

Sterlyn growled and stepped forward. "There was no *deal*. Only demands on your side."

"Oh, silver wolf, you have so much to learn." Allaya winked. "It doesn't matter if you agree to the terms—we made an offer, and you coming here is your acceptance. But you forgot one *critical* piece."

"A deal happens when you offer something of equal value." Mother stretched her wings out to the sides, making herself appear larger. It was an angel intimidation tactic. "You're asking for five people for the price of *one*."

Frikik smirked so wide that the corners of his eyes wrinkled. "That's technically not true."

Lungs not working, I blinked away black spots. I hated not knowing what we were up against. They were playing with us, and we were at their mercy. The urge to stomp and scream almost took over. *No, Rosemary*, I lectured myself. *That would only give them more power. Breathe.* I'd never had to talk myself down before, but this situation was worse than any I'd faced—other than thinking Levi had left me, but that was a different sort of worse that nothing else could touch.

"What do you mean?" Father asked raggedly.

"You're actually getting the better end of the trade. There are at least two hundred wolves and six witches in there in exchange for *five* of you." Allaya shrugged. "Which, I mean, you haven't fulfilled the bargain for."

"We brought who we could. Now, let everyone go. We aren't the ones who wronged you." Killian's wolf surged forward. He gritted his teeth to prevent the shift from happening.

He was right. The entire pack was just leverage to get us here. Unfortunately, they were my weakness, and the demons must have realized that.

"As long as they behave, they'll be fine." Frikik rubbed his hands together as his red eyes brightened.

They were hoping that the wolves and witches would do something to cause the fight to occur sooner.

"Here we are." Levi raised his hands. "So let's do this."

Allaya shook her head and waggled her brows. "No deal. We want Azbogah, too."

Her actions concerned me. Something was off, and a warning sensation buzzed through my gut, adding to my anxiety.

Fiddling with her ring, Mother mirrored my concern. She cleared her throat. "Then I guess we'll be off to get him since you're not willing to take the four of us instead."

The demons at the outer corner of the group stepped forward, and a branch fifty yards away snapped. My gaze swung over and landed on four humans with their phones pointed right at us, a red light glowing on each of the devices.

Humans were recording the altercation.

Levi's head swung in their direction, and he hissed, "You've got *them* recording us."

"It's more *fun* this way." Allaya smirked. "The princes of Hell don't have to stay hidden in Hell any longer. Fate gave them a sign that it was time to return to Earth."

All because I'd touched that damn skeleton key. I wished I could go back in time, but it wouldn't matter. I'd make the same decision because if I hadn't, Azbogah would have been in a position to take over the angels, and with Mother out of the way, he'd have targeted Shadow City. I'd made the best choice possible, given the horrible situation.

"And the best way to terrorize humans is by letting them know supernaturals exist." Frikik chuckled. "They will learn to cower and fear the shadows."

"You must have lost a lot of brain cells in Hell." Ronnie wrinkled her nose. "Is that what you think will happen? Because you're grossly misinformed."

A female demon tossed her bourbon-colored hair over her shoulders. "What do you mean?" Her red eyes darkened with concern.

"Because you're right. They'll *fear* us, but they won't cower." Ronnie pinched the bridge of her nose as her frustration bled through.

Placing a hand on his wife's shoulder, Alex glared.

"They'll *attack* us. Experiment on us. They'll do things to learn how to control us."

Allaya scoffed. "And we'll kill them. Easy solution. And I enjoy killing as much as terrorizing."

"You do realize there are substantially more of them than us, right?" Griffin asked, sounding bewildered. He flung his arm in the humans' direction. "We may be stronger, but they have the numbers to cripple us."

The female demon twisted her hair around her finger. "They've got a point—"

"Don't listen to them, Deseih!" Allaya spat. "They're trying to mess with us."

"No, we aren't." Sterlyn thrust out her chest. "All of this will get worse. We need to take those cameras away from them."

Frikik shifted into his shadow form. "It's too late for all that, and we aren't scared of anyone we can bring to their knees."

A loud gasp came from the humans, and one of them whispered loudly, "Did you *see* that? He vanished into thin air!"

It was too late to remedy the situation. That had to be why the demons had killed humans in the first place—to reveal our existence. With the number of humans who'd escaped on their own and been evacuated with Killian's pack's help, the news must have gone out days ago, and that was why people with video cameras were here now.

We couldn't let them distract us because every one of our lives was at stake. *They won't allow us to get Azbogah.*

I know, Levi replied, his dread slamming into me. *The demons want this captured on film to show the world what they're capable of.*

Terror was the coward's way of control. I'd rather be

respected for what I stood for than for some perverted sense of power. *For them to never feel safe in their own home.* Because they wouldn't know if they were truly alone or not.

You have to understand that to a demon, fear is the same as respect, at least for the fallen. Levi's disgust caused my blood to run colder.

I didn't understand, but it didn't matter. That was how they operated, and I couldn't change their desires, just like they couldn't force us to become something we didn't want to be.

The rest of the demons changed into their human form, and a petrified cry came from the woods. I had to block out the humans' terror; for now, they weren't in actual danger.

My gut screamed that these demons would be more formidable enemies than the ones within Shadow City. Preparing for battle, I spread my wings. With the humans already recording everything, including my parents and me landing here in the clearing, hiding them was pointless.

Cyrus pawed at the ground as he threw his head back and howled.

That told me everything I needed to know without looking in his direction. He had alerted the five silver wolves who had stayed behind to come forth. I'd hoped that he would wait, but I couldn't blame him. His mate was with the demon to whom her father had promised her.

Allaya charged first. Her eyes locked on Ronnie as she removed a dagger from her shadowy frame.

I flicked my gaze to Ronnie, making sure she was watching, and Ronnie didn't disappoint. She had her dagger in her hand, ready to engage.

I surveyed Sterlyn, Griffin, Killian, and Alex, who also had knives in their hands.

If you need me— I started.

But Levi cut me off. *Do* not *tell me that. When you got injured not even hours ago, you didn't tell me. I'm keeping an eye on you now.*

I'd done that without thinking. Now he might get hurt since he'd be focused on checking on me. *I swear to you, I'll let you know if I get injured. I didn't mean to hide it from you earlier. We were just at war.*

Like we are now. He growled as demons raced toward us. Four demons charged each of us, but I had suspected the strongest ones would be going after those of us the princes of Hell intended to capture. I could only hope they wouldn't kill them here—that the princes planned to do it themselves.

Frikik and Deseih, along with two others, charged at me. Soon, I wouldn't be able to tell them apart. Even Frikik was the same size in this form as the others, making it difficult to tell who I was up against.

All the demons wielded their weapons, not caring about revealing them right away, unlike the demons in the city who'd hidden their weapons until they needed them. This again reinforced that they were comfortable fighting.

"Be careful," Levi said loudly. "These are some of the top fighters in Hell."

Luckily, these demons didn't have strange weapons. Each one carried a small sword.

The four demons attacking me hefted their swords at the same time. They wanted to kill me, but they must not have realized or cared that my wings could protect me.

I lifted myself several feet off the ground, my feathers flipped to the sharp side. I raised my sword and spear and clanked blades with the two demons in front of me. As the other two attacked my sides, I shifted my wings, allowing myself to drop and block their thrusts. I knocked two of their swords to the ground as I kicked the other two demons in the stomach. They sailed backward. Taking the momentary reprieve, I swung around to help the others.

As expected, Levi's attackers weren't going hard on him like they were with me. Instead, they were distracting him from helping me or the others. As long as he was safe, I was more than fine with that.

Sterlyn, Griffin, Cyrus, and Killian were a whole different matter.

"*Pulsate in terra*," Eliza chanted as she lifted her hands. A hard gust of wind surged toward Sterlyn and Griffin and flattened the demons to the ground.

Circe rushed over to Cyrus and Killian, her four attackers following suit, and yelled, "*Ventilabis eos in caelum!*" She pointed her palm at each demon and tossed them a couple of miles away from us.

Apparently, I didn't need to worry. The witches had this handled. I flapped my wings and spun back around in time to find a demon on me, sword swinging toward the base of my wing.

The plucker was trying to sever my wing. It was a good plan. I'd be in intense pain and defenseless. A missing limb wasn't something I could heal, and they must have known that.

I swung the spear to block the blow. With as much strength as I possessed, I lowered my grip on the handle just as it clipped the sword's blade. I gritted my teeth and shook from the force, the demon trying to push through to stab me in the arm. If I shifted my weight to utilize my wings, I'd get injured.

There was only one choice.

I kicked the demon in the stomach.

Its eyes bulged as the sword dropped from its hand. It groaned loudly and deeply, completely in pain.

Maybe I'd hit it in its genitals, though that hadn't been my intention. I hated low blows; I'd rather win with my mind and hands. However, this move had done the trick, and the demon floated toward the ground.

The pounding of paws and feet informed me that our backup was nearly here. We needed as much assistance as possible, and I hoped that once we got inside, Killian's pack would be ready to help fight to get us out of here. Forty-two of us couldn't do it on our own.

Two demons surged toward me, red eyes burning brightly with rage. I lifted my spear and dagger. They attacked, one aiming for my chest while the other soared behind me. They were working together to exploit my blind spot. However, I turned so they were both at my sides and flew up a few feet. My momentum caught them off guard, and I swung at the one who had tried to stab me in the back and sliced my blade through its neck. Its nasty blue blood splattered all over me, but that wasn't anything new tonight. I was already covered in it from head to toe.

"Rosemary!" Mother screamed, and I spun in time to see a sword flying toward my shoulder.

Flames slammed into my enemy, and the demon lost its grip on its weapon. It dropped only an inch away from my body.

The strike would have caused a severe injury that likely would have resulted in my death, since I wouldn't have been able to protect myself in that state.

I blinked, almost in shock. The flames that licked over the demon held a sense of my mother's power, and it washed over me. Screeching, the demon flailed, trying to extinguish the flames, but the fire only brightened.

If Mother's ring could do that, I was beyond curious about what her sword could do. Tearing my eyes away from the flames, I focused back on the battle. Though our backup had arrived, no one but the silver wolves could see the demons. The witches cast spell after spell, and I raced toward the demon closest to me. I swung my sword, severing its head, then moved on to the next one. When its red eyes found me, it backed away.

"Come fight me, scoundrel," I said through gritted teeth.

The twenty that remained alive hurried back toward the neighborhood. If they retreated, they would warn the others. I was rushing toward them when Circe yelled, "Rosemary, no!"

CHAPTER SEVENTEEN

CIRCE'S SCREAM of warning rang in my ears, but before I could react, something slammed into me. The sensation of sludge coating my body overwhelmed me as my wings grew too heavy to keep me elevated. I flew backward and tensed, bracing myself for an impact with the ground.

Flying in an intense rainstorm had proven to be difficult before, but it didn't compare to this. My feathers felt as if they were clumped together.

Strong arms wrapped around my waist as I tumbled into someone. The buzzing of my skin immediately informed me who it was.

Levi.

However, he couldn't halt my momentum, and he succumbed, falling hard onto his back. Pain exploded inside me.

He'd cushioned my landing.

Gasping, he tried to take in deep breaths, and his hold went slack on my waist. He'd had the wind knocked out of him.

Levi! I exclaimed, hating that I'd hurt him. Though I wasn't injured, the evilness that covered my body had extinguished a large portion of my magic. However, I had to try something.

As I rolled off him, a strong hand grasped my arm, helping me to stand. The musky sandalwood scent was distinct among the other musky and floral scents swirling around me—Killian.

I'm fine! Levi wheezed. *I promise.*

I stumbled to my feet, wanting to check on him myself, but before I could, my attention turned to the immediate threat in front of us. I spread out my feathers, and despite them moving as they should, I felt as if they were hanging limply at my side. I had lost control of them. That shouldn't have been possible.

Fear constricted my heart. I'd never experienced anything like this before.

A woman stood in front of me, portions of her long, pale-golden hair spilling from the edges of a black hood and cloak that covered her entire body. Under the right circumstances, her faint blue irises might have appeared white. The sun was setting behind her as the moon ascended into the sky, casting a twilight glow around her that screamed *evil*.

Twenty-five more witches stepped from the woods in front of us, wearing the same garb. Each had a stark paleness to them that seemed unhealthy, reminding me of vampires who had lost their humanity and were sensitive to even moonlight.

The woman in front tilted her head jerkily, as if the movement caused her discomfort. "You were *not* granted permission to come inside." Her Gaelic accent was one that couldn't be found in today's world.

"That's my pack *neighborhood*," Killian spat. "That's my *home*. I don't need permission to enter."

A smirk filled the witch's face, displaying a cruelness that the demons' shadow forms usually hid. "Earth is *our* home now. Not yours. From here on out, you are all visitors permitted to only go where we allow."

Power pulsed from the coven as they moved closer together. Three skeletally thin males flanked each side, making up six of the twenty-six witches on site. In general, there were more female witches than male because of Mother Nature and her affinity for women. Only male witches who had a soul more aligned with nature than usual were blessed with magic. Unlike shifters, witches coveted women because they tended to have the strongest powers.

I tried to lower my wings. I didn't want them to enjoy the sight of my discomfort under whatever spell they'd cast on me. However, the more I tried to lower them, the higher they spread out beside me.

A tan witch chuckled. The contrast of her skin tone with an eerie pale coating on top made her appear more sinister than the woman in front. Her dark brown hair fell from the black hood and waved down her shoulders just past her breasts. With eyes resembling opals, she was breathtaking, even in this form. A vision of danger, alluring and savage. "Tabitha, I love your cunning. Look at the angel struggling with her wings." She had a French accent.

"They must have a reversal spell on you," Eliza whispered as she brushed the tendrils of hair away from her face. "Do the opposite of what you want to do, and your body will obey you."

I didn't have much to lose so I moved so my wings would spread wider, and they collapsed beside me. That was a pesky trick. If I couldn't get them to remove the spell, it would make it nearly impossible for me to fly, as they intended.

Be careful, Rosemary, Levi connected. *Tabitha is the oldest witch of the coven. She clawed her way up to become priestess of Hell, and she'll do whatever it takes to prove her strength and viciousness to those who would consider replacing her.*

Though that was problematic, maybe we could use it to turn them against each other. *I won't do anything to purposely upset them.*

"If we wanted her to know what spell we cast on her, we would've told her." A male from the back stepped forward. His amber eyes glowed faintly red, resembling the eyes of demons. His hood hid his entire head, and only his eyes and a fair-complected nose were visible.

Mother cleared her throat, drawing their attention. "My brothers asked us to come here, and we obliged."

"Brothers?" Tabitha's high-pitched laughter echoed. "Did you hear that, Greta? She called them *her brothers.*"

The lady with the French accent chuckled darkly. "If I were her, I wouldn't use that term. They don't think of you as family, not anymore."

"So I've been informed." Mother straightened her shoulders. "Which is why I want to see them."

"I wouldn't be so eager if I were you." Greta pointed to herself. "But *I'm* excited to see what tortures await you."

I swallowed bile, and it burned down my throat.

You have to understand—these are the worst witches in history since the demons fell. Levi stood behind me, his pain finally having receded. *The demons who could come to Earth undetected searched for the worst they could find. Anyone with any morality was either killed in Hell or, best case, wasn't brought there.*

I had no doubt that if Erin's coven hadn't aligned with Azbogah, the original priestess who'd cast the spell would have been down there, too.

Father placed a hand on Mother's shoulder as he said, "We understand, but it's time they hear the truth from our side."

The fact that Father thought the princes would care about what he had to say was foolish. Even with my evolving emotions, I knew better than that. But his willingness to try proved that Father had a bigger heart than I'd realized, now that his emotions had returned.

Mother mashed her lips into a thin line, an expression she showed when she sensed a threat. She usually reserved the expression for Azbogah, and now my body wanted to freeze from terror. Realizing she thought the situation was just as dire as I did provided no comfort.

"You heard them," the man in the back said. "If they want to see the princes, who are we to stop them?" The excitement in his voice added to my dread.

"Well, they only want Ronnie, Pahaliah, Yelahiah, and me," Levi said as he stepped beside me. "So there's no reason to force everyone to come."

What are you doing? I wanted to strangle him as badly as I had the first time we met. *I'm not leaving you behind.*

Rosemary, you can't say you wouldn't do the same thing in my place. If those princes figure out who your biological father is—and I bet Lucifer will—they'll want to torture you as much as they do Azbogah. Not one ounce of remorse poured from him, and he pushed his determination through our bond.

Pragmatic Rosemary surged forward. He was right. I *would* do the same thing, even though this newly emotional Rosemary was upset and wanted to call it a betrayal. He was doing it to *protect* me. *We're stronger together. Separating is wrong, especially if we can't talk telepathically.* Mates were meant to be together. That was why the price for abusing our power had been the severing of our preordained mate bonds. There was no way around it.

"Ah, Levi, always the bleeding heart." Tabitha patted her chest. "Which is even more reason for everyone to come inside, especially your black-winged little angel toy. I must say, after *all* the demons who desired you down there, this particular angel is *very* easy on the eyes. I'm sure they'll love destroying her face before putting a bullet between your eyes."

He lunged forward, but I caught his arm. They were goading him to make him act irrationally. *Don't give them more pleasure.* My fingers bit into his skin. *And I would like a chance to come out of this so we can form a family.*

Either my words or my touch centered him because he relaxed marginally, and our connection warmed with hope. *A family?*

I've always wanted at least one child. And I would enjoy all the sex required to conceive an additional one.

"Huh." Greta tapped a long, black fingernail on her mouth. "Maybe he liked the idea of her being abused. He could be turning after all."

A low hiss escaped him as his irises turned a dark coffee brown.

"Are you taking us inside or not?" Circe intertwined her fingers in front of her. "I'd like to check on my coven."

Though I believed her, I also knew there was more to it than that. She wanted to check on her *family*.

"If you're that eager, who am I to say no?" Tabitha snickered and lifted her hands, pointing them at my parents. "*Fac suas alas non operatur.*"

My parents' wings spread out wide beside them, and they stumbled. She'd spelled them the same way she'd done to me. Unease formed a knot hard in my stomach.

As the moon began its ascent, Sterlyn's hair began to glow, her skin sparkling slightly. The moon was only a sliver shy of being full, which meant the silver wolves were almost at full strength. During a new moon, they were only as strong as a normal wolf. We needed as much power as possible on our side.

A loud growl came from a bear shifter as the tallest one's teeth elongated. Once we stepped inside the perimeter, our chances of surviving would reduce drastically. The other shifters with us wanted to eliminate the threat, but they didn't have people they were emotionally tied to inside. Their animal would naturally fight against walking into a situation with these odds.

"*Non mutent,*" Greta murmured as she lifted her hands toward the bears.

The growl changed into a groan as the bear shifter's teeth went back to their normal human form.

"Now come, or we'll block your animal indefinitely," the amber-eyed man rasped, and five of the witches turned to lead the group.

Cyrus jumped at the opportunity and rushed toward the neighborhood. The enemy would use his desperation against him, but there was nothing we could do to calm his turmoil. Having been cut off from Levi before, I understood that. It wasn't something a mate could control.

Circe and Eliza were right behind him, both worried about Annie and the rest of their coven.

My wings inched upward as my focus shifted from controlling them while under the spell to getting to our friends who were in danger. I forced myself to pretend I was about to take off to keep them at my side. I didn't want the princes of Hell's first impression of me as being a weak person. It would make me an easy target.

A pair of witches took five of us, splitting us into groups to make sure there were equal eyes on every one of us. When Levi and I took up the rear, the remaining witches, including Greta and Tabitha, followed right behind.

As we stepped onto the cement road, a question that I should've asked long ago forged itself in my mind. *Lucifer was the angel of intelligence, and when he fell, his chief quality changed to pride. What about Wrath, Belaphor, and Asmodeus?*

Disappointment and guilt wafted from Levi as he took my hand. *I can't believe you don't know all this already. I feel bad for not sharing more with you, but it was something we always knew in Hell. I never considered—*

You don't need to explain yourself. At one point, I'd thought he was holding information from me, but I'd learned that hadn't been his intent. Most would never consider explaining things that were believed to be common knowledge. *But you have to understand that we didn't speak about the demons. Their betrayal—it hurt.* Which was ironic, since Azbogah was the true betrayer. He'd hurt the demons *and* the angels who had been left behind. *Even if it wasn't an actual betrayal, we were told it was.*

We'll fix it, he vowed.

I wanted to correct him, but that would have been futile. He couldn't promise anything right now. We could only hope we'd make it out alive.

Most of the princes of Hell are the opposite of what they were when they were angels. Wrath was...well...war, but it was for the good of the world. Belaphor was able to create things from the air, but after he fell, he focused on destruc-

*tion, and Asmodeus was the angel of love, which he
perverted to lust as a demon.*

As I processed the information, I couldn't imagine my
parents as the opposite of the way they were. Seeing them
differently was unfathomable, and I feared they wouldn't be
able to see the princes for what they were now.

As the Craftsman-style houses appeared ahead in the
woods, the witches veered to the left, away from the homes,
toward the wolves' training area.

Sterlyn, Ronnie, Alex, Griffin, Killian, and my parents
walked close to us. We glanced at one another. This was
one of those times I wished we could all communicate. I
wondered if they could talk to the pack now. None of us
dared to speak with the witches right behind us.

Out of the corner of my eye, I saw Mother remove her
ring discreetly and pretend to scratch her chest as she
slipped it into her bra. Father nodded as he slipped his
necklace under his suit jacket, which had once been white
but was now blue from demon blood.

A little of my tension eased, but not as much as I
desired.

Beyond the slight noises our larger group made, the
woods were silent. No animals scurried around. The only
sounds were our footsteps and the slight breeze that rustled
the remaining leaves on the trees. Every few feet, leaves fell
around us, and the disgusting sensation of the sludge
coating me became stronger.

Keeping the hostages in the training area was very
smart. They needed to guard only one side since the river
separated the Shadow Ridge training area from Shadow
Terrace and flowed around half of it. Unless someone was
in the trees or a boat came by, no one would see us.

When the group broke through the last line of trees, the

hundred-yard-wide open space came into view, and pure evil slammed into me. Despite the maliciousness weighing me down, the world still *looked* the same with the green fescue grass and the red roofs of the Shadow Terrace homes across the river, clearly visible through the thinning leaves of the oaks and redbuds. All three hundred members of Killian's pack were gathered in the center of the open area. The remaining sixteen members of the silver wolf pack stood to the right of Annie, with Sierra and the witches on her other side.

At least one thousand demons surrounded them with about fifty more witches. Over half of the demons were in their shadow forms, hovering in the air, so the wolves below didn't notice them. About two hundred demons circled them in human form, probably to make it more difficult to determine who was witch and who was demon. The only slight comfort was that about half of the demons didn't have red eyes—they were undecided.

Four demons stood in front of them, staring straight at us. Most of the vileness radiated from them as if they were the root of all things evil.

"Well, well." The tallest dark-haired demon stood to the far left, steepling his fingers and placing them against his lips as they stretched into a smile. His crimson eyes brightened, making his olive complexion seem darker. "Look what we have here, brothers."

That's Lucifer, Levi informed me.

The very one who'd sacrificed countless humans to scare the world. My stomach revolted.

Running a hand through his shaggy, ash-white hair, the demon on the far right sneered as his garnet irises flared. "The people I've been dying to kill."

"I get to kill my granddaughter," Wrath commanded with his scarlet eyes flaming. Unlike the others, he was bald, and his face twisted with anger as he glared at Belaphor on his left.

"Like *Hell* you will," Alex spat as he moved in front of his wife. "You'll have to kill me to get to her."

The corner of Wrath's lips tipped up. "And you think that will give me pause?"

"Since we're claiming individuals..." The demon standing between Wrath and Lucifer narrowed his blood-red eyes on Cyrus. The demon's midnight hair hung in his face, and his full lips were sensual. "I claim the silver wolf who's Annie's current mate so I can make her mine."

Sterlyn moved to Cyrus and touched his arm. They must have been having a conversation because Cyrus didn't charge, though his face turned red with fury.

They were grandstanding to dominate us with words alone, and we were allowing it. "Clearly, you had these conversations before we got here." I wanted to take the focus off my parents, Ronnie, and Levi, but more than that, I wanted them to know we were aware of their theatrics. My power was lower than I'd like, and I couldn't put up a good fight, but at least I could pretend. Besides that, I was searching for something...anything...to divide them.

What are you doing? Levi's anger roiled.

Trying to take control. Surely he had to see that.

"It's true." Sierra scoffed from where she stood just behind the demon princes. "That's *all* they've been talking about."

Wrath pivoted on his heel and smacked Sierra in the face. Her head snapped around as she stumbled back a few steps. He yelled, "Be quiet!"

White-hot fury slammed into me. Though Sierra liked to run her mouth, she hadn't deserved that. She'd been trying to help by confirming what I'd suspected.

"You bastard!" Killian bellowed as he charged toward the demon.

Tabitha lifted a hand. "*Frigidus eum.*"

Within a second, Killian stood frozen like a statue.

My breathing turned ragged, and I tried to push past my fear. That was what they wanted. Levi had said they coveted our terror more than our respect, so we couldn't give it to them. "We're all here, so it's time to make the trade." Somehow, my voice didn't shake.

Levi moved toward Killian, but I grabbed his arm. We didn't need him pulling out his demon sword yet. That would only escalate the situation, and the longer we stalled, the stronger I'd become.

"We aren't making a *trade*." Belaphor clenched his hands. "You didn't bring a certain someone with you."

My hair stood on end in warning.

"No, we have something that will actually hurt him." Lucifer rubbed his hands together. "I watched them while they were in Shadow City, and I know what *she* is." He nodded toward me. "We will kill her first so that Yelahiah—our *dear* sister—Levi, and Azbogah can feel the pain."

Levi grabbed my arm and tugged me behind him. As he stood in front of me, crouching in a fighter's stance, he said, "You will *never* touch her."

Lucifer snickered as he tilted his head. "It's so cute that you think you can make a difference. If Azbogah doesn't come, we'll do the only thing that can hurt him. We'll *kill* his daughter."

"What!" Annie gasped, and I realized the secret hadn't fully circulated until now.

Suddenly, wings flapped overhead, and I turned around to find someone I'd never expected to see charging toward us.

CHAPTER EIGHTEEN

I BLINKED SEVERAL TIMES. I had to be hallucinating. There was absolutely no way *he* would come here. He wouldn't risk himself for anyone.

However, the closer he came, the harder it was to deny.

Azbogah was here. But *why?*

The answer was right before my eyes because two demons flanked him. Two sets of all-too-familiar eyes—black diamond and golden brown—stared back at me in answer. Zagan and Bune had convinced Azbogah to show up.

There was nothing they could have promised Azbogah to get him here. His death was what the demons coveted most.

A strangled cry shifted my attention to Mother. Her forest green eyes shone with tears, which confused me. Was she crying over Azbogah's impending death? Their preordained bond had been broken. Then again...Azbogah had mentioned that he'd never lost all his feelings for Mother. Could those feelings have remained on both sides, fueling the hatred between them?

222 JEN L. GREY

"Who's leading the people back in the city?" my father asked.

Azbogah glanced at him and answered, "Jegudiel."

"I never thought I'd see the day," Asmodeus said with awe. "Azbogah is here, and he's brought two of our traitors with him."

Lucifer rocked on the back of his feet and smiled smugly. "I told you *she* was the key." He pointed at me. "Every time I saw them together, he was attempting to gain her attention. Apparently, he's had a falling out with his daughter."

"He's not *my father*," I spat. I didn't want them to get the wrong impression of my relationship with Azbogah.

A dark snort came from Wrath. "Lucifer, she's not lying. Maybe you got it wrong."

"But he's *here*." Belaphor lifted a hand at the dark angel as his brows furrowed.

Maybe this was the thing that could divide them. Clearly, Wrath enjoyed proving Lucifer wrong. They weren't as close as I'd presumed. *Have they always been this divided?*

I wouldn't say divided, but each one wants more power than the other. They work together to ensure no one challenges them, Levi answered, despite not turning to me. He continued to stand in front of me, making it clear they'd have to kill him to get to me. *Why?*

We need to drive a wedge between them, but we must be strategic. If Lucifer was as cunning as everyone claimed, we would have to be deliberately careful. We couldn't go about it too quickly; otherwise, the strategy wouldn't work.

His shoulder blades twitched. *Do whatever you think is best. Azbogah bought us more time, but they'll soon focus on you again. They know how much you mean to him, and they'll want to leverage that connection to cause him substantial pain.*

"Because of Yelahiah, you buffoon." Wrath rolled his eyes. "They are preordained mates."

For some reason, seeing that reaction from the demon of war made him less intimidating. Even with that amount of anger, he still held humanlike expressions.

"That might be, but she's with Pahaliah now, or is pretending to be." Lucifer examined Azbogah, then Mother. He turned his attention to me. "If Azbogah isn't your father, then please, inform us who is."

A lump formed in my throat. "No."

"I am." Pahaliah's wings folded in beside him. He had wanted to appear confident, but the reversal spell had resulted in the opposite.

"*You?*" Asmodeus's shoulders shook with silent laughter. "I know you've always held a flame for Yelahiah, even when she was bonded with Azbogah and allowed him to change her fundamentally. You turned on us, too, which I presume was for *her*."

My heart fractured, but I was partly thankful because part of the question I'd always been afraid to ask had been answered—why he'd decided to raise me. It was because of Mother and how he felt about her.

"No, I did not." Father nodded, and his shoulders straightened.

"So you turned on us because you wanted to," Wrath said through clenched teeth. "At least you're angel enough to admit it." His attention swung to Zagan and Bune. "I know why Levi changed sides, but what are your excuses?"

"None of us turned on you." Mother's hands relaxed at her sides. "We didn't know what happened. He didn't tell us. When things changed, I thought it was because *you* chose to fall and leave us behind."

"You thought we'd *chosen* this?" Lucifer motioned a hand in front of him. "To lose our wings and be separated from the lights of Heaven?" He scoffed. "You should've known better."

Belaphor flexed his fingers. "Oh, stop. We might not have chosen this, but you can't deny, now that we're back on Earth, that we're not unhappy with what happened. We don't have to worry about weak little humans any longer, and we can focus on our desires instead."

"Though we may have been in Hell for over one thousand years, that doesn't mean we've forgotten our time as angels." Wrath broke away from the group and moved toward me. He didn't pay Levi any attention as he examined me.

Instincts made me want to lift my wings, but with the reversal spell, I'd wind up doing exactly what Father had, and my wings would lie at my sides. Against all instinct, I forced myself to lower them...which made them do as I desired. I would not cower—that would only make the demons more vicious and confident.

Wrath frowned. "She is moving her wings like normal. I thought you spelled the angels so they couldn't fly away."

"I did a reversal spell." Tabitha's voice shook. "They're aware of it and can counteract it, but they shouldn't be able to fly. That would be more complicated than just lifting their wings. They would have to fight against nature."

I lifted my chin. "Or so she thinks."

The demon of war hissed.

Rosey, do not *antagonize him.* Levi's anger and fear surged through our connection.

I told you, we have to drive contention between them.

Though I'd meant the princes of Hell, I'd take any opportunity. Making them doubt the witches could fracture their hold, too.

"Between the color of her wings and her rudeness, there is no way she's Pahaliah's spawn." Lucifer looked down his nose at me. "Though she clearly does view him as her father. Azbogah, is she *your* daughter?"

The dark angel landed in front of our group, placing himself closest to the demons. He stood tall, not cowering, as if he were as strong as the princes of Hell. "Yelahiah, Pahaliah, and all the other angels had no idea what I did to you. Your antipathies should lie with me and no one else."

My eyes widened, and some of my animosity toward Azbogah splintered. Though he'd told me he wouldn't come, here he was, taking responsibility for his decisions.

Lucifer's jaw dropped. "Is that so?" He turned to the other princes. "Did you hear that? This whole ruse can end now. All we need to do is kill Azbogah, and things will be *just fine.*"

Even a fool could have detected the sarcasm.

"You're right." Wrath rubbed his chin. "It's not like the other angels *knew* us and every preordained mate who was forced to fall with us." He paused and looked Azbogah in the eye. "Oh, wait, they did. Yet they still chose to believe a proven pathological liar." His nostrils flared.

Belaphor's lips curled upward. "Whether they believed you or not, they destroyed our world and allowed you to trap us in a different dimension. We're here to return the favor."

"Those who stand aside and do nothing are sometimes worse than the person who *made* the choice." Asmodeus took a step back next to Annie. "And that's the real reason we wanted you here. It wasn't to kill you but for you to watch the death of everyone who stood behind you."

They didn't care whether the other angels knew what had happened. There was no fixing that, and in a way, I understood. If my friends and allies had turned their backs on me, it would be hard to forgive, especially when everything inside me would've been searching for a way to channel my rage.

The only way to resolve this situation was to kill the princes. They'd gone so far that even reason wouldn't allow them to let go of their hatred. I wished my magic had more time to recharge, but as long as I focused on physical strength and didn't use my healing powers, I should be okay.

Annie whimpered as she rubbed her stomach and focused on her mate.

"Ah, don't worry, pet," Asmodeus cooed as he caressed her cheek. "You won't perish, nor will your children. You can still be of good use."

Growling, Cyrus charged.

"*Pin—*" Tabitha paused as she raised her hands.

A voice called out from behind us in the woods, "*Fac eam mutum!*"

Erin?

Shock immobilized me. The Shadow City priestess *came*.

Tabitha's mouth continued to move, but no sound came out. Azbogah punched Lucifer in the jaw.

This was the best opportunity we would have. "Now!" I shouted, hoping everyone understood.

I tried to take off, but instead, I crashed to the ground. Mother *plucker*, that stupid spell!

Rosey! Levi linked as he stooped next to me. He wasn't paying attention to what was going on around him.

I'm not hurt. Though that was true, my body had taken a slight beating. With my already depleted magic, this was less than ideal, but there was nothing I could do about it.

With clenched teeth, Eliza appeared beside me. She pointed one hand toward me and the other at my parents. She chanted, "The Witches of the Pentacle release their hold on the angels."

Something caressed my skin, and soon, my feathers worked as intended. Eliza knew their coven name and could take away their power despite being outnumbered.

"There, you three should be okay now." She turned her attention to the other shifters and shouted, *"Ne transeatur!"*

And just like that, Cyrus raced toward his mate.

"No!" Greta screamed as she and the other witches from Hell lifted their hands.

Erin and ten of her coven members joined the scene, spouting off the words, *"Fac eum mutum!"*

Immediately, the voices of Hell's witches were gone. Erin's coven was silencing each witch who attempted to cast a spell.

Though I'd been surprised that Erin and the others had joined Azbogah, I realized they must have known if we didn't win this battle, their coven would be next on the demons' long list of retribution.

Thankfully, Sterlyn and the others raced toward the demons in their human form, with Ronnie transitioning into her shadow form.

One bear's voice turned growly, and I yelled, "Not everyone should shift!"

"We know. We're staying in human form," a girl fox shifter rasped. "Killian, Cyrus, and the witches kept us well informed."

Good. They'd been working together during the past week, so it made sense that they'd shared that knowledge.

"*Sit liber*," Eliza said as she flicked her wrist at Killian.

He unfroze and charged behind the others.

The demons shifted into shadow form, and Killian and the other nonangel descendants paused in their tracks. They couldn't see them. "Circe!"

As the demons ran toward us, Circe yelled, "Now!"

Cordelia, Aurora, Herne, Lux, Aspen, and Kamila reached under the necklines of their shirts and yanked what had to be a container of Levi's blood and mine. They all tossed them on the ground and stomped on the glass, shattering it, then chanted, "*Daemones omnibus revela!*"

We needed that spell to work quickly. The wolves who had been taken captive were fighting the visible demons and being killed by the ones they couldn't see. In the blink of an eye, there'd been ten deaths on Killian's side.

I'd moved toward them when I noticed Wrath's attention latch on to Ronnie, and he soared toward her. He was focused on getting his dagger. She was already engaged in battle with three other demons, and he was going to stab her in the back, quite literally.

As he flashed past me, I pushed out my wings and slammed into his side.

Rosemary! Levi shouted inside my mind. *What are you doing? They want to kill you!*

He's focused on Ronnie. I had to protect her. I shoved him into a nearby oak, hoping to knock out his breath so I could easily behead him, but he didn't flinch.

Instead, he laughed, and my blood froze.

"Did you think I'd be that easy to defeat?" He turned to me, removing two short, double-edged swords from their sheaths. "That's fine. Lucifer wanted to kill you, but you've forced my hand."

Without taking another breath, he aimed both swords straight at my heart. I swung my sword up, blocking one side while spinning so my wing thwarted the other. With the weapon that I'd hindered with my sword, he flicked his wrist, spinning the weapon over my sword and lodging it in my right shoulder.

Pain exploded throughout my body, whiting my vision. That was my previously injured side.

He grinned as he yanked the sword to the side, damaging my shoulder even more as he removed the weapon. My eyes burned with unshed tears, but I swallowed down a grunt of pain.

When I died, I'd go down like the warrior I was.

"Did you forget that I was in charge of training the warriors before you all abandoned me?" Wrath sneered. "I *created* the program."

Probably the very one we still taught today since angels didn't like change. I needed to employ Sterlyn's fighting tactics, though they weren't ingrained in me. The wolves used weakness to their advantage. I'd always refused to implement that strategy, but we couldn't allow the demons to win. If they did, Earth would change forever, and the poor humans would face infinite terror.

I went to lift my sword but pretended to struggle more than I needed to. With the amount of pain surging through me, roiling my stomach, it wasn't hard. *I'm injured, but please keep an eye on your own battle,* I linked with Levi. I didn't want to die and have Levi be upset that I hadn't been honest with him again.

I'm on my way, he replied.

Wrath's eyes glowed in what could only be delight as he

raised his sword. It dripped with my blood. Just as I prepared for him to attack, his eyes shot upward.

Sparkles of Levi's blood and mine sprinkled over the demons and made *all* of them visible. I didn't understand why the spell had taken so long, but it provided the perfect distraction.

Gritting my teeth, I aimed my sword at Wrath's neck. We'd be down a prince of Hell in moments with only three remaining.

When the blade was five inches from his neck, he ducked, and I caught only air. He swung a blade at me, and I flapped my wings, elevating myself high enough that it breezed under my feet.

The movement intensified the pain in my shoulder, and before I could react, Levi, in his demon form, barreled into Wrath.

No! I linked, but the damage was done.

Go heal yourself, he instructed as he ducked Wrath's first attempt with his sword. *Now!*

If only it were that simple. I landed a few feet back, only for five demons with bright red eyes to charge at me. I guessed that since I was no longer fighting Wrath, the demons were free to attack.

At least the shifters could now see their attackers, and the odds were more even.

The witches were trying to out-spell one another, each side wanting to control the situation and give their people the advantage. A few more witches from Erin's coven appeared, and my nerves tingled. Who might be left to defend Shadow City? However, what was done was done.

Two of the demons in front of me had human-colored irises, jade and light hazel. The other two had eyes almost as red as the princes'. The two red-eyed demons attacked first while the other two hesitated. They didn't want to be here.

A red-eyed demon removed a knife from his pocket while the other pulled out a sword. I hated to switch my sword to my left hand since it wasn't my dominant one, but the spear weighed less and would be easier to move on my injured side. My shoulder throbbed twice as hard as I lifted the spear. If I didn't use it, however, I'd be in worse agony.

The demon with the sword aimed for my right shoulder. He had the longer weapon and could inflict more damage. I pivoted and threw my left hand up, using the sword to block the blow as the second demon raced toward me with his knife aimed at my side.

I'd never feared death before, but my gut screamed it was imminent.

I'd fight until I took my last breath.

When the demon reached me, I kicked its extended arm. The world spun from my blood loss, and my grip on the handle of the spear slipped from my blood.

Levi, I need you to know I love you. I didn't want to say goodbye, but I needed to say those words to him.

His panic wafted through our bond. *Just hold on. I'm coming.*

If only things were that easy.

"Someone help Rosemary!" Levi screamed in torment.

I hated that I'd made him feel this way. Our relationship had begun in turmoil, and that was how fate planned for it to end, too. At least we'd had some nice moments in between.

The sword demon chuckled as he aimed his blade at my throat. He swung hard, but he was too confident. I jerked back, the blade missing me, and launched my own attack. I severed his head just as the knife demon reached me once again.

He paused and glanced at my injury, and then at his friend's body as it fell to the ground.

He inched backward, intimidated that I'd taken out Sword Demon while injured. Good. I'd take him out, too. The world spun faster, and I imagined this was what it felt like to be inebriated. Since gaining emotions, I'd begun to understand a lot more about human behavior than before... except for *this*. Who would purposely want to feel this way?

The demon blurred into four. My time was running out. I had to act now. I screamed as I swung the sword with the last remaining strength I had, but dark spots marred my vision. My only comfort was that I heard the cracking of bones. I'd injured him somehow.

But then I crumpled right in the arms of someone who smelled of honeysuckle—*Azbogah*.

"Hang on, little one," he pleaded softly, then yelled, "Pahaliah, get your ass over here *now*!"

No, they all needed to keep fighting. We couldn't afford the distraction. I had to do something.

But what could I do when I couldn't even open my eyes?

CHAPTER NINETEEN

EVERY SECOND, my eyes grew heavier. I'd always thought death would be peaceful, but this was horrific. How could I die when everyone I loved and cared about was in danger? Fate couldn't be that cruel...surely.

Levi's terror mixed with mine, making my body feel heavier. But the terrifying part was that despite the horror, my heartbeat slowed.

The preordained mate bond was cooling, and I was helpless to stop it.

I'm coming, Rosey, Levi vowed as if his presence would stop death.

But no one could stop death when it was time.

"Heavens, she's fading." Azbogah sounded broken.

I wasn't sure which was more peculiar—his concern about my well-being or me hating that I was putting him through it.

Somehow, he'd broken through my defenses, and it had taken death for me to see that I cared. I would have laughed if I could. The angel I'd detested my entire life had changed a millennium of hatred into caring in mere weeks, even though he'd abandoned me, his child. I truly believed he'd thought he was unworthy, and in a way only he could, he'd shown how much he loved me.

The pain and heaviness became so overwhelming that I couldn't even chuckle at the irony. Just expanding my lungs was tiresome.

"You aren't going to die on me," he said gruffly as his magic flowed into me. "You'd better hang on."

His magic surged through me, and I finally understood why it felt so familiar. He was my biological father, and my own power was made up of components of his. When he'd healed me during the Wolves' Den fire, I'd thought I was hallucinating due to the severity of the injuries I'd sustained and the trauma from my fading preordained mate bond with Levi when I'd thought Levi had left me for Hell.

Some of the pain ebbed, enough for me to groan, "No, you can't do this." Healing me would require a significant amount of his power, and he needed to reserve it for his own fight.

Levi's and my connection warmed, and soon, I felt Levi on my other side. Though I couldn't open my eyes, his presence was undeniable, and when he touched my arm, the buzz of our bond sprang to life. He linked, *Let him heal you. Please.*

He'll die if he keeps focusing on me and draining his magic. I tried to nudge away, but my body didn't budge. My arms and legs hung limply as if the world were weighing me down to suffocate me. "Stop. You'll get hurt."

He chuckled warmly. "The fact that you care means more to me than you'll ever know."

If the smell of honeysuckle hadn't been swirling around me, I wouldn't have believed that this being was the dark angel I'd always known.

The pain receded more, and my heart pumped again loudly, forcing blood to flow through my body. When I tried to open my eyes again, they actually fluttered in time for me to see Father racing toward me. His irises were almost cobalt, significantly darker than I'd ever seen before. The blue demon blood splattered on his face had hardened him, and he appeared like an angel of war and very unlike the one I knew.

I blinked hard. That couldn't be the angel who'd raised me out of the kindness of his heart.

When I opened my eyes again, Belaphor was charging toward him.

Father! I connected with Levi. *He's—*

A bolt of light surged between Father and Belaphor. The prince of Hell crashed into it before he could counter his movement, and he screamed, "Yelahiah! How did you get your..." He swung around, and his gaze locked on the gold ring she wore. "Those are supposed to be guarded. The other supernaturals took them away from you!"

They'd expected the other supernatural races to still be at odds with the angels. In fairness, we'd come together only this past week because of the demons, but they must have thought their arrival would fracture us more.

"Are you scared now?" Mother snickered, goading the prince as Father reached me. She was going to hold them off, but I wasn't sure what Father thought he could do.

Belaphor scoffed and changed into his demon form. His red eyes narrowed, and the power radiating from him grew stronger. It was easy to tell that he was a prince of Hell. He rasped, "Of course not, and I won't make it easy on you."

"Make sure she doesn't die until her daughter perishes," Lucifer commanded as his eyes locked on me, then flicked

236 JEN L. GREY

to Azbogah. A sinister expression crossed his face as he hurried toward us. "I'll take care of her now."

Dropping his hand, Levi stood and changed into his demon form. "You two do whatever the hell you have to do, but make sure she doesn't *die*."

"She won't." Azbogah pushed more of his magic into me. "I won't allow it."

My chest shook with quiet laughter. "Only you would think you could outwit death."

"Angels can heal," he retorted kindly.

Until now, I'd thought his concern for me had been a ploy, but he was risking everything by healing me.

Father took Levi's spot beside me, and I managed to turn my head to see Levi stand protectively in front of the three of us, his mother's sword at his side.

"Your demon sword doesn't scare me." Lucifer sneered as he pulsed from human to demon shadow. "You aren't nearly as strong as I am."

Please be careful. I wanted to ask Levi not to fight, but that wouldn't be right. If I were in his position, I'd be doing whatever I could to save him. *I can't lose you.*

You won't. He lunged forward.

The more magic Azbogah funneled inside me, the stronger I became. Taking a moment, I surveyed the area. All the malicious demons were engaged in battle, but most of the undecided stood idly on the sidelines. Asmodeus was engaged in battle with Cyrus, while Wrath fought Ronnie. My solace was that everyone was scraping by.

My lungs moved more easily, and the pain lessened to mild discomfort. My head began to clear, and the world stabilized once again. "I'm good enough. You can stop."

I tried to sit up, but Azbogah held me against his chest.

"No. You had an injury that you didn't completely heal, which nearly killed you. You're getting back to normal."

"Then both of us will be depleted magically and be at risk." Though he was older, he must have used at least half his magic, if not more, by healing me like this.

Father pulled his necklace from under his button-down shirt. "That's why I'm here."

"I understand you're a fighter. I see that now. But you can't fight the princes all on your own," I said. Father had shown me during the past week of training that he was more than capable. It wasn't surprising since he was an archangel, but he still wasn't a Fate-chosen warrior. The princes had trained hard their entire time in Hell for this moment, whereas we'd grown complacent, not realizing there was a risk of interdimensional war.

"Wait until I've healed her before you use it." Azbogah grunted as his forehead lined with concentration.

I recognized that strained look and had been in this very position several times. His magic was more than half-depleted. I attempted to sit again, but Azbogah grabbed the scabbed spots where my wounds had been and pushed larger amounts of magic inside.

The last of my discomfort vanished.

When I tried to sit up, he didn't fight me, but instead sagged against me. He was drained.

"Azbogah, no." I couldn't believe he'd been so foolish. Of all the times to care about someone, he'd chosen *this* moment to prove he'd changed.

Father leaned forward, cupping his necklace in his hand. His eyes glowed, reminding me of the shifters, and then the pendant in the palm of his hand shimmered. The light started out bright white, and then the iridescent swirls of color swarmed around us. Immediately, the magic inside me began to recharge.

"How...?" I asked, but I couldn't formulate a more coherent sentence. Magic swirled around me, making the surrounding chaos feel less threatening...as if Heaven were on our side.

"I'm the archangel of humanity. Heaven's light is my natural gift, engendering my need to protect Earth. I helped create the magic of the glass dome that protects Shadow City." With the light swirling from his necklace, there was no word to better describe him than *angelic*. I'd always thought he was soft, but now that Earth was at stake, his protective side was in full force, and it was beyond impressive.

The magic wafting from him was stronger than the light of the dome, and within seconds, I was fully recharged.

I stood, ready to fight alongside my mate, mother, and friends. I couldn't sit back while they fought for their lives. But first, I spun around and looked at both men...my fathers. Something twisted inside my chest, and it had nothing to do with an injury. "Thank you both."

Though they smiled back at me, Azbogah's face was strained. He wasn't yet replenished. I'd been the one directly in Father's light.

When Father shifted closer, I realized he was going to heal Azbogah, too. He was truly a righteous angel, even when dealing with the love of his life's former preordained mate.

I gazed around, determined to protect them. I needed to assist the others with the princes of Hell. If we cut off the heads of evil, that would leave the rest of the demons unsure of the next steps.

"Everyone, fight now, or I'll kill you all when this is over," Wrath spewed as he swung his sword at Ronnie.

The undecided inched closer to their nearest battle. A few pulled out their swords hesitantly. They didn't want to fight, meaning they would be less inclined to kill.

My gaze landed on a silver wolf who'd been thrown halfway across the clearing. I forced my attention to the demon who had thrown it, and my stomach soured. Asmodeus clutched Annie's arm as he announced, "We're leaving."

Glancing at the silver wolf, I was surprised to realize it was Cyrus. He'd landed on his back, his silver eyes wide with rage. However, blood poured from his shoulder.

I would help Annie.

As Asmodeus yanked her toward the edge of the clearing, I flew toward them. Annie growled and pulled against the demon's grip, but she barely moved. When she noticed me, she screamed, "Rosemary, help! Don't let him take me!"

"Where do you think you're going with her?" I asked through clenched teeth.

He snarled, "Do you think I'd tell you anything?" And he continued to drag Annie toward the trees. She was so large now that her shirt inched above her round stomach, revealing skin.

I didn't expect him to say much, but talking might slow him a little.

"You've been chatty the entire time," Sierra said, shocking me as she walked in front of the prince of Hell. She held a knife, and her hands shook slightly. "Why stop now?"

My heart swelled. She'd been training hard and had improved so much, but even I wanted to pause while fighting these demons. Her bravery in confronting

Asmodeus to help Annie humbled me. The princes held power that everyone could sense.

"And *you* and that other blonde are annoying." Asmodeus removed a sword from his side. "Killing you will bring me more pleasure than normal."

He aimed for Sierra's heart, making sure not to miss the mark. As he swung, closing the distance between his blade and her chest, a golden wolf lunged at them from behind a large oak.

Luna.

For a second, I was stunned, but as her teeth sank into the unsuspecting prince of Hell's wrist, reality crashed back over me. Now was the time.

I pushed my wings harder and raised my sword. As I swung at Asmodeus's neck, Levi connected, *Rosemary, watch out!*

Something hard slammed into me, and I tumbled sideways. As I plummeted to the ground, vile sludge covered me.

A prince of Hell had to be on me.

At the last second, I rolled, catching the demon off guard and removing him from my back. *Which one is it?*

Lucifer, Levi answered as he landed next to me.

I jumped to my feet and faced the demon.

"It's unfortunate that you impress me." Lucifer examined me. "Not only do you have Azbogah acting selflessly, but you are more cunning than the average angel. I wonder if your persona is only that. A persona."

I lifted my chin. He wanted to play mind games, and I wouldn't fall for it. "And you realized that Asmodeus would sneak off with Annie at the first opportunity instead of staying here to fight alongside his brethren."

His irises dimmed as he squinted. "What do you mean?"

"Look at our location." I gestured to how close we were to the tree line. "And Annie."

The prince of Hell obliged, and he examined the hold Asmodeus had on Annie's arm. "You were running away."

"She's pregnant," Asmodeus said. Then he headbutted Luna. "I want to protect the babies."

Luna whimpered as her jaw went slack, and he tossed her to the ground.

"*Babies?*" Annie squeaked.

Sierra's jaw clenched as she stared at Luna, but the wolf's Caribbean-blue eyes stayed open without any sign of disorientation. She had to be playing the injured card. That was something shifters regularly did.

"You're planning to hide from us." Lucifer's eyes brightened. "And breed your own demon and silver wolf army to kill us so you can rule by yourself."

Asmodeus shrugged. "Lust is my superpower, and it is stronger than any of yours individually. Why should I settle for anything less than complete domination?"

I watched out of the corner of my eye as Sterlyn crept up behind Asmodeus. This familial rift was a great distraction.

I'm going to attack Lucifer. Anything to keep the attention off Asmodeus so Sterlyn could slit his throat.

Wait— Levi started, but he was too late. I was already swinging my sword as Luna jumped to her feet. She hadn't been knocked out after all.

Levi's displeasure surged through me. *Damn it, Rosey. I almost lost you, and now you're fighting a prince of Hell alone. I'll be the first demon to ever die of a fucking heart attack.*

That's not possible. You're an angel. Sometimes, I didn't understand why he thought things were so dire. Angels didn't die of human-like causes.

Blocking my blade with his sword, Lucifer kicked at my stomach. It was a move I'd make, so I'd anticipated it. I flew higher and lifted my feet to my chest. His leg sailed underneath me, and I spun, forcing his weapon to his side as I kicked him in the face.

Silver fur flashed past me as Cyrus joined the attack against Asmodeus. I was glad he and Sterlyn were fighting together since Annie couldn't fight.

But I had to remain focused on Lucifer. Though he wasn't the strongest fighter, he was intelligent. He would use strategy and not brazen strength to hurt me. I would have to trust my instincts instead of my observational skills, which I'd been trained to never do, but he'd do the unexpected.

He fell back several feet, and I took a moment to check on the others.

Luna had bitten Asmodeus's other wrist above the hand holding Annie, and Sierra had her knife in the demon's back. Cyrus dug his claws into the prince's chest, and Asmodeus's face scrunched in agony. When I blinked, Sterlyn swung her knife, severing the head of the prince of Lust. However, a demon with a large dagger soared at Sierra.

"Sierra, watch out!" I commanded as Lucifer barreled toward me.

I braced myself. Levi stood next to me, demon sword drawn, ready to attack Lucifer.

Remember, we're stronger together, Levi linked, echoing my words.

Then let's kick the feathers off him. I winced due to the

irony of the situation. Technically, he'd already had his feathers removed, but semantics didn't matter.

"I need help!" Lucifer called, and within moments, a demon flanked his side as two others faced Levi and me. "Levi is mine."

Apparently, killing Levi and me was more of a priority than before, or he viewed us as more formidable.

The two demons drew their weapons. One held a scythe, while the other had a mace. I smiled, my grin broadening as their steps faltered. I'd battled demons who had used these weapons before.

Scythe went for the base of my wings as Mace aimed for my sword. I waited a beat, pretending not to know what they were planning. Swinging my sword up at the last second, I blocked the mace as Scythe snickered darkly.

He thought he had me.

As he flew over my shoulder, swinging downward, I spun to the side and speared his neck. His scythe dropped as he reached for the spear to dislodge it from his throat.

That was all the time I needed to move my wings. I flipped over, kicking Mace under what had to be his chin. I had to guess since they were in their shadow form, but with the location of his eyes, I had to be pretty close. Mace hit the ground on his back as I landed back on my feet, slitting Scythe through the neck. His blood splattered me, but I was already drenched. Fresh blood wouldn't make a big difference.

Azbogah appeared beside me and began helping Levi. My throat tightened, and I had to blink back tears. So much had changed in such a short amount of time. I wanted to ask Levi if he was okay, but there was no pain coming through the bond. I had to trust him to inform me if he was in trouble. Besides, Azbogah was there, helping him fight.

I focused on Mace, wanting to end it. He soared toward me, his gaze jerky. He was nervous, which boded well for me. I'd made an impact.

He screamed as if he hoped it would affect me. Though I wanted to cover my ears, I forced myself to ignore the ringing. As he charged with his mace extended, I waited until the last second to fly over him. I landed directly behind him, and as he turned to face me, I severed his head.

I scanned my surroundings. No demon was focused on me, so I turned to Levi and Azbogah. Lucifer stared at Azbogah as if he was going to strike. But when he thrust his sword, it was to the left, at Levi's heart.

"No!" I screamed, and launched myself at them, but it was too late.

CHAPTER TWENTY

EYES BLAZING, Lucifer laughed in delight.

My world crumbled around me. I pushed myself toward Levi, but I couldn't move fast enough. There was no way I could reach him, and an exploding heart was something no one could come back from.

Azbogah spread out his wings, barely making it before the sword. The blade bounced off his midnight feathers, and tears of relief burned my eyes. Once again, my biological father had come through for me. Not only had he saved my life, but now my preordained mate's life as well.

For a millennium, I'd believed people could never change. But after my own transformation, I knew they could. And Azbogah had just reinforced my belief. If *he* could change, anyone could.

As Lucifer's sword ricocheted off Azbogah's feathers, he jerked it toward Azbogah's side. Azbogah swung his sword down, but he was too late.

Lucifer stabbed the dark angel deep in the side.

Terror pumped through my veins, making me fly faster.

As Lucifer yanked the sword free, Azbogah groaned and stumbled forward.

I lifted my sword, aiming for Lucifer's neck, as Levi pivoted around Azbogah's wing, his demon sword lifted for an attack. However, Lucifer thrust the sword up and into Azbogah's heart an instant before my sword lopped off his head.

The prince of Hell had been so focused on killing Azbogah that he'd forgotten about the threat behind him. But I didn't feel victorious. Rather, I flew over the body of the still-standing Lucifer and landed beside Azbogah.

"Let me heal you!" I said as I tapped into my magic. He'd healed me, and it was only fair to return the favor.

No. It wasn't returning the favor. I *wanted* to save him.

Blood pooled at the corners of his mouth. "You...can't..."

"I have to try." Maybe it was futile, but I couldn't just sit here. Nausea swirled inside me as fear gripped my heart.

"Little one," he said through gritted teeth, "the sword is in my heart. If you take it out, my heart will shred apart, and I'll die in seconds, but you can't heal me while it's in."

A lump formed in my throat. *Levi, get Mother.* Even if they weren't together anymore, Azbogah was her preordained mate. She needed a chance to say goodbye.

"There's got to be a way." Warm liquid dripped down my face, and now I knew it was tears. "I...I don't want to lose you." If he was dying, the least I could do was let him know I cared.

The fighting continued around us, and Sterlyn and others circled Azbogah and me, protecting us while we had the final moments of his life together.

"I'm sorry," he rasped. His face twisted in agony, but his gray eyes stayed locked on mine. "My biggest regret in life is walking away from Yelahiah...and you."

For a moment, I wished I could turn back time and not believe what he was saying. It would have made *this* easier, but here I was, holding on to his every last word. "Was it all worth it?"

His face paled as his body began to fail. "No, it wasn't. It wasn't until the truth came out and I got to spend time with you that I truly realized everything I'd sacrificed. I wish I could take it all back. But I can't. Not now. It's too late."

My throat constricted. The sincerity of his words added to my own confusion and heartbreak. The truth was, I didn't want to lose him, and the realization shocked me to the core.

We're heading back to you now, Levi linked.

Good. I'd been worried that Mother wouldn't make it here in time. "Keep your strength. Mother is on her way."

"No, listen. I need *you* to understand." He licked his lips. "Of everything in my entire existence, you're the one thing I tried to do right by. I gave you up because I wasn't worthy of being your father, not because I didn't want you. I tried to keep my distance from you...but I couldn't, and I took out my anger and hurt on your mother." His chest heaved as his breathing became labored. "I...I love you, little one. I always have, and I always will."

I wished I could take back all those times I'd hated it when he'd watched me. He had desperately wanted to be in my life, and he'd done it in the only way he'd known how. My breath caught, the surge of grief nearly incapacitating. "I wish we could've gotten to know each other better."

"Oh, sweet child, I know you." He paused, wheezing as he filled his lungs. "You're the perfect balance between your mother and me. You have my determination and can see the larger picture, but you also have her incredible sense of right and wrong. You bridged the gaps among shifter, witch, vampire, and demon in a way no other angel could." His hand shook as he clasped mine. "You're the light to my darkness. Every time I acted upset with your decisions, it was because I wished those were the decisions I had made long ago. I felt trapped and grew bitter. You're the balance Fate brought into this world to counteract *me*."

Someone flew over us, and I readied myself to fight. However, Mother's face, lined with worry, came into view as she landed on Azbogah's opposite side. My bond with Levi warmed as he stepped up beside me.

Mother didn't say anything, but no words were needed.

Azbogah turned his head as his eyelids lowered. His heart was slowing as he neared the end. "I love you, Yelahiah. I never stopped, and I wish I had never done any of the things I did. I hate myself for it all—"

"Stop." She took his other hand and squeezed it tightly. "You need to save your energy." Her hands glowed as she tried to heal him, but I knew the moment she realized the same thing as I had because her eyes glistened.

"There's no point." He barely squeezed our hands, and he winced. "Listen, Jegudiel should take my place on the council after he has had time to acclimate. He's yet another person I love who I've wronged. But right now, you need to fight. You've spent enough time here."

"You rascal!" Mother's nostrils flared. "This isn't fair. You can't say all this now."

"If not now, Yelahiah, then when?" Azbogah asked as blood trickled from the corners of his mouth.

She didn't respond. There wasn't much she could say.

He gurgled as his lungs stopped working, and I laid my head on his chest. I had to say these words before he perished or I'd live with a lifetime of regret. "Father, I love you."

"Love..." His chest shook. "...you." And then his heart stopped beating.

A sob racked my body as the angel I'd only just realized I loved stilled beside me. Out of every possible scenario, I never would have dreamed *this*, yet here I was, desperately mourning the death of an angel I'd only begun to know despite having judged him my entire existence.

He'd been broken. Yes, he had done it to himself, but he was broken nonetheless. And no one had been there for him until his death.

Arms wrapped around my waist, anchoring me. The buzzing of our connection comforted me, but even Levi couldn't stifle the turmoil raging inside. Any chance I had to know Azbogah better was gone.

A loud howl pierced the night, bringing me back to the present. I was wasting energy grieving when there were still so many lives at stake, including the lives of everyone else I cared about.

The last thing I wanted to do was release my hold. I wanted to cherish his smell and warmth while they remained, but life continued even when a heart had been shattered. I'd learned that when Levi had left me behind.

I forced myself upright and watched Mother kiss Azbogah's forehead. She stroked her fingers through his spiked hair almost reverently. She still cared for him, though she had moved on. She'd learned to live with his presence; now, she'd have to adjust to life without him in this world.

Scanning our surroundings, I noted we were actually winning, but two princes of Hell were still fighting. The war would rage until they were dead.

Even with Azbogah's death, I despised killing. It was a

necessity I didn't cherish. However, these two demons were set on vengeance, even though no one left alive had been involved in the decision that had caused them to fall. They didn't care. They'd nurtured their hatred, and it was like a disease that spewed from within.

I pushed away my hurt to focus. Wrath still sparred with Ronnie, with Alex and Killian flanking each side. Ronnie's forehead was beaded with sweat as she blocked Wrath's blade once again, but the prince of Hell kicked both men in the face, knocking them back several feet.

Father must have taken Mother's place in battling Belaphor. Two demons were fighting beside the prince of Hell, which meant he needed help as well.

While Mother moved to my side, Sterlyn, Griffin, Sierra, Luna, Darrell, Mila, Emmy, and several silver wolves broke the circle as they raced back to help the others. I hadn't even noticed everyone who had been protecting me until now.

The demons weren't nearly as deadly when everyone could see them, so their numbers were thinning. Half of the witches from Hell were dead, which surprised me. I'd thought they'd be stronger.

"I'll go help Pahaliah while you two fight Wrath," Mother instructed as she nodded at Levi's demon sword. "We need to end this before there's more"—she broke off as a tear ran down her cheek—"death."

She was more impacted by Azbogah's death than she wanted to let on.

"Okay," I said.

Let's go. They're struggling, Levi linked as his arm brushed mine.

The buzz shot through me with a chill from him being

in his demon form. He must have changed to retrieve Mother.

I'd just spread my wings, ready to take flight, when the strange urge not to leave Azbogah overwhelmed me. It was irrational, especially since he couldn't be hurt worse in his current state. These were times when emotions hindered logic. Forcing my wings to move, I joined Levi, and we jetted across the clearing toward Ronnie.

Killian and Alex had just reached her side again when five other demons swarmed them. We had to get to them. I refused to lose anyone else.

Unlike Lucifer, Wrath glanced over his shoulder as if he'd sensed us. He had a strong sense of self-preservation, and I wondered why Lucifer had been so narrowly focused on Azbogah. However, none of that mattered. They were both dead.

Death was the one thing you could never come back from.

As Wrath spun toward us, the other five demons swarmed Ronnie, Killian, and Alex. The three of them fought side by side while the Prince of War turned his hate-filled eyes on Levi and me.

If he thought he could intimidate me, he'd soon learn otherwise. I lifted my sword, not feeling the least amount of discomfort because Azbogah had healed me. A sob built in my chest, but I swallowed it and moved forward. I could mourn his death when this was all over. For now, I needed to channel that emotion into the fight. Otherwise, it could overtake me.

Wrath lifted his sword in response, ready to battle.

Be careful, Rosemary. Levi's concern wafted through me. *He's physically stronger than any other demon.*

That's why we'll fight him together. Though I might be

hurting, I wouldn't do something irrational. *We're stronger that way. I'll distract him so you can stab him with your mother's blade.*

Swirling iridescent lights filled the surrounding area, and Wrath paused. His head snapped toward Father, who was using his necklace to power the space around us. The demons grew more disoriented, and both princes of Hell were distracted.

Mother shot a lightning bolt at Belaphor, blasting him back several feet.

That was enough for Wrath to turn his attention back to me and lift his sword in time to block my blow.

I gritted my teeth, trying to hold his weapon in place. *Now!*

Following my command, Levi swung his demon sword at Wrath's neck from the other side. The prince of Hell spun away from my blade, and my arm dropped as Levi missed him.

As he finished his spin, he continued the movement, aiming his sword at my side. It wouldn't be a kill move, but it was the same tactic Lucifer had used to kill... I trailed off. I couldn't overthink and needed to react.

I blocked the blade with my wings, something Azbogah hadn't been able to do at that moment, then kicked Wrath in the face. His head jerked to the side, but I couldn't get cocky. That was exactly what could get me killed.

Levi hissed, *I bet I have gray hairs by now.*

I frowned, nonplussed. I was surprised he didn't know that angels didn't age like mortals, but that lesson would come later.

With the spear, I stabbed Wrath in the neck, but before I could go deep, his weapon hit the midway point of the handle, slicing the tip of my thumb where I gripped it.

Adrenaline coursed through my veins, and I felt no pain. However, he knocked the spear from my hand, leaving me with only one weapon to defend myself. That was fine. I had something better on my side—Levi.

My mate jerked forward, using Wrath's downward momentum to stab his shoulder. The dagger sparked as it flowed into Wrath's skin. I'd never seen anything like it before.

Pain exploded on the right side of my face, and it took a moment for me to realize that Wrath had punched me while I'd been transfixed by Levi's sword.

Even adrenaline couldn't stop this sort of agony.

"You *bastard*," Levi rasped as he pulled out the sword, ready to strike Wrath again.

Wait. Don't— But it was too late. He'd already yanked it from the Prince of War's arm. *I think he did that so you'd remove it.* He was desperate to get the weapon out of his body and attack me.

However, the damage was done. We had to move on.

Blue blood oozed from his shoulder, and the overly sweet, metallic smell made my stomach churn. We had to end this.

Wrath moved the sword to his left hand. Since he favored his right, that would tip things in our favor.

I kicked his left wrist before he had a good grip, pivoting without pausing, and aimed for his chin. He managed to keep a grip on his sword, but I'd forced him backward.

Preparing, I waited for him to attack again, but instead, he spun toward Ronnie. The five demons were down to two, none of them fighting as easily with the lights flickering around them. They weren't used to Heaven's light. Not anymore. It was pure and probably coated their skin like their vileness did mine.

But that wasn't what worried me. It was the look in the Prince of War's eyes. He blurred toward Ronnie, who was fighting alongside her mate. As she used the dagger against the demon, Wrath's eyes focused on the weapon.

He was desperate to kill her, aware that time was running out.

I hadn't used my connection with Levi in this fight, not wanting to pull energy away from him when he might need it most, but Ronnie's life was in peril.

Flying faster than ever before, I reached Wrath just as he stabbed at the spot in her back where her heart beat. Realizing that my wings would be most effective, I twisted. Turning your back on your enemy wasn't smart, but I was listening to my gut. My wings were an extension of me, and my sword wasn't. I had more control over them.

When my wings cut through bone, my breathing evened out. The risk had paid off.

As my feet touched solid ground, I released the tug from our bond, allowing Levi to regain his power. Wrath's shadow head lay at my feet, but all I could focus on was Ronnie. She wasn't injured, but her emerald eyes widened as she realized what had almost happened.

"You saved my life," she murmured.

"I protected my sister." Maybe my former self would've said something like, *of course I did*. But I wasn't the same angel anymore. Sterlyn, Ronnie, and everyone else in our group, including the men, were my family. It had taken me a while to understand that, though I'd felt it from the start.

Alex pulled Ronnie into his arms, a tear running down his cheek. He looked at me and said, "Thank you."

I averted my gaze, an odd sensation coming over me. "There's no need to thank me. That's what family does."

He laughed, and I involuntarily looked at him. My cheeks heated, and the urge to run almost overwhelmed me.

"We're definitely family, Rosemary." He nodded.

My heart grew larger despite the pain still wafting inside me.

It's over, Levi linked. *I...I can't believe it.*

Glancing at my parents, I found Belaphor at their feet, dismembered. Every single witch with ties to Hell lay lifeless around us. But at least fifty of Killian's pack were dead, too, and my heart fractured more.

If these were the casualties here, what would we find in Shadow City?

A hundred red-eyed demons soared away while about fifty undecided stood frozen in place. As we'd figured, we'd killed the princes, and the rest had crumbled.

"Should we go after the demons?" Zagan asked, his black diamond irises on Levi and me.

All the demons turned to Levi.

Why are they looking at me? Levi linked as he reached my side.

Realization washed over me. *Because you're Marissa's heir and a full demon.* They were looking at him to take charge.

Disbelief surged through him, so I decided to come to his aid. We needed to leverage their trust before they turned to someone else. "We don't have the capacity. Even if we tried, they would split up and go different ways," I told Zagan. Though I hated to admit it, there was no way we could capture them without alerting more humans. They had a head start. I could only hope they would lie low, not wanting to pop back onto our radar, or that they were rushing back to Hell, where they'd be protected.

"What happened to all the witches?" Sterlyn asked as she looked around. "How did they all die?"

"That's because—" Eliza started.

Erin cut her off. "Once the demons who had extended their lives died, their magic left their bodies, causing them to age to their true years."

Now that she'd said that, I noticed how skeletal their faces were. Some of them even had a dustlike appearance, as if they were already becoming part of the Earth.

"You do realize I was speaking," Eliza bit out. "You didn't need to interrupt."

And I'd always thought that shifters were ornery about proving their dominance. The witches might have them beat.

"I was only answering the silver wolf's question." Erin pushed her hair behind her shoulder as her attention landed on Azbogah's body. She stilled, and her face twisted into agony before she smoothed it back into a mask of indifference. She did care about Azbogah, though I wasn't sure if it was for his well-being or for all the things he'd promised her.

"Which Eliza was *trying* to do," Circe said through clenched teeth.

"Your coven tries a lot but never actually comes through." Erin shrugged and smiled condescendingly. "Well, as fun as *all* this was, we need to head back and see how Shadow City is faring." Erin waved a hand. "Come, members. Let's alert the city to the good news." She spun on her heel and marched off toward Shadow City.

Mother avoided looking at Azbogah's body and said, "We'll go with her." She took Father's hand, tugging him toward the city. "We don't want her to take too much credit for what's done, and we need to ensure that the demons realize the princes are gone."

That was probably for the best. I wanted to go with them, but I needed to stay back to deal with the dead and help Levi with the demons looking at him as their leader.

Eliza's chest heaved, and her nostrils flared as the Shadow City witches left.

I didn't have the energy to empathize with her. The loss of Azbogah crashed over me once more.

"Guys!" Sterlyn called out, her iridescent purple eyes glowing. "Cyrus needs us. It's Annie."

CHAPTER TWENTY-ONE

THE MEMORY of Asmodeus dragging Annie away sickened me. "Is it a demon?" Having more information would be great before we raced into danger; however, I readied myself to fly.

As the last of Erin's coven left the area, Sterlyn gnawed on her bottom lip. "It's *time*," she said vaguely, and flicked her gaze to her stomach.

Even though I usually didn't pick up on insinuations, this was crystal clear—Annie was in labor.

"My goddess." Eliza clutched her chest. "Take me to her. I—no...Circe needs to be there to help since she's..." She trailed off.

The last silver wolf alpha heirs to be born were Sterlyn and Cyrus. The memory of how Eliza had spelled newborn Cyrus to appear dead and given him to an enemy must have still haunted her.

"No, *we* should go together," Circe said, and took Eliza's hand.

Though the demons surrounding us appeared willing to follow Levi, they hadn't gained our trust, and I was glad

Eliza hadn't finished her sentence. Her coven had been at the bedside of every silver wolf alpha heir's birth since the wolves had left Shadow City. The coven had taken on the role themselves since the birth of alphas was strenuous on a wolf shifter's body, albeit they were usually regular wolf shifters and not an alpha demon wolf themselves. However, we couldn't be too careful. Technically, Cyrus wasn't the true silver wolf alpha, but Annie was the alpha of the demon wolves, and they wouldn't want to take any chances.

We need to get to Annie, I linked to Levi. Though I was sure Eliza could handle the labor, I needed to be there as well. If something went drastically wrong, I could heal her and the baby.

Levi's shadow head nodded. He turned to Bune. "Father, can you please coordinate the cleanup and burials here? Even our brethren who chose vengeance deserve a final resting place."

Warmth exploded within me. He was already setting a good precedent: even though some of his people had chosen to fight against us, all demons were our brethren.

"Yes, son." Bune flickered back into his human form. He smiled proudly. "I can do that. Go help Rosemary and her friends."

Are you sure that's smart? I hated for him to leave when things were unsettled. "Please take care of Azbogah. He did wrong, but he regretted it...at the end."

Bune nodded.

"All of you, go on," Darrell said from his position between his daughter, Emmy, and his mate, Martha. They were spattered with blood, and I saw red mixed with blue, but they didn't seem severely injured. "Billy and I can take it from here."

Billy. Killian's beta.

In all the chaos since Levi had come into my life, I hadn't spent much time with any of the wolf packs. I knew only a few of the wider members. Perhaps I would have a chance to get to know more of them now.

Billy rubbed a hand over his bald head and reassured Killian, "The rest of the pack is heading this way."

I realized that not even half of their people had been here. "Where were they?"

"At the university," Killian responded. "Half of our fighters were inside, protecting the building in case the demons came back—we placed anyone not trained for battle inside the main building. We split up, not wanting to put all of us at risk in one location." He glanced down at his arms, which were thickly coated in blue blood. "Cordelia, Kamila, and Eliphas stayed there in case they needed to perform the demon-vision spell."

"Cyrus is freaking out. He needs us now." Sterlyn ran in the direction Cyrus and Annie had gone after we'd engaged Asmodeus in battle.

We could talk on the way. "We'll be back as soon as we can."

"We will all go to Annie," Circe assured us. "The others are coming to help. Herne and Aurora, help with the burials and aftermath. If you need us"—she looked at Eliza —"then get Sterlyn or Killian to let one of the shifters here know, and either Mom or I will be back as quickly as possible."

All of our reservations dissolved as our group hurried toward the pack neighborhood. As we got closer to Azbogah's dead form, I focused elsewhere. I couldn't see him that way again without falling apart. At least Mother had that one drawing of him that would serve as a memory of his appearance.

Glancing to the side, my attention landed on yet another sight that added to my agony.

Luna.

She lay several feet away from Azbogah, a dagger lodged in her chest. Sierra leaned over her, tears running down her cheeks.

"Is she breathing?" I asked as I hurried over to her. As long as she wasn't dead, I could try to heal her.

Sierra shook her head. "Yes, but barely. Please save her. She jumped in front of the dagger and saved me."

"Is the dagger in her heart?"

"I...I don't know." Sierra's tears dripped onto Luna's face.

Not wanting to waste any more time, I raced to Luna's other side. I placed my hands around the dagger and felt her heart gently beating against my palm. Somehow, the dagger had missed it. "I think I can heal her."

"Thank gods," Sierra cried brokenly. "We were *just* becoming friends." Sierra petted her golden fur. "I didn't even get to tell her that I forgave her."

That sentiment was all too familiar.

I pushed my magic inside Luna, healing the internal injuries. When her heart beat more steadily, I pulled the weapon from her chest and then placed my hands over the wound. I wasn't going to lose another person today. She'd risked her life to save someone I loved, which made her family now.

I felt Levi's hands on my shoulder. He pushed his magic into me, strengthening my power. Within seconds, I'd healed Luna enough that she'd survive, but I didn't want to risk doing more in case another threat appeared. "She'll be fine, but she needs rest."

"This is all my fault." Sierra broke down more, despite

Luna being in better shape.

None of that made sense to me. *Why is she still crying?*

Because she feels guilty. Levi stepped back, giving me a moment with Sierra, but I didn't want him to move away. I couldn't leave her like this, and he had better mortal skills than I did. I still needed training.

Just comfort her and speak from your heart, Levi connected.

I wasn't sure how to do that. I inhaled deeply. "Sierra, I understand the guilt you're bearing, but her sacrifice speaks volumes. She wanted to save you. She wouldn't have done that for someone she found unworthy, so the best thing you can do is not blame yourself. She didn't die, and she'll be awake soon. She'll be fine."

She rubbed her nose with her palm and sniffled. "I never thought about it that way."

Though having emotions made things difficult, I'd lived without them for so long that it was slightly easier for me to see things in a different manner. "That's why you have..." I trailed off, trying to get used to being supportive. "Friends."

Snorting, Sierra pulled me into her arms. "Rosemary, ever since you met Levi, you've been full of surprises. And I gotta say, I kind of love it."

I tensed for a moment before wrapping my arms around her. Though it didn't feel as awkward, my butt was sticking out, and my back was at a weird angle.

"But you're still weird about physical gestures." Sierra laughed, though more tears poured down her face.

What should I do? I wasn't sure if I was making this worse or better.

Levi pushed comfort toward me. *You're doing exactly what you need to. You're being yourself.*

Mother plucker. I was being self-conscious. When had I

264 JEN L. GREY

turned into *that* person?

"You guys need to go." Darrell groaned from nearby as he lifted the body of an older man from Killian's pack. "Annie's close. It won't be much longer. I'll take Luna to one of the other houses so she can rest. Annie needs you all right now."

"Right!" Sierra fisted her hands in front of her. "Baby. Now. Let's go." She leaned down and kissed the top of Luna's head. "Thank you, my friend, and I'll be chewing your ass out shortly." Then she turned and ran toward the pack housing.

Levi and I were right behind her, flying through the woods. I could go faster, but I didn't want to leave Sierra alone, even though I was certain we were no longer at risk. I paced myself to fly close to her, dodging the trees as they came along since I wasn't willing to risk flying above them with humans around, trying to capture more supernatural activity.

That was a whole other issue we'd have to contend with, but right now, Annie birthing a healthy baby was top priority.

This time, when the Craftsman-style houses came into view, I landed and pulled my wings into my back before stepping out of the tree line. The humans had been near here last time, and I didn't expect them to have gone very far.

Griffin, Alex, and Killian stood outside Killian's hunter green house. They had their hands on their heads and looked pale.

Something was wrong.

I rushed over, wishing I had kept my sword. I would kill anyone who threatened an unborn child without hesitation. "Where's the threat?"

Rubbing a hand down his face, Killian rasped, "There isn't one."

"Speak for yourself." Griffin shivered. "Seeing Annie on the living room floor, pantsless and in that kind of pain, was definitely threatening."

"Oh, stop." Alex rolled his eyes. "All you saw was her side."

"Then, please"—Griffin waved a hand at the white door —"go back in and help the ladies."

Tugging at his once-white collared shirt, which was now nearly all blue from demon blood, Alex cleared his throat. "I'd hate to get in the way."

They were squeamish over her labor. I pushed past the three buffoons and opened the front door. My gaze immediately landed on Annie, who was in the position they'd mentioned. Her face was drenched in sweat as Cyrus and Ronnie each held her hands. Eliza had Annie's head cradled in her lap with her hands on Annie's shoulders, and Circe placed her hands on Annie's belly. They both moved their lips, casting a spell for the birth.

No one was between her legs, helping.

I rushed inside in such a hurry that I almost slipped on the hardwood floor. "What can I do?"

I could hear the guys outside. "Levi, I'm telling you, you don't want to go in there," Griffin said. "I will if Annie needs us, but I think it's safer out here."

"You four are idiots," Sierra said as she followed behind me and shut the front door.

I positioned myself between Annie's legs and got ready to work.

266 JEN L. GREY

Twenty-four hours later, I was still reeling from everything that had happened. However, holding a brand-new baby girl who smelled like the perfect balance of angel and wolf helped mend a part of my heart that had broken. I sniffed Lizzy's silver hair, trying to sear it into my memory as I caressed her cheek. Her dark purple eyes opened and tried to focus on me. She had the hair of a silver wolf and the eyes of a demon wolf.

You look even more breathtaking with a baby in your arms, Levi linked beside me on the couch.

I tore my eyes away from her and beamed at Levi. He was holding the firstborn, Arian, who had the dark hair of a demon wolf's fur and sterling silver eyes that were a mirror image of Cyrus's. A demon wolf with the silver eyes of the alpha bloodline of the silver wolf.

The twins were a *balance* of the two angelic shifter lines, born after Azbogah's and the princes of Hell's deaths. Lizzy, named after Eliza, who had loved them so much she had sacrificed herself, and Arian, named for Sterlyn and Cyrus's deceased father, whom he'd never met. There was no doubt in my mind that Fate had planned this ending and new beginning.

One day, I hope to be holding our own child. I'd always dreamed of having a child, and now that dream had grown into being a family—something I hadn't wanted until Levi.

Holding these babies was a miracle. They were a sign of everything we had all gone through to get to this place.

Though Annie was fierce, birth was no easy feat, especially when giving birth to twins. She and Cyrus were resting in Killian's late sister's room. It was still a shrine to Olive due to his guilt over her and their parents' deaths. Though he hadn't been responsible, he blamed himself for attending a party instead of checking out a threat against them.

Sterlyn and Ronnie entered the room, wearing tender smiles on their faces. Every single one of us, including Griffin and Alex, was completely in love with these little ones.

"Give us the babies!" Ronnie whispered loudly. "And you two get out of here."

"What?" She'd caught me off guard. Normally, they were always asking me to come here. They'd never asked me to leave before. But I squared my shoulders—they were right. "I should go back and help the angels now that we know Annie and the babies aren't in danger." Levi and I should've left hours ago.

Actually, I've already talked to your parents and my father, and they're fine holding down the fort for a few days, Levi linked as he passed off Arian to Sterlyn.

The fort? Maybe, at one point, Shadow City could have been called a fortress, but not anymore. The crystals had stopped working, and humans were infiltrating and videoing the city that had been hidden from them for centuries. *It couldn't protect us from a feather right now.*

That's not what I meant. Levi scooted to the center next to me. *I meant they want to handle things while we go away for a few days.*

Away...? But I can't. Every time I left this area, it angered my parents and the council.

Levi tilted his head. *Why not? The demons aren't a threat anymore.*

My breath caught. He was right. There wasn't a reason I couldn't leave.

"You two better go while you can." Ronnie laughed, taking Lizzy from me.

"But the humans..." I hated to leave with all the turmoil.

"Oh, they'll still be a problem in a few days. Don't worry." Ronnie patted my shoulder as she sat on the loveseat parallel to me. "In fact, by that time, you probably won't be able to go, so you two *go* now. Take two days and be alone while you can. You know chaos always finds us shortly after any reprieve."

Let's go to the beach, Rosey. Levi stood. *I haven't been, either. Let's dip our toes in the ocean while the sun rises. Let's go experience something together, just you and me. Two full days. That's all I'm asking.*

I opened my mouth to say no...and that's when I knew my answer. I regretted the time I'd never spent with Azbogah. Having those types of regrets with Levi...well, that was something I wouldn't recover from. *Two days.*

Our life is too chaotic for more. Levi held out his hand. *But let's take what we can.*

Like Ronnie had said, the humans would be here when we got back.

When I placed my hand in his, his shoulders relaxed. He hadn't expected me to say yes.

I'd travel anywhere as long as you're the one beside me. I kissed him, not caring that Ronnie and Sterlyn were there with us. *I love you.*

I love you, he replied. He pulled back as happiness radiated through our bond. *Our bags are already at the door. I can't wait to get you naked...I mean, once we get there.*

I laughed. *I feel the same way. Maybe we can find a deserted spot for some sex on the beach.*

Uh...what are we waiting for? He dragged me to the door. *No better time than the present.*

He had a way of making everything fun and right. I typed out a text message to Eleanor, asking her to help

Mother and Father in the city since I would be away. It was too much of a burden for only two people to handle the cleanup and reorganizing, especially after our history had changed so suddenly.

When she texted back that she'd be honored, I stared in disbelief, shaking my head at how things had changed. Then I smiled. I had no other valid reason to stay.

The two of us walked out of the house, ready to travel to the beach. And for the next two days, I'd get to understand what it was like to be a mortal in love.

THE SUN WAS SETTING behind the ocean, painting the water in reds, golds, and pinks. Looking out into the vastness made me feel insignificant. Levi's side pressed against mine as we sat in the sand, close enough to the water that when a wave rolled in, it washed over our feet.

We'd traveled to Mexico because of the warmth and clear waters the country was known for. Luckily, back when I'd been approved to attend Shadow Ridge University, before all the chaos, I'd received a monthly stipend to pay for things I might need outside of Shadow City that I had rarely used. Spending mortal money was proving to be a lot of fun.

This is amazing, I linked. It was a magical view, especially here. The fresh, salty air caressed us as the waves crashed like a lullaby.

I never wanted to go home.

He wrapped an arm around my shoulders. *I'm just sorry we haven't been able to find a vacant enough spot to make love on the beach. The hotel room has been good enough, though.*

We'd divided our time equally between here and our room, and we'd experienced two of the most perfect kind of days that I'd never known existed.

The sun dropped behind the water, and twilight descended upon us.

Come on. Let's go back to the room. Levi winked.

My body warmed. Every time we made love, it was better than the last. I'd assumed that at some point, things would cool slightly between us, or at least not feel so urgent, but so far, it hadn't happened. I could ravage him time and time again.

Couples walked hand in hand past us, and families came out with flashlights, buckets, and nets, searching for nocturnal creatures to catch and admire.

I stood eagerly, trying to remember not to move too quickly. We didn't need to alert anyone that we were different. As of now, our secret was still secure.

My skin buzzed where his touched mine, and we both cherished the walk back to the hotel. We'd secured an ocean-front view on the bottom floor, so it wasn't long before we were entering our room.

Levi's mouth crashed onto mine, and I slammed the door shut as I slid my hands under his shirt. His rock-hard abs greeted me, and I traced their curves. He groaned.

The television flickered in the background. We'd forgotten to turn it off before leaving. We'd been watching to see the news footage the humans had videoed during the war, but in this moment, I didn't care what was being shared.

I'd pushed Levi onto the king-size bed when a familiar voice drifted from the television.

I froze.

What's wrong? Levi stilled.

Turning around, I found Killian on the screen, standing in Shadow Ridge in front of a brick building downtown. My heart leaped into my throat, and I choked on a gasp. His dark chocolate eyes were warm, but the tightness in the corners told me everything.

He cleared his throat. "Yes, supernaturals are real. We exist. But we won't harm anyone."

My phone buzzed, and I reached over to grab it.

I found a message from Sterlyn: We can't contain it. News stations have swarmed us. I just wanted to let you know before you found out another way.

That would have been helpful to see an hour ago.

"Holy shit," Levi gasped. "I thought we had more time."

But we both knew our time was up.

"One last romp before we leave?" He waggled his brows.

His sentiment surprised me. "You want to wrestle?" I'd figured he'd want sex, not play, before we headed back to the others.

He chuckled and kissed me. He linked, *We can wrestle as long as we're naked. It's not like an extra hour will change anything.* He took the remote and switched off the television.

But we'll head back right after? I hated to cut our time short, but it wouldn't be by much. We'd planned on leaving early. *Because we do need to get back to them.*

Promise, he vowed as his finger ran up my side. Enticing shivers followed. *I need your undivided attention for a little longer.*

And I succumbed because I *wanted* to. We'd get back within a few hours, and we'd determine the next steps together—with my friends and my family.

The way things were always meant to be.

ABOUT THE AUTHOR

Jen L. Grey is a *USA Today* Bestselling Author who writes Paranormal Romance, Urban Fantasy, and Fantasy genres.

Jen lives in Tennessee with her husband, two daughters, and two miniature Australian Shepherds. Before she began writing, she was an avid reader and enjoyed being involved in the indie community. Her love for books eventually led her to writing. For more information, please visit her website and sign up for her newsletter.

Check out her future projects and book signing events at her website.
www.jenlgrey.com

ALSO BY JEN L. GREY

Shadow City: Silver Wolf Trilogy

Broken Mate

Rising Darkness

Silver Moon

Shadow City: Royal Vampire Trilogy

Cursed Mate

Shadow Bitten

Demon Blood

Shadow City: Demon Wolf Trilogy

Ruined Mate

Shattered Curse

Fated Souls

Shadow City: Dark Angel Trilogy

Fallen Mate

Demon Marked

Dark Prince

Fatal Secrets

Shadow City: Silver Mate

Shattered Wolf

Ruthless Moon

Fated Hearts

The Wolf Born Trilogy

Hidden Mate

Blood Secrets

Awakened Magic

The Hidden King Trilogy

Dragon Mate

Dragon Heir

Dragon Queen

The Marked Wolf Trilogy

Moon Kissed

Chosen Wolf

Broken Curse

Wolf Moon Academy Trilogy

Shadow Mate

Blood Legacy

Rising Fate

The Royal Heir Trilogy

Wolves' Queen

Wolf Unleashed

Wolf's Claim

Bloodshed Academy Trilogy

Year One

Year Two

Year Three

The Half-Breed Prison Duology (Same World As Bloodshed Academy)

Hunted

Cursed

The Artifact Reaper Series

Reaper: The Beginning

Reaper of Earth

Reaper of Wings

Reaper of Flames

Reaper of Water

Stones of Amaria (Shared World)

Kingdom of Storms

Kingdom of Shadows

Kingdom of Ruins

Kingdom of Fire

The Pearson Prophecy

Dawning Ascent

Enlightened Ascent

Reigning Ascent

Stand Alones

Death's Angel

Rising Alpha

Printed in Great Britain
by Amazon